Love and Loss Series, Book 2

LAKE FOG

CLAUDIA
WHITSITT

Claudia Whitsitt

ISBN: 978-1-7375073-1-4

For MACY JOANN, who brings light and laughter to my life each day.

CHAPTER ONE

KENDRA KELLY HAD BEEN SQUINTING AND STARING AT a blank page for hours when she heard the sound. She listened hard, certain it had come from the back bedroom. But when she rose and investigated the entire house, not for the first time today, all remained quiet. The cries had been so real. So Joey. She let out a ragged sigh.

Disoriented and unnerved, she returned to the office chair, determined to get something down on paper and not waste the entire day, but her mind remained full of shadows and ghosts. Despite a looming deadline, which had formerly motivated her writing, Kendra recognized that today was not one filled with words. She gazed outside and decided on the only option that made sense—kayaking.

Snatching sunglasses and a ball cap, she scoured the kitchen for the water thermos, frantically opening and closing cupboards, checking the table, counters, fridge, everywhere. She'd just had it.

Where the hell did it go?

Annoyed beyond frustration, she marched outside into the late July heat, tromped across the lawn, and blindly reached out to yank the kayak down from the rack. Kendra's knuckles scraped the sharp edge of the empty rack.

"Dammit." She shook her fingers in a feeble attempt to reduce the sting, turned, and searched behind the trees and the boat rack.

Did I not replace the kayak after yesterday's paddle? Did I drag it up onto the bank and get distracted?

Kendra peered over the landscape, the yard, and the lakefront, finally spotting the boat in the water, its tether looped around the dock cleat.

I don't do that. I've never done that.

Sinking down to the grass, she held her head in her hands. Every day brought more disturbing evidence. Nearly six months had passed. She should be better by now. Yet she'd obviously left her kayak in the lake. At least she'd discovered this fumble alone. There weren't witnesses, charting her continued inability to function.

The best course of action was to climb in the damn boat and paddle. Paddling usually helped to center her back into reality. The first ten minutes of rowing would make her biceps scream, but she knew from previous paddles, the pain would soon disappear, and muscle memory would take charge. Besides, a little muscle pain would serve as a welcome distraction from an otherwise waste of a day and distract her from the ghosts that made her feel she was never alone. A damp mist hugged the air, firmly rooting her in the memory of another misty day not long ago—the recollection as clear as if it'd happened yesterday.

Kendra had rocked Joey as he nursed, glancing out at the heavily wooded yard, at the myriad of tulip, oak, and elm trees— the buds forming on their branches were as much a sign of new life as the one she nestled in her arms. Joey gazed at her with such intensity, her heart filled with warmth. Her life had never been so complete. She counted numerous blessings—meeting Joe as her biological clock had ticked wildly toward the finish line of her child-producing years; the whirlwind romance; the intimate, idyllic wedding; the surprise but welcome pregnancy; and the success of her debut novel. The stuff of fairy tales. She'd also had the privilege of being home with Joey, and although exhausted, like any new mom, she'd relished the fact that she, rather than some stranger, spent every waking minute with this perfect miracle of a baby boy and soaked up every bit of his wakefulness with the same exuberance he did.

The memories brought tears. Then deep, heart-wrenching sobs. Splotches rose on her face, and immediately, her eyelids began to swell. She reached under the boat's seat—an involuntary movement—for a drink. After taking several cool, long gulps, Kendra dropped the bottle as if it had caught fire.

How is my thermos in my boat? And filled with ice-cold water? Didn't I just ransack the kitchen, trying to find it?

Her nerves frayed to shreds.

"You all right there?" A voice echoed from out of the mist.

Kendra jumped a mile and almost tipped the boat. Focused on Joey, she had completely missed the paddle slap of another boat on the hazy lake—her nosy fisherman neighbor Russ Jameson. She muttered a curse, pulled her cap further down on her forehead, and pushed her sunglasses up her nose in a weak attempt to hide her tearstained face, her raveled sanity.

"Fine." Kendra refused to offer Russ the satisfaction of acknowledgment. She just wanted him to vanish.

"I worry about you, you know. You should wear that life preserver. Sitting with your back up against it won't be a bit of help in an emergency."

Even though Kendra had rebuffed Russ, she pictured his expression of concern and sympathy. If she had a dime for every time someone offered a sympathetic gaze …

Heat rose up Kendra's neck. "I'm fine. No need to worry, Russ."

But Russ's kayak held steady at her side. "You don't seem so good."

She peered in his direction. "The water helps."

Russ shook his head. "The water ain't necessarily a good place to take your troubles. I'll leave you be, but I'm keeping my eye on you."

He didn't know her story, and in the coming moments, despite Kendra's irritation, she recognized he was genuinely concerned. He must think she was about to do something rash.

"Missing my family, is all."

Russ curved his boat away from Kendra's and muttered something under his breath about, "Watch yourself."

After at least an hour of hard paddling, Kendra eased the kinks from her brain, body, and heart. By the time she reached the shore in front of her home, dragged the kayak through the yard, hoisted it back onto the rack, and stepped toward the house, she realized she needed to hurry. A thought niggled at her; she'd forgotten something, and she had no idea of the time. She picked up the phone to check her calendar and discovered a message from Molly Muldoon, her best friend.

Just a reminder. Grief group tonight.

Thanks, Mom. Glad you're keeping track of my life.

I know you don't want to go, but it will help.

How the hell do you know what's good for me?

'Cause I'm smart.

Kendra sent a devil emoji back to Molly. She loved her best friend but had to admit that Molly had a tendency to get into her business far more often than she was comfortable with. All the hovering and pushiness should have fallen away by now.

Grief group. What the hell was Kendra going to do in a grief group?

Six months ago, she'd never dreamed she'd wind up living

alone at Pleasant Lake. No one lost both members of their family within the span of four days, nor should they be expected to discuss such a profound loss with a bunch of strangers.

Chills crept along her limbs. She'd be expected to share her story. But telling others would make it real, and Kendra had no desire to face reality.

Kendra mused over the possibilities. If she were lucky, there'd be too many people in the group for everyone to have a chance to divulge their story. If Kendra was forced to put her losses into words, she'd crumble. Voicing them would make it too keen, ice-pick stabs into her already-bled-out heart.

She stored the thoughts and shut off feeling until another time. She'd already cried enough today. If not for having promised Molly …

A half-eaten sandwich and a cursory shower later, she backed the SUV out of the garage and headed east to the corner and then south through the country roads filled with majestic farms and landscape, which provided great distractions from her destination—the church where the grief group met. You'd think she'd be happy to be out of the house, but the thought of getting out of the SUV and into the building once she arrived paralyzed her. She talked herself in and out of going inside for a full five minutes before she finally climbed out of the driver's seat.

Just go and get it over with. You don't have to talk. You just need to check the box. Tried a grief group. Hated it.

She'd parked at the rear of the lot, feeling less conspicuous there. As she made her way to the door of the church, she noticed others heading inside, and even though the sense of being observed stayed with her as she crossed the parking lot, she rationalized it beautifully. This was her first time out in quite a while. It made sense for her to feel a bit paranoid. She wasn't alone and being watched. She was out with others. Maybe they were there for choir practice or something. People going about their normal lives. Just because Kendra was attending a group didn't mean they were there for the same reason. She recognized her neurosis had taken over and tilted her head down and entered the building.

A sign indicated the group met in the basement. Kendra descended the stairs, inhaling a musty aroma as she trailed a couple of others, and took in the dismal setting—the exposed overhead light bulbs and the stiff metal folding chairs, which screeched across the drab army-green linoleum floor as the leader placed them in a circle.

Kendra thought about faking. *Oops, sorry, I'm in the wrong place.*

She turned around hoping to make a quick exit, but an older gentleman sidled up next to her. "Not a breeze, coming here, is it?"

Taken aback, Kendra answered without a second thought, "Did you spot me looking for an easy exit?"

His eyes twinkled. "Sorry to say, not my first time attending one of these. I know where you're coming from. A little advice from an old man? Give it a chance." He pointed to a long table along the back of the room. "Follow me. Tea and coffee are over here. It's worse than fast-food sludge, but it gives you something to do with your hands."

Kendra traipsed across the room with him. "I'm Kendra."

"Gary."

After filling their cups, they wandered back to the circle. Kendra had already decided to take a place directly across from the leader, musing it would give her the best advantage in terms of avoiding talking. But once she and Gary took their seats, she realized she had a bull's-eye view of the facilitator and already felt onstage.

Gary seemed to read her thoughts. "It'll be all right. I promise."

Molly must have called ahead and warned someone of Kendra's reticence to attend the group. She wouldn't put it past her.

Once the circle of six chairs filled, the room went quiet but for the hum of a fan.

"Welcome to Grief Angels. I'm Mary London, your facilitator. You are all here because you've lost someone near and dear to your hearts. That's hard. I've experienced grief myself, so I, too, know what it's like. As far as rules, confidentiality is the biggest concern. I will not share your journey with anyone, and although I can't control what you say to anyone outside this group, I'd ask you to do the same. Do any of you have rules we should consider?"

As Kendra perused the gathering, she noticed the discomfort of all the members. Some gazed into space, some stared at their hands, and some fidgeted. But no one spoke.

Mary continued. "Let me help. One concern is often respect. No one's journey is harder than anyone else's, so let's not say, *My loss is worse than yours. My friend's death was more traumatic.*" She scanned the room as group members nodded. "I'll be taking notes, just so I can remember things more easily.

"First, we'll do an icebreaker. I'd like you to describe yourself with an adjective that starts with the same letter as your first name, so for instance, I'll be Moderator Mary. Then, we will go around the room and each repeat everyone else's name. That will help us remember each other."

Mary glanced at a young woman to her right—slight with deep-set brown eyes, who wore a woebegone expression along with a boxy T-shirt, sweater, and baggy jeans.

"I'll be Chatty Cathy."

Mary chuckled. "Okay. Chatty Cathy." She wrote the name on her notepad.

Cathy nodded.

"So far, we have me, Moderator Mary, and Chatty Cathy." She looked to the next member.

A tear slid down Kendra's cheek, and she swallowed hard. She didn't think she could even utter her name without falling apart.

A thirty-something guy with thick, shoulder-length blond hair, striking blue eyes, and a muscular build with tattooed biceps said, "I'll be Bossy Brendan."

Mary remained stoic and repeated the names so far. Kendra wanted to laugh aloud.

The next guy was tall, maybe six-four, and broad. "This is awkward. My name is Nathan, and it's tricky to find an adjective that starts with N, other than *nice*."

Kendra burst out with, "Noble," before she realized it. But that was how he appeared to her. A decent, noble man. She sucked in a breath, realizing she'd overstepped. "Sorry," she mumbled.

But other group members nodded.

"You like it?" Mary asked.

Nathan shrugged. "Okay with me."

"I'll be Guilty Gary," the elderly gentleman next to Kendra said.

"I'll be Kayak Kendra."

And there they were: Moderator Mary, Chatty Cathy, Bossy Brendan, Noble Nathan, Guilty Gary, and Kayak Kendra.

"We will use these titles for this session only, just to help our brains remember. Now, I'd like us to get to know each other. If you can, tell us even a little about your story—about the loved one you've lost, how long it's been, mention their names and how they passed away. Maybe talk a bit about the emotions you felt at the time."

Each member went around the group, briefly telling their stories void of emotion. Chatty Cathy had lost her best friend, one she'd had since kindergarten, to drowning at the age of seventeen. Bossy Brendan had lost his forty-year-old brother to a motorcycle accident. Noble Nathan had lost his dad to Alzheimer's. He was the only member whose eyes welled with tears when he talked.

Kendra went fifth and surprised herself with a rote script even if she clasped her hands so tightly that they turned parchment white. "I lost my baby when he was only three months old and my husband four days later. It's been six months, and I still miss them terribly. Most days, I think I'm losing my mind."

Guilty Gary, sitting next to Kendra, spoke about the agony of losing his wife to a sudden stroke and being unable to know if she'd even recognized him in the end.

After the introductions, Moderator Mary changed the topic to self-care. Startled, Kendra realized, other than Molly nagging at her, she hadn't really considered caring for herself in the months since she'd lost her family. Sure, she went kayaking and did feel some relief after paddling furiously, but what simple acts did she do to make herself feel better? When she was out on the lake, she went with purpose. She didn't stop and take in her surroundings, watch the herons, or search for an eagle or a sandhill crane. She didn't notice turtles rise to the surface of the water. She didn't inhale the smells of the lake or appreciate the sun hitting her back and shoulders.

Long ago, life's simple pleasures had recharged and refreshed her. She'd lost all that.

Kendra left the group meeting with a sense of sadness but couldn't deny feeling a small sense of relief at the same time. Moderator Mary had been right when she spoke about not feeling alone, when she referred to the strength in sharing aloud, helping to "take the power of death away." Somehow, Kendra felt as if putting the words out into the world and acknowledging the truth gave the deaths of Joey and Joe less control over her rather than consuming her, as they had. Only time would tell.

As she drove home, she pondered a future for the first time in months.

CHAPTER TWO

KENDRA HIT THE REMOTE BUTTON FOR THE GARAGE door a quarter mile from home. She had a thing about zooming into the garage and promptly closing the door behind her, so she wasn't accosted by neighbors, curious about how she was faring. But as she rolled into the driveway, she noticed Molly's car parked on the apron. Her heartbeat calmed as she parked and walked to the front yard to greet her friend.

"Wow," she said. "You really don't trust me, do you?"

Molly blew her off. "I wanted to see you." She held up a bottle of wine. "Plus, we should celebrate. Tonight was the beginning of your new life!"

Kendra arched her brows. "That might be a stretch."

"Let's go out on the deck, and you can tell me all about it."

The women wandered through the back door, and Kendra pulled two wineglasses from the cabinet while Molly opened the bottle. Molly poured, and they strolled out to the deck, Kendra grabbing a bag of chips on the way. The evening was perfect—a light breeze, birds chatting in the trees, and even a humming-bird drinking from the feeder Kendra had attached to the family room window.

Moderator Mary's advice floated into her brain. *Notice. Care. Fill the hole.*

"Look how tiny that little bird is."

Molly smiled but stared at Kendra with concern.

Kendra sipped her wine and stared at her friend. "What?"

"I'm anxious to hear how things went tonight. You seem calm, so I'm trying to decide if that's good or bad. You're still a master at masking your feelings, and then after … well, you know, I've noticed different struggles. I'm wondering how you really are."

"I'm a ping-pong, honestly." Kendra relayed her hesitancy to go into the meeting. "Once I got inside, it was better. An older gentleman took me under his wing. Sad story. His wife died of a stroke. Just so unfair. They'd been married just short of fifty years and planned a huge party. He planned a funeral instead."

A ring of the doorbell interrupted their conversation, and Kendra peered toward the sound.

Molly patted Kendra's knee. "I'll get it. You sit."

Kendra's eyes followed Molly as she opened the front door in direct view of her chair.

"Hello."

"Hi, I'm Nathan Nash. I believe Kendra Kelly left this behind at church tonight." He held up a straw crossbody handbag. "I found it when I was putting away the folding chairs. I looked inside her wallet to find the address. I hope it's all right. I didn't think she'd want to be without it. Her cell phone, wallet …"

Nathan glanced over Molly's shoulder and peered at Kendra, whose eyes went wide. She set down her wineglass as heat climbed onto her cheeks.

"Oh, you're in the grief group," Molly said.

"Oh my goodness," Kendra said, hopping out of her chair and

hurrying inside. "I'm an idiot." She patted her pocket and began to babble. "I put my keys in my pants pocket when I changed after kayaking earlier. I take them out on the water, so I can lock up the house. And I never go out anymore, so I never take my purse. Thank you so much." She smacked a palm on her forehead, as if to knock in some sense.

Molly handed Kendra the bag.

"I didn't remove anything. It's all there." Nathan, indeed a noble man, proved deserving of his title.

"Of course," Kendra said. "Thank you so much."

Nathan nodded and shifted uncomfortably. "Well then, have a good evening. See you next week."

Kendra rattled on, profusely thanking him as he ambled back to his truck. Finally, Molly shushed her and dragged her back outside.

"He's cute," she said.

"Now, here's an idea: you go to grief group and hit on Nathan, and I'll stay home."

"You need to consider dating again," Molly said.

Kendra scowled at her friend. "You've lost your mind. Not only am I uninterested, but I'm also unwilling to risk losing everything. Once was enough." She lifted her glass to her lips and took a healthy slug.

Molly inhaled sharply. "You feel that way now—I get it—but you won't always."

"Goddamn it. Stop. No more." Kendra slammed her stemmed glass down on the table. It shattered into a million little pieces, wine trickling over the edge of the table.

She cursed and stormed inside, unaccustomed to such spikes in her mood. She forced a deep breath and went back outside. Molly was busy, mopping up the mess with a beach towel she'd found in the deck box.

Kendra laid a hand on Molly's shoulder. "Oh my God. I'm sorry. I shouldn't have lost my temper."

Molly stayed busy, cleaning, focused only on the task at hand.

"I'll clean up my own mess. I hate you hovering, treating me like an invalid—or worse, one of your unmanageable students."

"Sit," Molly commanded.

Kendra obeyed.

"It's been six months since you lost Joey and Joe. I've been with you every step of the way. I'm not a therapist. I'm your friend. But I know this: you've changed. It's not just that you're grieving. You've decided your life is over. I can't accept that. I want to see you through this, but I never know who I'm going to run into when I come over here. You're not yourself."

Kendra's eyes welled with tears. "Would you be?"

Molly plopped down next to her and held her hand. "No, but I'm not sure it's normal to have such abrupt personality changes."

"You think I'm losing it." She recalled hearing the baby's cries that morning. She recalled the sense of being watched continually. The kayak. The water thermos.

Molly might have a point.

Molly narrowed her gaze. "I don't know. What I do know is, I care about you. I want the best for you. I know what you've been through is profound. I can't imagine … but you've lost your spunk, your optimism. You used to be able to function."

"I functioned today. I showered, ate, and went to grief group. All by myself."

Molly eyed her suspiciously. "Did you write?"

Kendra studied the lake. "I tried."

"That's a step." Molly sank back in her chair. "I have an idea. Why don't I arrange a get-together with the girls? For coffee? You haven't seen them in ages. Maybe seeing everyone will give you a sense of normal."

Kendra set her head back and stared at the clouds. "Don't you see? My life isn't normal. I don't know if it ever will be again. I'm trying to put one foot in front of the other. It's not easy. Seeing people throws me off-balance. Tonight was hard enough, and I don't even know those people. If I have to see friends, they'll just remind me of everything I've lost. I have to do this on my own schedule. If I go to group once a week, that might be all I can muster."

"You're right. Going to group tonight was a huge step. I'm probably rushing you. Shit, how do I know? I could just set something up. Maybe out a week or two. It's just that I remember after Paul broke our engagement, you put up with my depression for a long time before you just laid it on me and told me I was stuck and had to move ahead. I recognize your situation is different, and you're entitled to grieve, but I want to see you recover and live again. Do you even feel alive?"

Kendra stretched her arms overhead, the knots in her neck practically strangling her. She shifted in her chair and took a sip of Molly's wine. "Not yet. But tonight, for the first time, I did think about doing something to take care of myself. And see? I just took a sip of your wine. Normally, I would never do that. I'd sit here, dying of thirst, too lazy to go inside but not bold enough to do what I wanted to do."

Molly laughed. "You're a fucking headcase."

"I know. Now, I'm going to get myself a glass. Open the chips. We need a snack."

By the time Kendra came back, she felt a shift in her mood. Joking with Molly was a small but welcome step. Maybe she was doing a little better.

"How are the nightmares?" Molly asked.

"Better," Kendra lied, unwilling to let Molly into more of her darkness.

"Thank goodness. So, what do you think? Should I set up something with the girls?"

Kendra shut her eyes and sighed, tired of Molly's nagging. "Go ahead."

Molly patted her arm. "You're going to be fine, you know."

Kendra scowled. *Fine.* Such a stupid word. People said it all the time, even when they weren't fine. And what did fine mean anyway? A garbage word, a catchall. If you slept all night, you were fine. If you tossed and turned till morning, you were fine. If you had a stomachache, you were still fine …

She caught herself before she went further down the rabbit hole. More than anything, Kendra wished she could control the ricocheting moods.

Mary's words revisited her mind. *Self-care.* What did that look like?

While Molly went on, droning about her summer tutoring gig, Kendra made a mental list. *Go kayaking. Listen to the birds. Gaze at the sky. Paddle on one side of the lake rather than down the middle. Be adventurous. Have a cup of tea. Or better yet, an ice cream cone.* She couldn't remember the last time she'd indulged in a treat.

"Molly," she shouted.

"What? What's wrong?"

"You're right. I'm not myself. I want to get better. This is a fucking nightmare, and I need to wake up and have it over." Tears poured down her cheeks, and the ache and pain she'd been carrying for six solid months returned with a vengeance. Huge, racking sobs consumed her. "All I do is cry."

"It's okay. It's going to be all right." Molly led her inside. "Maybe some rest would do you good. Why don't you wash your face, and I'll find your pajamas?"

Kendra nodded, hating these jags of desolation that consumed her from out of the blue.

Where is normal? Does it even exist anymore?

Not five minutes ago, an inkling of a simple, fun trip for ice cream had delighted her. Now, she needed to be put to bed.

Molly came up behind her and rested a hand on her shoulder as she finished washing her face.

Kendra turned and wrapped her arms around Molly's shoulders. "I'm scared."

"I know, honey. But you're making progress. Put things in perspective. You left the house today. You talked to strangers. This is serious work you're doing. I know I'm being tough on you, but you're being hard on yourself too. Let's slow down. One day at a time. And when that doesn't work, we'll slow things down even more. Want me to spend the night?"

Molly had spent many nights at the lake with Kendra.

"No. I need to be able to say I made it through a rough night without my crutch."

"Well then, I'll leave you to get some rest. Remember, I'm a phone call away."

Kendra gave Molly another long hug. "Thank you for putting up with me."

Molly kissed her on the cheek before leaving. "Sleep tight."

CHAPTER THREE

KENDRA ANSWERED MOLLY'S EARLY MORNING TEXT. *Feeling fine.*

She chuckled to herself after reading the missive. *Fine.* A new trigger word.

She brewed a strong cup of coffee and listened as the phone rang, the sound an annoying white noise. As a habit, Kendra didn't answer her phone. Not since the … well, not in a long time. Texting put more distance between her and the world and became a preference she'd adhered to over the past months. She used email for most everything else. Only the most urgent matters were handled with a call. Or a conversation with Molly.

Today, the phone rang with urgency. As soon as the ringing stopped, it started again, nagging and insistent. The incessant ringing interrupted her coffee and mindful time out on the deck. Now that she'd decided to focus—or at least try to concentrate—on self-care, Kendra was determined to thwart interruptions. She needed to silence the ringer.

Kendra spotted her purse on the coffee table, and a brief flash of a man standing inside her entry came to mind.

Did that really happen?

He was tall, maybe six-four, and broad, sandy-haired with … eyes. Of course he had eyes; she just couldn't recall much about them. Kind eyes. Yes, they were kind. He had spoken to her. The conversation wouldn't come back to her, but he was nice. Soft-spoken. Yes, he was nice. Oh my. Nice, noble Nathan. She rationalized her forgetfulness with the excuse of having had an overwhelming day.

She supposed her anxiety had peaked after attending the grief group last night, and she recalled the exhausted expression on Molly's face. Kendra could no longer deny that Molly had reached her breaking point. She hadn't said so, but Kendra had noticed the abbreviated sighs, the edge Molly fought to diminish in her tone as she spoke to Kendra about moving on and having a life in spite of the fact that Kendra had lost everything she loved.

Molly had shepherded Kendra through the funeral as if she were disabled. Unable to accomplish even the smallest task. All that was true but normal—in Kendra's mind. Then, Molly helped her find this house, helped her sell the one in town, packed her entire home, arranged the move, and settled Kendra in at the lake. Kendra had never experienced that kind of paralysis. She'd always been self-reliant and strong.

A part of her knew she wasn't herself, but she continually rationalized her reactions to be completely understandable.

Along with that, there couldn't possibly be a timetable for this kind of grief. She tried to think of a friend whom she'd accused of grieving too long after a death. She couldn't. So, how could anyone judge her?

If nothing else, Kendra acknowledged it was time to give Molly back her life. She owed her friend that much.

Kendra barely glanced at the phone as she silenced it, carried her tea outside, and drank up the morning sun. She reminded herself that today was about self-care first and then writing.

Self-care. How to begin?

Showering, eating, breathing a full breath, for a start.

Journaling, meditating. Those were harder steps.

Clouds rolled in, heavy gray mammoths that threatened to dump at least an inch or two of rain. The winds, as if on cue, joined the threatening chorus as it howled through the lake's valley. Kendra remained outside a few more minutes, releasing her hair from a ponytail and feeling the rush of air as it whipped tendrils of hair around her head. She inhaled the damp smell of humidity and the heaviness that accompanied it.

There, she'd done it. Spent time in the moment.

An unrelenting pounding interrupted the short revelry, and Kendra glanced over her shoulder at the window next to the front door. At the time she had purchased the house, she had loved the idea that you could see straight through the house from the front door to the lake, especially with the translucent windows on each side of the entry. Now, not so much. She detected movement—an adult holding something. Must be a delivery. She wished he hadn't spotted her through the window. Now, she had no choice but to open the door.

Kendra pulled open the heavy door and gaped at the man in front of her. Her mind became a web of confusion—the man's facial expressions, his mannerisms, his "Joe-ness," his presence from out of thin air. All of it sucked the breath from her lungs. Her legs wobbled, and white noise filled her head. Her mind disconnected from her body, and she involuntarily strode out onto the front porch. Reaching for his neck, she ran a finger down his throat, searching for a belt. He smiled at her. Joe's smile. Lost in the moment, she wrapped her arms around his neck and inhaled his scent.

He shifted back and forth—a total Joe move. A slight

nervousness accompanied his hesitant smile, and he eased himself away from her.

"Hi, I'm Jake Kelly. You must be my sister-in-law."

Kendra, glued to the spot, was unable to move. Instinctively, she wrapped her arms around her chest and rocked. She blinked back hot, stinging tears, embarrassed that she'd mistaken this man for her dead husband. But his gaze, it was Joe. She could barely stand.

The sky darkened further, and a clap of thunder sounded in the distance.

Jake laid a hand on her shoulder. "Look at you. Joe never told me how gorgeous you are. I'm so happy to finally meet you. You're family." His pleasant demeanor became suddenly pensive, and he furrowed his brows in the same fashion as Joe.

Kendra couldn't take her eyes off him. He had so much in common with Joe besides looks—the friendly babbling, the mannerisms, the pride and devotion that radiated from his eyes.

But Joe had said his brother was dead.

So, is this guy for real or a figment of my shaky imagination? Why would Joe tell me his brother was dead if he wasn't?

Kendra had known Joe was estranged from his family, so she didn't think much of it. More pointedly, she hadn't been thinking at all then.

"Who are you?" Kendra gripped the sides of the porch rocker and eased into the chair.

The man took another step back and raised his arms, as if his identity were obvious. "Jacob Kelly. Jake, Joe's brother. You all right?"

"Fine."

"I'm sorry I didn't make it to the funeral. I didn't learn about Joe's death until a short time ago. When he hadn't called, I was concerned. I saw his obituary in the paper. What a shock. I'm sorry I wasn't here."

"But how …"

"Did I find you? I had your old address, and the new owner told me you had moved out here. A little Googling here and there, and, well, here I am." He glanced around. "I've never been to Michigan. It's pretty this time of year. We don't have much change of weather in California."

Finally, the building clouds unleashed torrents of rain. With blowing winds assaulting her, Kendra rushed inside, leaving the door wide open. Boneless, she slithered down the wall onto the floor.

Jake followed and gazed absently around the house. "Can I get you some water?"

Kendra pointed to the kitchen.

Jake returned moments later and delivered a glass of cool water to Kendra. She sipped, blinked, studied Jake, and then shook her head.

"You're surprised to see me."

"This isn't a good time," Kendra finally uttered and tried unsuccessfully to stand.

Jake glanced at Kendra's clothing, forcing Kendra to do the same. No, she didn't look as if she were going off to an appointment or something.

"I, um, have to work. We'll do this another time."

"Let me help you to a chair." He put a hand beneath Kendra's elbow, eased her up, and guided her to the sofa.

She leaned back and covered her face with her hands. Her ribs felt as if they'd snapped, like dead wood from a tree. She clutched her chest.

"You're pale. You're in pain. Should I call a doctor?"

Kendra shook her head in disbelief. "Please go."

"I tried calling this morning. Joe had given me your number a couple of years ago and made me promise never to use it unless there was a dire emergency. I figured his death, even though it was a while ago and no one bothered to let me know, well, I decided this was a tragedy and you might need some support. I even left you a voice mail. I didn't mean to startle you or show up unannounced, but when you didn't answer, I thought I'd take a chance and stop by." He hesitated, stepped toward the door, then stopped, and gazed at Kendra. "My number is on the voice mail. Call me. I really want to talk. Get to know you. Maybe share some memories of Joe. Sorry I came at a bad time." Jake dipped his head to the floor after setting something on the mantel and left, closing the door behind him.

Kendra clasped her fists to her chest and waited for the cramping to subside. Her breathing finally slowed, and the trembling in her fingers evened out a bit. Her mind shot from scene to feeling, feeling to scene. Jake. Joe's brother. Joe had told her Jake died a long time ago. Was this man a ghost? An impostor? She *was* losing it.

Kendra leaned forward. Combed the room for a sign. The unlocked door was a clue that he had been here along with—her gaze traveled from the entrance—the wet footprints on the wood flooring. Kendra shuffled over to a footprint, measuring her bare foot alongside it, just to be sure. No, this print was bigger than hers and had left the mark of a shoe bottom.

Relieved she hadn't imagined the stranger, Kendra took stock. This man, Jake, had been here. He'd claimed to be Joe's brother. She didn't have reason to believe him other than the fact that he was Joe's twin in every possible way. If she were sane and able to think rationally, she might trust he was telling the truth. Then again, he might not be.

A teensy nook in her brain admitted the scene was like something from an episode of *The Twilight Zone*. She knew her PTSD had kicked into overdrive the past day or so. She questioned imagining all kinds of things. The visit from the man last night, the visit from this stranger this morning. And here she'd thought she was making progress. Molly had suggested she was doing better, and maybe Kendra had believed her because that was what she wanted to hear. Maybe she was losing her mind all over again.

The glimmer of a memory came back to her. Jake had placed something on the mantel before leaving. Kendra squinted as she inched over to the fireplace. Sure enough, she found something. A photograph of two young men in their teens. Kendra studied the image hard, sure to within an inch of her life that the guy on the right was Joe. Photoshop? A ruse? She hated that she could no longer trust herself.

She couldn't afford to retreat to the horrible, dark hole that sucked her in and refused to let her out. It would consume her if she did. It almost had. It still could.

Slowly, questions, confusion, and anger rose to the surface. She hated how Joe had left without answers. She loathed his abrupt absence, loathed being alone and adrift, grieving the two most important people in her world. Hated that she couldn't blink and have the horror of the past six months disappear.

CHAPTER FOUR

Although Kendra hated to bother Molly, she craved grounding. But rather than call and set off alarms, she sent an innocuous text.

Someone dropped by this morning.

The purse rescuer, Nathan? What did he want?

No, not him. Want to stop by after work today? Might stop raining. We could sit on the deck and have happy hour. I can tell you about it then.

Be there by 5.

As the pounding in Kendra's ears relented, a thought came to her. *Do something. Prove to Molly that you can function outside of her watchful eye.*

Plus, Kendra couldn't stand thinking of herself sitting in a puddle on the floor. Why everything continued to reduce her to melting was starting to piss her off.

She marched into the office and woke the computer. Might as well Google Jake Kelly. Joe had shared how he had grown up in

San Diego and told her Jake had passed away from a drug over-
dose when he was in his teens.

*What the hell is going on? Jake was supposed to be dead, but he
showed up on her doorstep?*

She searched Jake's name and that location first, and then she
paused for a moment before adding the word *obituary*. Nothing.
She ran a search without a location. Hundreds of Jake Kellys lived
in the States but not a single obituary even remotely similar to
Joe's brother—neither Jake's age nor the disastrous circumstances
under which Jake had reportedly died.

Would Joe have lied to her? Why?

There had to be a reasonable explanation—Jake was the one
who was lying.

The search continued. Finding a specific Kelly in San Diego
proved similar to searching for a Starbucks receipt from ten years
ago.

Fifteen minutes later, an article caught her eye. In 2006, Joseph
David Kelly Sr. and his wife of thirty years, Sarah, had been found
brutally murdered in their home but in La Jolla, not San Diego.
Their son Jacob, fifteen years old at the time, was listed as the
chief suspect. Reportedly, Jacob had been treated for emotional
issues since first grade and was a suspected illegal drug user—
the perfect combination for a psychotic episode. After a lengthy
trial, the Kellys' son was acquitted. Sarah Kelly's mother, Marcy
Walker, assumed custody of her troubled grandson. Their older
son, Joseph David Kelly, a college sophomore—and most likely
Kendra's future husband—hadn't attended the trial.

Kendra's mouth hung open in disbelief. Tingles shot down her
arms. This explained so much. She blew out a jagged puff of air.
So many details matched her husband's life. His parents' names,
his brother's name, the college Joe had attended. Joe's age at the
time of his parents' deaths.

Is this my Joe? How?

In a split second, Kendra raced out the door, grabbing her purse and keys almost as an afterthought. She headed to the nearest town, which was nothing more than a Stop sign less than five miles from the lake, and hurried into the former gas station—now a shabby local liquor store—where she marched up to the counter and purchased a pack of cigarettes.

Halfway out of the place, she headed back to the counter and snatched a lighter from a rack next to the register. She handed over a twenty-dollar bill, outstretched her hand for change, and motored on home.

As if overcome by alien forces, Kendra lifted a discarded soup can from the garbage bin and took it to the deck with her. She kicked up her feet and lit up the first cigarette she'd smoked since her dad's death.

With the first drag, she felt her mind clear. If she backed away from this morning's discovery about Joe's family, she could be more objective. A rush of energy zipped down her spine—maybe a good sign. She hadn't felt anything other than numb for months.

Kendra stubbed out her cigarette and marched to the garage. She grabbed her gardening gloves and the weed puller. Columns formed in her mind. One listed possible explanations for Joe's suicide, considering the recent research to be true. Another column measured reasons Joe might have omitted his past. Kendra made a point to divorce emotion from reason at this juncture and assumed a researcher's stance. She yanked out the soft weeds and then thrust the puller in the ground with such force that she uprooted some iris bulbs.

Joe had been distraught after Joey's death. If he had already suffered the tragedy of his parents' murders, he might have been a bit like Kendra, believing he didn't deserve happiness. Maybe he'd worried he'd be a bad father, and fear had turned into reality. Maybe he could no longer stand to face Kendra, the mother of his child, the woman who had been in charge when Joey died.

She stormed to the deck, lit a cigarette, and inhaled a stiff drag. This thought was tough to swallow. Her mind switched to easier possibilities as she walked back to her flower garden.

Maybe Joe had neglected to share his past because he was ashamed. Maybe he supposed Kendra wouldn't want to be involved with someone with such a troubled past. Maybe he had been too sad to talk about it. She was certainly too sad to talk about Joe's and Joey's deaths. Maybe a similar devastation had dragged down Joe for years. His parents' murders weren't natural deaths, like her parents. Maybe he felt guilty about his parents' deaths even though he wasn't responsible. Maybe he'd worried she'd hold him responsible. She worried her friends blamed her for Joey's death—she had been a bad mother, delinquent in her duties.

As Kendra crushed her second cigarette on the edge of a railroad tie and grasped the weed puller in her hand, reality crept in. Joe had lied. True, she could turn the facts around and give him an out, say her husband had omitted his past for just cause. He had been mortified, devastated, and not wanted to revisit that horrible time in his history. Lord knew, she had shrouded herself in *if onlys* since the loss of Joey and Joe. Joe must have done the same. Maybe this explained his suicide. After Joey's death, maybe Joe had guessed he didn't deserve happiness, only tragedy. She pitched the weed puller across the lawn, where it stuck into the grass like a dagger.

She could hardly wrap her head around the fact that Joe had kept so much from her. Part of her wanted to deny his secretiveness, but it was difficult to refute this evidence. Another part of her fumed at the edges and left her guilt-stricken. If she had known, she might have been able to help. If she had known, she could have prevented his suicide. Tears rushed down her cheeks like a river.

Her chest ached. Her fingernails ached, for God's sake. Her head pounded, and a knot tightened in her stomach. She screamed so shrilly that she scanned the landscape for a response.

You son of a bitch, how could you?

He could have at least been honest with her. She tried to tamp the sparking anger, but the flame caught fire. How dare he leave! How dare he cop out after Joey died! He'd promised to be with her through thick and thin, yet when the worst possible loss devastated them, he had taken the easy way out. He'd lied before their marriage. He'd said he trusted her implicitly. In the face of all these secrets though, Kendra had to face facts. He had not.

She ground her teeth, stormed across the lawn, and snatched the discarded tool. Weeds were everywhere.

Maybe none of this was true. Maybe this Jake guy was an impostor. Maybe the sky wasn't blue. She glanced up just to check. Maybe orange was a Christmas color.

She desperately needed Joe to come back to life, even for fifteen minutes, and straighten out this confusion. But she was a mystery author. She did this for a living.

She'd solve this on her own.

Kendra sat down on the lawn and held her head in her hands. After a good five minutes, she rose and strode to the deck, picking up her pack of smokes from the steps.

Kicking her feet up onto the table, Kendra smoked two more cigarettes and then headed inside.

She wouldn't have judged Joe if he'd chosen to confide in her. She wouldn't have avoided a relationship with him. In spite of what others thought—tragedy was as contagious as the flu—Kendra knew in her heart that tragedy was part of life.

So, why did she feel her life was over? Why did desperation fill her every minute of every day? Why did tears consume her? Sap her energy? Leave her as a shell of her former self?

She'd never move on. Hell, no one would ever want her. Her guilt weighed more than a camel on safari. The shame she carried? Insurmountable. She'd had one job. Watch over her baby and keep him safe. Joey wasn't even mobile, and he had no blankets in his bed, just a sleep sack on. She'd followed every possible safety protocol, and despite all her best efforts, she couldn't keep him alive. She deserved every year of penance. She was a failure in every conceivable way.

By the time five o'clock rolled around, Kendra had somehow managed to set snacks on the table along with a good bottle of cabernet and two glasses. The deck heater blew warm air near the seating area, taking the sudden chill off the late afternoon. Kendra hid her makeshift ashtray in the shrubbery, preferring to keep this slight regression from Molly. As she lifted her head from the bushes, she heard Molly's voice.

"Lose something?"

Kendra's heart stuttered. "No, just … playing in the yard."

Molly raised her eyebrows and shot a questioning eye at Kendra but continued up the steps to the deck. "Thank God. Food. And wine. I didn't even have time to eat lunch today, just wolfed down a protein bar during my prep."

They toasted and sipped their wine. "Mm, nice choice," Molly said.

Molly's head lolled back in her chair as she tipped her face to the sky. "This place is heaven. We lucked out, finding it." She turned to face Kendra. "Are you okay? You're pale. You look a little lost."

Kendra hated how well Molly knew her. "Just fitting pieces together. You know how confused I get since, well, you know …"

"Did you write today?"

"Yes, if thinking about writing is writing."

Molly chuckled. "We call that the prewriting stage at school."

"That."

Molly sat back and munched on some crackers, thinking and

clearly choosing her next words carefully. "I had the weirdest dream the other night."

Kendra shot her a puzzled look. "And?"

"You were in a therapist's office."

Kendra's head snapped around. "What kind of therapist?"

"The regular kind. You know, lady in a chair, you on a couch. Her taking notes, you telling her how you really feel. So weird though. The therapist looked like your mom."

Kendra's arms prickled. The thought of a therapist scared her shitless. A professional would have her locked up in a heartbeat. "I'm off-balance, no matter what I do, where I go. I don't fit anywhere. I mean, here I am, at this grief group with all these regular people who've lost loved ones, just like me, but not a single person lost both members of their family and by no means did anyone lose a family member to suicide."

"If you wanted, you could go to a suicide group. Would that make you feel better?"

"God, no."

"There you go."

"Something else happened."

"Are you changing the subject because you're uncomfortable? You do that, you know."

"Drink your wine and be quiet," Kendra insisted. "This guy showed up today ..."

Kendra continued to relay the story of Jake's visit and her subsequent research.

"He could be a conman, looking for money, or maybe a cousin or something."

"He might be the real deal too."

Molly sipped her wine and nodded. "He might. I say *Scarlett O'Hara* him. Think about that another day."

"Don't you want to know why Joe killed himself?"

Molly's face crumpled. "How can you ever know? Sometimes, it's best to let things go."

"Doesn't this Jake guy showing up make you question Joe?"

Molly bit her bottom lip with fury. "I want this to be over for you."

"I need answers." Kendra pursed her lips.

So often, she kept secrets from Molly. If she had to guess, she'd say she only revealed about half of her days to Molly. She coated most days with fresh paint, sharing acceptable experiences but not how she'd melted on the floor when Jake appeared or the number of times her body had disconnected from her mind. While Molly had witnessed Kendra at her worst, she didn't know what a train wreck Kendra still was. To tell her or not, that was the question.

Faced with admitting a shaky grasp on sanity or continuing to pretend that she was improving even though times were still rough remained a quandary. Kendra couldn't grasp reality. Not full-time. Maybe not even part-time.

Am I getting back to normal? Am I on schedule?

Whoever had decided a year was the magic space of time within which the bereaved would recover seemed awfully optimistic. The thought that she only had six more months to move past her grief seemed an impossible task.

Molly interrupted her. "Hey, you in there?"

"Just wondering how long I'll be a mess."

"Hopefully, not much longer."

CHAPTER FIVE

EVERY TIME KENDRA PICTURED JOE, SHE ENVISIONED HIS lifeless body. The flashbacks struck like lightning, and no matter what tactics she used, the terrors ceased to leave her alone.

He'd left for work.
I tried to write … to block out the world.
Rumble of the garbage truck …
Shit.
Trash day.
Hurry.
Joe, her husband and best friend, dangled from a belt, lifeless, in his freshly pressed gray suit, starched white dress shirt, and polished oxfords.
Grabbed a utility knife. Snapped up the blade. Climbed onto SUV roof.
"You're going to be all right. You're going to be fine."

Sliced through shiny belt leather. He toppled like cement rag doll. Slid to icy concrete floor. My head throbbed.

Stark contrast of an SUV's gleaming rims against the weight of a slack body.

No!

Dead weight.

Forced breath.

Tears. Horror.

Inched out from underneath. Rolled him onto his back.

Welt around neck.

"You'll be okay, baby. Stay with me."

Straddled and pumped his chest. Blocked his nose. Forced air into his lungs.

Purple lips. Swollen head. Dusky as chalk.

"Breathe, dammit!"

Pumped fisted hands on his breastbone. Blew air into him again.

"Wake up. Not you too."

How she'd finally managed to call 911, she had no idea.

As if former training had kicked in, she'd realized she couldn't breathe life into Joe, couldn't bring him back. She needed help. Medical help. No. A miracle.

While sirens wailed in the distance, she could only sit with her husband, hold his head in her lap, clutch him to her chest, and wail, "I love you. Don't leave me."

Frozen to the concrete floor, a chill traveled up her back and down her extremities, she'd been overtaken by shock and impossibility. She heard faint cries, not recognizing them as her own.

She had just dialed 911 four days ago. Not about Joe. Even a week ago, he'd been the happiest man on earth. In fact, up until then, the couple had lived a year of pure bliss.

Turned out, all those expressions were true. Life turns on a dime. Life is short. Happiness is fleeting.

A fireman led her into the house, taking charge. He knelt in front of her, calmly repeating instructions, "Inhale through your nose and exhale through your mouth." He modeled the behavior.

Breathing was no longer voluntary. It required effort. And a coach.

Kendra had no desire to breathe. Joe could leave her, but he never would have left his son.

Why breathe when your life is over?

The firefighter refused to give up. He lifted her chin, directed Kendra to lock eyes with him, breathe with him. Over and over again until the room stopped spinning and her feet hit the floor in a perceptible sense.

After several long minutes, gravity met matter. Solid ground. But her brain refused to function. As soon as she took her eyes off the man, she held her breath. Dizzy, disoriented, a heart battering against tattered ribs.

No, there was no one he could call. Mom and Dad had been gone a long time. No, there was nothing more he could do for her. No, she didn't care if they took Joe's body to the local funeral home.

No. No. No.

Her life was one big no.

No, I'm not married.

No, I don't have a child.

Chills consumed Kendra as she struggled to push down the flashback. The peace she'd treasured seconds ago turned out to be as fleeting as the cover of walnut leaves on her deck. Kendra watched as they blew away with the next gust of wind.

Back inside, she checked her phone. Three messages from Jean, her agent. In the midst of an otherwise awful day, she placed a FaceTime call. Jean picked up on the third ring. Surprising since she hated FT calls as much as Kendra. But when they gave in to their need to see each other, it always lifted both their spirits. Jean had one of the most pleasant voices and a nice smile to go along with it. Kendra had titled her as Fairy Godmother since they'd met three years ago at a writing conference in California. Jean had a way about her. Honest, tough, but compassionate at the same time.

"If you've been trying to reach me this morning, it must be something serious," Kendra said.

"Nothing other than the usual. You've been on my mind, and I feel better when I see your face. I like to keep track of you, make sure you're eating and not losing yourself in the blackness of life."

"Actually, it's been a rough couple of weeks."

"Tell me," Jean said.

"There's just so much craziness going on." Kendra came clean—explained the hallucinations, the fact that she constantly, maybe obsessively, looked over her shoulder with the foreboding sense she was being watched. The depth of her grief, the flashbacks, the anger, the forgetfulness. And she also mentioned Jake and grief group.

"Let's take a step back," Jean offered. "Part of what you're going through is completely normal. New moms are always on alert for their baby's cries. The fact that you think you hear Joey is simply a leftover from having an infant. And maybe the sounds you're hearing are real too. A neighbor perhaps or the fact that you're in a completely new environment and you're unaccustomed to the sounds of living in the country. It's a pretty remote spot, right? You've mentioned this older guy, Russ, before. He sounds like one of those oddballs without boundaries. Those folks are unnerving. They make your skin crawl. No wonder you feel a bit frenzied. It's a ton to get used to."

"Do you really think so? You'd tell me if you thought I was losing my mind, wouldn't you?"

"I worked with a number of patients who experienced anxiety and depression after a significant loss. If this persists, I'd recommend an antidepressant, just to take the edge off."

"Sometimes I forget you were a nurse and a police dispatcher before you became a literary agent. You have such a vast range of knowledge and experience. In any case, I always feel so much more normal after we talk."

"I'm glad," Jean said. "Now, tell me how often you're getting out in the world. I certainly understand the inkling to hide, but you also need to push yourself. You'd be surprised what a positive impact interacting, even if it's only on a superficial level, has on helping you move forward. You don't want to become housebound on top of everything else. Remember that class you taught at the conference a few years back?"

"Oh my goodness. The one about the loneliness trap that writers experience. How we become insulated and fearful when we spend too much time alone."

"Maybe watch the TED Talk again."

Kendra exhaled. "Great idea. You know what I'd like? If you moved in with me and reminded me how to do life."

Jean chuckled. "You know how to do life, sweetie. You've just lost your way for a bit. Trust me, it'll all come back to you. Just remember to force yourself out of your comfort zone. I know it's impossible to know what that means right now, but inch forward. Doesn't have to be big leaps. Little steps are fine."

After they ended the call, Kendra decided to ingrain an image of Jean in her brain. Her super-short gray hair and dark brown eyes that sparkled like agates. Not only did Jean have a smile that lit up a room, but she also had an impish quality about her that let you know she was both fun and wicked smart. Seeing Jean's face was like healing medicine. Maybe she'd even print out a photo and tape it on the edge of her desktop as a reminder or a kind of touchstone to center herself when she felt cliff-edged frightened.

Whatever works.

CHAPTER SIX

ENDRA KNEW SHE STRUGGLED WITH A SERIOUS CASE of regression. The grief group sounded great in theory, but in reality, it caused Kendra's PTSD to surface in old and disturbing ways.

In the hour before she had to leave for group, she'd heard a voice say, "No belts!" and shaken her head, as if she were trying to loosen water from her ear.

She struggled to put one foot in front of the other to enter the building and fought unsuccessfully to find something distracting to focus upon. Irony oozed—grief group met in the basement of a local church. She'd long ago given up on God. He'd delivered her nothing but loss for quite some time—since her parents' deaths in fact. Yet here she was supposed to heal, move on, and return to living.

Kendra forced herself to descend the stairs, held the railing for support, then grabbed a metal folding chair from the rack, and joined the circle. The basement smelled even danker than last time, the musty air somehow melding with the late August humidity. The starkness of her surroundings felt more like a place to crumple and wither rather than sprout new wings.

She spotted Gary and offered him a wan smile, and then she wandered over to the coffee station, needing something solid to hold on to. Mary had either lost count, or new members were showing up tonight. Two of them, according to Kendra's calculations of the extra chairs.

Trapped like a caged animal, Kendra darted her eyes to the staircase. Her legs went to jelly. The thought of having to repeat her story filled her throat with bile. She couldn't run. Didn't know how to hide in plain sight.

She glanced up and saw two new pairs of eyes upon her. Kendra dipped her head in shame. No one else's loved one had chosen to leave them. None of their family members had given them the finger and hanged themselves in the garage, where they would be certain to find them. No one had lost their precious infant, their single hope for a bright future.

If only she could signal Molly, like she had in the dating days. Hit a previously written text that read *help* and receive an emergency phone call seconds later.

As the thought left her, Moderator Mary brought the meeting to order. She explained that the two new members had been members of another group, but their moderator had a family emergency out of state, and so they were offered the option to join this group. Hurrah for them.

Mary went through the same damn elementary school icebreaker, asking everyone to give their name and a brief description of their loss.

Fuck Mary.

Gary leaned over and brushed Kendra's arm. When she glanced up, he winked and whispered, "It'll get easier each time you have to tell the story."

What the hell does he know?

The first new guy decided he'd be Terrified Trevor. He'd lost his younger sister to a brain tumor. He broke down while describing her last moments, and Kendra found herself tearing up as well. It was new to her—tearing up around someone else's loss. She felt hopeful. Maybe her heart hadn't totally blackened after all.

The second new member named himself Just Josh. "When I lost my Joseph, my world ended. And I can't stand the comments from friends and family. How the hell do they know what I'm going through?" His anger simmered, his cheeks glowing crimson. He stayed quiet, but a slow burn seemed to consume him.

After solid understanding in the form of universal nods of support, a litany of callous comments spilled out from all the members. They could have pinned a giant poster board on the wall and filled it within minutes.

"God has a new angel now."

"Your sister earned her wings."

"He's in a better place."

"There's a reason for everything."

"At least she's no longer suffering."

"You need to move on after all this time."

"This too shall pass …"

Mary interrupted after a few minutes. "We have this in common. No matter who we've lost, we have anger to protect our hurt. The depth of grief could consume us if we didn't have distractions from our fury. Anger provides us a safe place, somewhere to just get pissed off, to shield us from the depth of our tragedy. A good coping skill when the sadness becomes overwhelming. Let's take a few minutes and go over our homework from last week. How did everyone do with self-care?"

Kendra toyed with her bracelet, surprised Mary had led the conversation in a different direction. While Mary was spot on about anger proving to be a great outlet, Kendra wasn't ready to let go of the topic. Up until this moment, she hadn't allowed but a tinge of anger to take hold, and she was ready.

She thought about God. He'd dealt her an impossibly steep mountain to climb, forcing her to deal with the loss of her entire family at once. The idea that she could start over and simply replace Joey and Joe—the pressure she felt from Molly to "move forward"—was ludicrous. A knot formed in her stomach and radiated to her extremities; she fisted her hands and tensed her lips into a thin line. As much as the anger was uncomfortable, it also proved to be reassuring. She had the capacity for more than the undertow of grief. She wanted to sit with it for a while. Savor it.

Her mind wandered while the rest of the group discussed the self-care steps they had taken during the week. Kendra thought about the vows she'd taken eighteen months previous when she and Joe married. He'd promised to stand by her in sickness and health, yet when Joey died, Joe chose death over his vows, ultimately abandoning Kendra when she needed him most. He'd deserted her in her time of need. White heat ran from her toes to her head. She was beyond angry with him.

What would she do with this rage?

She knew, more than expected, that he'd lied to her about his past. *Why? What was his motivation?*

She'd have to figure that out if she ever wanted closure. Moving on didn't seem possible. Maybe that was where everyone had misled her. She couldn't imagine carrying on with life after her loss. To desert her past was like saying Joe and Joey didn't matter, like committing an act of treason. Although she hadn't had them long, the promise of having them forever had been taken away. Her entire future erased. How the hell would she resolve that and move forward? She'd have to unearth Joe's secrets. Or shove them deep underground.

"Kendra?" She heard her name from the periphery. As if in a

dream. She heard her name once more before she realized someone was speaking to her.

She looked up and blinked, reestablishing herself in the room. "We were sharing self-care from last week."

Kendra cleared her throat. "I found it helpful to think about what I used to do before I lost my family, things that helped me center myself in times of stress. I used to take moments of mindfulness and just be in my surroundings. I tried it this week. It was so different than how I'd operated since my loss. I have to admit, it calmed me, made me feel closer to normal than I'd felt in a very long time."

"This week, I'd like to suggest another tip to add to everyone's grief arsenal toolbox," Mary said. "I encourage you to seek good company this week. We all have those friends who are tired of seeing us grieve, those who expect us to *get over it*. Let's all make an effort to embrace some old friends we haven't seen in some time or make new ones. People who are comfortable letting us sit with our grief. Those who aren't trying to push us in one direction or another. Sometimes, we need company without expectations."

Kendra's resentment fueled her. "Easier said than done."

As she glanced around the circle, she noticed heads bobbing in agreement.

"True," Mary said, "but still a valuable exercise. It might be as simple as going to a coffee shop and interacting with the barista. A light conversation with someone who doesn't know your situation. Someone who treats you as a normal individual and chats about something other than loss—the weather, a recent read, something light and breezy. Can we all sign up for that?"

Hesitation hovered over the group.

Finally, Gary offered to give it a whirl. "I can go to the hardware store and chat with all the retired guys who work there. I haven't been there since Sally died. If there was ever a group of guys who knew how to shoot the shit, they do." He chuckled as he thought about it.

Mary leaned forward and smiled at Gary. "No pressure on making a decision about how to do the exercise, but I love your idea, Gary. It's exactly what I'm suggesting. Either something you used to do and have abandoned since your loss, or something entirely new."

"Can we go back to anger for a minute?" Kendra surprised herself with her forthrightness.

Mary nodded.

"Thank you for understanding," Kendra said. "The thing is … my husband died four days after my son. I'm still shell-shocked, and it's been six months. I'm barely able to do my job. I sold the house and escaped my physical hell, but I can't seem to move on or forward—whatever that means … and as we spoke of earlier tonight, I recognize I haven't allowed myself to be angry. Tonight, I'm furious."

She expected mouths to fall open or gasps from her fellow grievers, but she only saw heads dipping with understanding. She relished their compassion. Nevertheless, the hair on Kendra's arms rose as a chill traveled through her limbs. She was always cold. Always.

Nathan, who Kendra now knew was a firefighter along with being a purse savior, spoke next. "Just waking up every day is a challenge. I'm still a mess after losing my dad, and I knew his death was imminent. Frankly, I'm pissed off most of the time. Why my dad? You're an incredibly strong woman to have made it through the last six months. I don't know if I would have had your strength."

Kendra's face scrunched with confusion. "It doesn't take strength to wake up each day. In fact, I sometimes see it as a sign of weakness. I'm still here, and they're gone. In some ways, I see myself as a coward. If I were stronger, I'd have checked out by now."

"Suicide doesn't require strength. It's an act of weakness," Just Josh spat.

"Or desperation," offered Brendan.

"Suicide?" Kendra asked.

"Yes," Just Josh said. "Only the most desperate take their own lives."

Kendra shifted in her chair. "It's awkward for me, talking about suicide."

"Then, maybe *you* shouldn't be here," Josh added. "My partner killed himself. I'm going to talk about it."

Gary leaned forward. "I'm not a fan of suicide, but there are a few people I've wanted to take out in my lifetime."

Mary stepped in as people adjusted uncomfortably in their chairs, not because of Josh's disclosure, but because of the strength of his spite, directed toward Kendra. "We're getting off track, and it's time to close for tonight. Would you like to add anything, Kendra?"

"Maybe next week. But thank you for listening. For not making me feel stupid for feeling the way I do. For letting me share my anger. None of you swept in and tried to talk me out of being mad. I just need you to be with me, and you are." Kendra folded her arms over her chest as exhaustion engulfed her.

Nathan offered to rack the chairs after the meeting. Kendra escaped to the restroom and threw water on her face—she needed to change gears before driving home. As she exited the ladies' room, Nathan stood near the door and held it open.

"I know I'm being presumptuous, but would you like to go for coffee?" he asked.

"I'm exhausted, but thanks. And thanks again for returning my purse. I can't believe I still have a hard time keeping track of things." Kendra bit her lip. "I'd better head home before I forget where I live."

"Actually, I'm thinking about a quick beer instead. I can drive and then drop you off back here if you'd like."

Kendra's impulse to beg off was replaced by a desire for companionship. After revealing more than expected, she realized she didn't want to be alone. And spending time with someone who understood through experience held a ton of appeal. Plus, her homework would be done way early.

"I have no idea what's close by. I've lived in the area for six months, but I don't go out."

Nathan nodded. "I'm pretty familiar. There's a place close by. Stick with me."

Kendra decided to follow Nathan rather than drive with him. Getting into a near stranger's car seemed a bit risky. She trailed behind him down the county road for about two miles, where he turned right and parked along the main drag.

Kendra had passed through the little burg of Clinton once before. A homey little town, which still sported a local movie theater and an old-fashioned ice cream shop. It also had a neighborhood bar. Nathan led her inside.

Immediately, she loved the rustic atmosphere of the place—the long oak bar, the wood-fired pizzas, patrons dressed in jeans and T-shirts or suits and ties in a city where anything went. The place was obviously a town fixture.

Nathan motioned to two empty stools wedged between other customers, and they snagged them quickly, before someone else could.

"I can't talk any more about death or my personal losses," Kendra warned, "so we'll have to discuss the weather, like Mary suggested."

Kendra noticed the brief lift of Nathan's eyebrows. He proved to be just as observant as she'd suspected. As she took a closer look at him—the military-style close-cropped blond hair, striking blue eyes, and biceps bunching out of his short-sleeved shirt—she decided that even if she hadn't known, she would have easily guessed his occupation.

They ordered two beers, and Nathan offered the next bit of conversation. "Supposed to be a milder winter since we've had such an unseasonably warm August."

"Usually, the leaves begin to turn in August, but they don't even suggest changing yet."

Nathan chuckled. "Weather is a tough topic, maybe more so when you plan to talk about it. Do we sound stilted or what? Can I ask what you do for a living?"

Kendra went on to tell him about her writing, humbly describing the success of her debut novel, the pressure to write the next book in the midst of loss, and a recent move. She glossed over the hard parts.

An intuitive man, Nathan changed the subject. "So, I had this call today," he started. "Believe it or not, all those stories about people calling the fire department for nonsensical reasons are true."

He gestured to the bartender to bring Kendra another beer. Another beer and any semblance of normal were precisely what she needed. She rested her elbows on the bar, settled her gaze on Nathan, and listened intently to his story.

"We were called to rescue a bird from a tree."

Kendra couldn't resist leaning toward him, surprise widening her eyes.

"You're right," he joked. "Birds are commonly found in trees. But this poor turkey vulture had gotten caught in fishing line, out on that little lake west of town. Pierce Lake, actually."

Kendra listened with her chin on her fist, rapt by his story.

"He was trapped upside down, sad fella." Nathan's eyes glazed over with tears.

Kendra narrowed her eyes. "Are you crying?"

Nathan wiped his eyes with his fists. "Something in my eye," he said.

"Were you able to get him down?"

His eyes sparkled with humor, aided by tears. "We positioned a ladder but couldn't reach him because of the way he was tangled in the tree. Had to call in a ladder truck. When we got the truck situated, a Humane Society worker went up with me. We cut the tangled line and carried the poor frightened guy back to solid ground. The Humane Society will check him out and then release him back into the wild."

"You're an animal lover." *And a softie*, she thought.

He swiped a tear from his eye. "Anytime I save a living thing, I call it a win."

Truer words had never been spoken. In the midst of feeling like a colossal failure at every turn, Kendra admired his outlook. Maybe she should spend a little more time with Nathan. He seemed to understand more than Molly and more than anyone else she'd had occasion to talk to in the past six months.

All those false sympathies and the idiotic advice from the well-meaning supporters drove her nuts. Her friends still had children and spouses. They had no clue what she was going through, and they certainly didn't want to stare down the same possibilities. They thought of her as a pariah, as if they could catch loss from being in close proximity. Kendra was far better off in a room of strangers than she was with friends.

She wasn't sure of much these days, but of that she was definite.

"I hope you don't mind me changing the subject, but I want you to know I'm sorry for your losses. You lost your son. And your husband died too." He shook his head, as if overcome by the depth of her losses.

"A suicide," Kendra blurted out before she had a chance to swallow the words.

Nathan stopped and turned toward her. He gazed into her eyes, which glistened with tears. "That's just not fair."

Kendra lifted her brows. "No, it's certainly not. I already felt guilty enough about Joey, but then Joe hanged himself days later. I'd missed all the signs. He didn't seem any more despondent than me. He didn't let me know he wanted to die. I mean, I had the same fleeting thought. It seemed as if my life had ended with Joey's, but I held on. I held on to Joe. For Joe. I'd thought we were strong enough to get through anything together. Or maybe, in hindsight, it was more a hope than a promise."

"You need another beer."

Kendra tossed her head back and guffawed. "At least. But no. I have to drive home safely."

"Isn't it odd how we walk around, pretending everything is fine, all day, every day, when the reality is, we're barely able to put one foot in front of the other?"

Kendra clinked his glass. "That's for damn sure. No one truly understands, except one who's gone through it. Before, I always looked at people who'd suffered a loss and admired them for their strength. Now that I'm stuck in their shoes, I know it's more like they moved through thick fog for months. Pretending they were surviving. In truth, they probably hoped if they playacted long enough, the act would take hold. I'm not finding any consolation in that right now. If I allow myself to grieve, I might never crawl out from this cave I've created. I'm trying harder than ever, for sure, but every day is a monumental struggle. It's a weird dynamic. It's as if I'm holding grief at bay, but in doing that, I'm making it harder on myself."

"True that."

Kendra locked eyes with Nathan and smiled. She welcomed his offer of friendship and support. "You're more a friend than many of my friends."

"I hope so."

As they sipped their beers, Kendra felt a crack in her armor, as if a little life was seeping back into her veins.

CHAPTER SEVEN

THE FOLLOWING DAY, KENDRA NOTICED SOME COLOR HAD returned to her life. The weather was unseasonably warm but pleasant for a late August morning, so she decided to kayak for a while and enjoy one of the few nice days before the long months of cold settled in. She made it a mile down the lake before the slap of oars startled her. At least this time, the usual paranoia didn't set in. She knew who'd crept up on her. Russ Jameson, the resident fisherman extraordinaire, floated up next to her.

"Mornin', Kendra."

"Morning, Russ. How's the fishing today?"

"Just starting out, but I snagged a twenty-two-inch bass yesterday. Great fishing in this lake."

Nothing made Russ happier than fishing. He had a reputation for knowing all the secret spots, catching the largest bass, the only pike, and the most perch. He also held the title of Neighborhood Watchman. He could recite the history of every lake inhabitant—when their families had moved in, how many generations had lived there, and who the newcomers were.

Kendra successfully avoided Russ's multiple questions by asking him about himself. A widower, perhaps in his mid-sixties, he'd lived on the lake his entire life, his parents having raised him there. After his parents "left this earth for a better place," as Russ put it, he and his wife raised vizslas—Hungarian hunting dogs—while he worked for a local pharmacy. He had retired early to care for his dying wife, who lost her battle to brain cancer a few years back, and he'd recently decided to turn the in-law apartment above his garage into a short-term rental. He liked having visitors on the weekend. Said it kept him from going stir-crazy, having people around. Kendra could tell the guy spent hours remodeling. For a senior, his biceps and shoulders resembled those of a bodybuilder.

"I'm about to head back, so you have a good day."

"You too, young lady."

Kendra paddled toward home, hit the beach, and corralled the kayak back on its rack.

Kayaking fueled her brain, and Kendra spent the next four hours writing the first decent pages she'd laid down in months. Writing had saved Kendra in times of confusion, self-deprecation, upheaval, you name it. After discovering the next good starting place, she shut down her computer, realizing that while she felt good about the pages now, tomorrow, they would likely take on a different appearance.

Kendra took a quick shower and dressed. Today, she'd agreed to drop off books at the local coffee shop in her previous locale, if they arrived on time. Yet she startled as the UPS man, arms laden with boxes of books, trooped up the walk. One of these days, her old calm would return. It had better.

Isaac Smith was a kind man. A brilliant smile grew across his face whenever he saw her.

"Put these in the garage for you, or would you like them in

the back of your car? I hate to see you lift heavy packages when I'm able to do it."

"In the back of the car, if you don't mind. Thanks, Isaac. You're such a sweetie."

"If I'm not being too forward, you look lovely today. Got a hot date?"

Kendra rolled her eyes. "Funny. You know full well I've sworn off members of the opposite sex."

"Pity." Isaac winked. "Pretty girl like you shouldn't be alone."

"I like it that way."

Isaac shrugged. "You're the boss."

"Thanks for that."

Kendra liked Isaac. Not only could she count on him to say sweet things, but he also didn't overstep boundaries. They bantered like this every time they met. Come to think of it, he was just what Moderator Mary had assigned for homework. Twice this week, she'd completed her assignment. He knew nothing of her past but accepted her at face value—an upcoming author with a focus on her career. Kendra didn't hold his gentlemanly, old-fashioned notions against him. Plus, he'd offered to shovel the roadkill from the road in front of her house on his last visit. She'd forever be indebted to him for his good deed.

Maintaining the lake house meant dealing with the occasional mouse that preferred a warm place inside with readily available crumbs, and she'd run into a garter snake more than once this summer when she tended the flower garden. If Isaac offered, she'd gladly accept his help in any form. In the past, she'd been able to rely on her husband. Joe had chuckled at her lack of bravado when the odd spider crawled up the kitchen wall or when she climbed on top of the counter after spotting a cricket on the bathroom floor. Their life had been so normal then …

Kendra turned and checked her makeup in the mirror. As a local author, she had a certain image to keep up—a blessing and a curse. Thank goodness the local coffee shop owner was a friend who'd suffered her own losses and wasn't the kind to judge or offer lame sympathies.

When she made it outside, she discovered the boxes loaded in her car, Isaac gone, and energy still pumping through her veins. Maybe today was a sign. She was finally on the mend.

Before Kendra entered the shop mid-afternoon, she'd intended to sit in the car and sign books, drop off the autographed copies, then purchase some whole beans, grab a cup of fresh-brewed coffee, and head home. Kendra bounced inside when she realized she had forgotten an ink pen, a noticeable lightness in her step. She spotted her friends Amy Scranton, Jill Newton, Kathy Popper, and Erica Calhoun at their usual table by the window. Her heart sank. Here she was, struggling, and they carried on without even inviting her. True, they were probably sick of inviting Kendra and having her refuse their gestures. Still, it stung to see them together.

They had been best friends since kindergarten and gone through elementary and high school together. How could death break them apart? Molly had always been the leader of the pack, in charge of organizing get-togethers. Had she really exerted total control when she asked everyone to give Kendra space? Were they simply Molly's pawns?

Amy, mild-mannered and diminutive, was certainly more passive than the rest of them, married to a bossy guy who insisted she stay home and raise their child. Jill, tall and strong, the debate queen, certainly wasn't a pushover but was definitely the smartest and most pragmatic of the group. Kathy, pretty but shy, had always been the quietest, an observer sort, so Kendra wasn't all that surprised she hadn't heard from her. And even Erica, the constantly busy and chronically late person because she was nonstop distracted by shiny things, had joined group texts occasionally but not reliably. If Kendra had more time, she could delve more into their dynamic. She had other things on her mind.

Waving at them as if she wasn't offended, she stepped up to the counter and ordered coffee beans and a large mocha, telling the barista she had books in the car, and borrowing a pen. Part of her wanted to make an excuse and shirk back home, but her belligerent side wanted to show her friends she was doing better.

Amy's baby, Emma, sat in a high chair at her side, and Kendra assumed the empty seat beside her. Emma cooed and reached for the hair swinging from Kendra's shoulders. Kendra smiled and cooed back at the seven-month-old, her heart clenching. Joey would have been nine months old now.

"Can I hold her?"

Amy glanced worriedly at the other women at the table. Kendra recognized the meaning of the gesture. She hadn't held a child since Joey's death. She wondered if Amy's expression just confirmed her surprise or if she was nervous Kendra would cast a mortality spell on Emma.

"I won't hurt her. Honest."

"Of course you can hold her. Please. She'd love that."

Kendra lifted the baby from the chair and stood with her, bouncing the girl on her hip and stroking her stubby little fingers. Glancing at her friends, Kendra watched as they eyed each other. She wished she could do one damn thing without being judged.

She imagined their thoughts. *Kendra might kidnap my child since she lost her own. Hopefully, Kendra's misfortune isn't contagious. I hope she doesn't drop the baby.*

A piece of her recognized how unreasonable the train of thought was … another piece didn't. In a startling moment, Kendra realized how off the rails she'd been over the past six months, but she didn't fully trust these new emotions. Didn't trust her friends. Didn't trust herself.

"Thank you, guys, for sticking by me since … well, you know what. I've been doing better this past week. I thought you should know." A little piece of Kendra wanted them to feel guilty for not including her. Instead, she'd offered false words of gratitude and explanation. *Why does life have to be so complicated? Why couldn't I just say I was hurt to see them together without including me?*

Skeptical eyes gazed back at Kendra, and for a moment, she wanted to run. Reason kept her rooted to her spot. Of course the friends needed time to trust Kendra's ups. She hadn't had any in so long—they were right to be a tad cynical.

"Molly suggested I attend a grief group," Kendra said as evidence of her recovery, gazing at her friends for some indication they agreed with her process. *How ridiculous*, she thought. *I don't need their approval.*

No one looked up at her. Mostly, they seemed uncomfortable, shifting in their chairs.

"When are we going to have a girls' night out?" Kendra asked.

"We were just talking about that when you came in," Jill said.

Kendra knew full well the girls had gone to the local Irish pub, Connor O'Neill's, without her last weekend. Molly had let it slip. Kendra understood but still felt like an outsider—or worse, a nemesis. While Molly didn't have a husband or kids either, she still belonged to the group. She hadn't been cast out because life had dealt her two devastating blows, just days apart. Only Kendra carried that burden.

Funny how major losses triggered the loss of friendships—not just the friendships, but also the ease of conversations, the hugs at the grocery store, the quick phone calls or texts. All of those had died with Joey and Joe. And the effort required to worm her way back in was … well, still an unanswered question.

Kendra tempered her annoyance, worried it might morph into anger. Anger, especially the recurring sparks she'd been experiencing lately, left her prickly.

"Maybe next month," Amy said as she passed a private glance to Kathy. "My dance card is full the next few weeks. Kevin will be out of town, and my mother-in-law is coming to help out." She rolled her eyes.

"Let her watch Emma then. A perfect excuse to get away for a few hours," Kendra suggested.

Amy tilted her head. "You might have something there."

Emma burped and spit up on Kendra's shoulder. As she headed to the front of the shop for a napkin, she realized she had to rejoin society. She needed old friends as well as new.

Kendra wiped the baby's mouth and handed her over to Amy. "What do you say? Next Friday?"

Her friends agreed. Jill needed to check with her husband, but of all the women, Kendra could count on Jill. The girl loved beer and always needed a break from the kids.

Erica grasped Kendra's arm. "It's great to see you doing better, doll."

Satisfaction overwhelmed Kendra, a new and welcome centering of her gut.

At that moment, a hand gripped Kendra's arm. She about jumped out of her skin.

"Is that you? Kendra! It's so good to see you."

Instantly, her feet stuck to the floor, her legs turned to jelly, and she had to grab on to the chair in front of her and sit down in order to avoid puddling up on the floor. When she looked up, she gazed into the eyes of her former neighbor, Donna McNaught.

"I'm sorry I startled you. Are you okay?"

Kendra nodded absently, not at all okay.

"Did your brother-in-law find you? He seemed like such a nice young man. And the spitting image of Joe. I'm surprised he didn't know you'd moved out to the lake. You need to let family know where you are, dear. Seems a shame he was unable to attend the funeral. Why didn't you let him know what happened to

Joe? I know suicide is a shameful end, but you should have talked to him about Joe. They were brothers after all. It's so tragic, what people go through these days. All the suffering. Life is hard on everyone though. We all have our crosses to bear."

All eyes landed on Kendra, burning a hole into her forehead.

She wanted to run, but her legs wouldn't cooperate, and in an instant of clarity, she remained seated and found the wherewithal to change the subject. "Hi, Donna. How are the new neighbors? Do you like them?" *Are you into their business like you're into mine? Does anyone have neighbors who keep to themselves, or does everyone find it their personal mission to delve into other people's lives?*

Kendra lifted her eyes from the table and realized she'd spent a decent amount of time distracted and focused only on her friends. Right up until Donna showed up and flung her back into a deep, dark cave from which there was no escape.

Abruptly, Kendra glimpsed up at the wall clock and pulled herself up from her seat. "Look at the time. I've got to run. See you all later."

She dashed from the shop without another glance, forgetting entirely about her original mission to drop off books.

CHAPTER EIGHT

As soon as Kendra climbed in the car to head home, it happened again. That feeling. Someone was watching her.

She felt eyes on her as she buckled her seat belt and pulled out of the parking lot. *Dammit.* She drove west on Michigan Avenue and studied her rearview mirror. Silly, everyone was going in the same direction. Home. From work. From the gym. From sports practice. There was no way to tell if anyone was following her. Still, she couldn't shake the shadow.

She tried to tell herself she'd ventured out of her comfort zone by spending time with old friends. This was the expected aftermath—an anxiety attack. Made perfect sense when she put it that way. But as she turned onto Austin Road and headed into the country, she couldn't rid herself of the foreboding, like a thunder-cloud pressed down from above. Her arms tingled, and she tapped her thumbs on the steering wheel out of sheer nervousness. Even checking the rearview mirror and seeing that her car was the only one on the road did nothing to assuage her fears.

The garage door opened at the touch of a button, but Kendra didn't pull inside. She peered into the space, studied, and tried to discern if anything had been moved, if there were any signs of an unwelcome visitor. She'd had it happen once before—she'd stacked a basket of clothes for a donation, and it was overturned. She'd passed it off at the time, and maybe all these new activities were overwhelming her nervous system, but a single woman couldn't be too careful.

The garage was long-standing with timbers sixty years old and gave her the willies on a good day, as if she were stepping into a dank morgue. While this bare lumber had supplied much of the charm when she purchased the home, it had turned into another tormenting factor in the past few months. It reminded her of an abandoned building.

She pulled inside and parked, resting her head against the steering wheel and centering her breath. She hated this shit. She was tired of being scared, tired of not knowing what was real and what wasn't.

It took a solid, painstaking three minutes, but Kendra pushed down her fear and left the car. She made doubly sure that the garage door closed tight behind her, locked the entry door to the garage, and scurried to the back door, key at the ready. She entered the house and removed her light jacket, racing to secure each and every window lock. She pulled every blind, turning day into night, and crept into pajamas. At last, Kendra marched into the kitchen, uncorked a bottle of cabernet, and poured a hefty glass. She just couldn't quell her uneasiness.

As she cuddled up on the couch, she texted Molly. *Thanks for being my BFF.*

Molly answered. *Home? Jill said the girls ran into you at the coffee shop.*

Yep. Drinking wine.

That's my girl. Read a love story. Watch a Hallmark movie. I'll check in with you in the morning.

Instead of following Molly's advice, Kendra thought about a conversation Molly had most likely had with Jill, about Donna showing up and how Kendra had turned from calm and collected into a trapped animal.

She pulled out the photo album she'd created nearly two years ago. For the first time in months, she devoured snapshots of her and Joe when they'd first met, their dates, their wedding. Finally, she let the snapshots of Joey's birth, his first smile, and his first spoonful of cereal pierce her heart. Eyes welled with tears, she flipped through pages of memories. A hazy mist shrouded her vision. The most precious moments of her life, recorded for posterity, flooded her with sorrow. Her heart ached.

She missed Joey—holding him in her arms, feeling the warmth of his little body against her skin, nestling her face in his hair, inhaling the scent of baby shampoo, all of it. If only she could re-create those moments of pure bliss, complete and total contentment.

Kendra went to the bedroom and reached under the bed. In a box covered with baby-boy gift wrap, she unearthed the blanket she'd wrapped her baby in when she brought him home from the hospital. She carried the soft square to her place on the sofa and snuggled it, drew the cloth up to her nose and inhaled deeply. Maybe imagined, maybe not, Joey's scent seemed to linger and fill her with a momentary sense of peace. From that night on, she vowed to sleep with this memory—to keep Joey alive in her mind, to treasure the special three months they had spent together.

She cursed Donna and Jake for disrupting her earlier calm.

From there, Kendra drifted to memories of Joe—a different matter altogether. Kendra reasoned tackling one loss at a time made sense. When she had tried to deal with the loss of both Joey and Joe over the past months, she'd struggled with the enormity of their tragic deaths. She couldn't set a clear path to even begin to wrestle with her sadness. She'd dart from one vicious nightmare to the other—rolling over her blue-skinned baby, seeing Joe's lifeless body hanging from the rafters.

Maybe the decision to attend a grief group had been a good one in the end. Maybe focusing on sweet Joey was the answer.

Heavy cloud cover allowed Kendra to sleep past eight, a decent night despite the chance meeting with her friends, Donna's abrupt words, and the grief prompted by her memories. She rolled onto her back and listened to the birdsong. A jay here, a swallow there, a killdeer trailing on the edge. This place was a haven. A safe house. Untouched by drama, tragedy, or death.

But then again, was it? She carried the losses wherever she went—the haunting dreams at night, the imaginary sounds she heard during the day, the sense of being followed whenever she left the house. Could you create a sanctuary when your heart was broken and you saw ghosts everywhere you turned?

She'd do her best to make this lake house her savior. Still, Kendra couldn't open the door this morning without being haunted by last night's pall. Couldn't crack any windows but the transom ones in her bedroom.

Anger rose in her chest, and her fists tightened as she strode to the kitchen to brew a pot of coffee. Kendra had allowed a swarthy bite of anger to creep in lately. That was different. In the past, she'd spent a boatload of energy tamping down the ugly feelings, but since they'd come up the other day, she sort of rolled with them. Maybe she needed to embrace them and see where they led.

Kendra lifted the blinds in the family room and caught sight of the swan family floating in front of the dock. Their purity and stately forms calmed her. She'd be damned if she gave up this contentment. To hell with her demons.

The rich smell of coffee filled the tiny house. Kendra poured a cup, threw on some sweats, and trucked out to the deck with her Dad's binoculars. A breeze chilled the air, and Kendra crossed her arms, sipping from her mug as she took in the scene. Despite the soft wind, the water stilled, as if it were frozen. Birds trilled, and the strong but silent neighbor three doors to the east started his leaf blower. His presence allowed Kendra a welcome sense of well-being. As long as Chuck was outside, she didn't have to worry.

Kendra tilted the binoculars up to her eyes and scoped out the lake, taking in the geese and the osprey diving for breakfast, finally resting her gaze on Russ Jameson fishing in his rowboat. Having Chuck and Russ around gave her a sense of security. It might have been a false sense of safety, but for now, it worked.

Her phone rang in the distance. She'd probably left it on her nightstand. No reason to answer it now. Saturday meant a day off.

Kendra reentered the house, dumped her coffee into a thermos, and headed out to kayak. She paddled out to Russ with thoughts of enlisting his neighborhood watch skills.

"Morning, Russ."

"Hi there, Miss Kendra. Beautiful Saturday morning."

"It is. Hey, Russ, just wondering if you know who's home for the winter. Is everyone gone yet?"

"The Normans leave tomorrow and Chuck Goodwin next Wednesday. Most start to disappear after this Labor Day weekend. I have a new renter for the winter, but other than him, looks like the neighborhood will be thinned out within the next week. If you need anything over the next few months, give me a call. It can feel pretty desolate here once the cold settles in."

New renter? Kendra's anxiety spiked. "You found someone to stay over the entire winter? That's unusual, isn't it?"

"Nice young man. An author, like yourself. Looking for a place to hole up and write. Maybe you know him."

Kendra chuckled. "Lots of authors out there. I can't say I know them all."

"Hey, just thought of something. Not sure why it didn't occur to me before, but you two have the same last name. His name's Jake. Jake Kelly."

Kendra's heart caught in her chest. She couldn't find her breath.

"You all right? You're white as a ghost."

"Just remembered something. Sorry, Russ, I have to run."

CHAPTER NINE

KENDRA APPROACHED THE ARRIVAL OF JAKE ON THE lake as any normal woman who had recently lost her husband and child. As any woman who suspected the man she'd married had lied to her for the entire time she knew him. As any woman who suffered from a severe case of PTSD and imagined she saw things and assumed she was being followed. She freaked out.

Peering over her shoulder, Kendra dashed into the house after putting her kayak away. She double-checked the lock on the rear entry door. Goose bumps rose on her flesh. Even after pushing her arms through the thick wool sleeves of her warmest sweater, bumps rose to hives on her limbs. She pulled the blinds in her office and then draped a throw over her legs as she considered her options.

She chastised herself for not letting Russ know of her concerns, but if she had, she would have had to explain her life. By moving to the lake, Jake threatened to steal her anonymity, and she'd be damned if she let him. But more than exposing her ob-scurity, he made her vulnerable. She resented him. And, she re-alized, she resented Joe for not protecting her. As if someone had peeled back her skin, Kendra was bare and raw in a new and even more frightening way.

Panic wasn't the answer. But how could she make the dread disappear?

In the past—before she'd lost her family and her mind—when Kendra's anxiety had peaked, she'd clean house, weed out closets, pitch away old papers. When sad, she isolated her-self from others. When energized, she called friends, exercised, wrote, and read. In a brief moment of clarity, she realized that when reaching out, weight training, writing, and reading, she felt stronger, invigorated, and ready to tackle tough situations. She needed to pay attention and get busy.

Kendra entered the guest room and lifted weights for an hour—squatting, puffing hard through a myriad of chest presses, shoulder presses, lunges, and burpees until she worked up a drippy sweat and felt renewed and fortified.

She fried up two eggs and three slices of bacon, arming her body with protein. She showered and donned a favorite outfit.

Thankfully, the short walkway to the garage was shrouded by trees, a high row of lilac bushes on one side and a six-foot fence on the other, making it easy to escape to the garage unno-ticed. As she backed out of the driveway and then drove down the road, she considered purchasing a new vehicle but soon dis-carded the idea. If Jake wanted to get to her, he would. She was jumping ahead of herself. Then again, she'd have to stay a step ahead of him and make sure he was who he'd claimed to be.

Kendra spent the rest of the long weekend on high alert, poised for a visitor who never came. She tightened screws, dou-ble-checked dead bolts, and installed chain locks on the doors. A chance encounter with her dead husband's brother and the fact that he'd randomly chosen to rent Russ Jameson's loft, considering the circumstances around Joe's secret, shouldn't necessarily be cause for alarm. True, according to what Joe had shared, the guy reportedly had mental health issues, but this wasn't the first time she'd had a crazy in her life.

Soon after her debut novel had hit the shelves, she met an attorney at a book fair. Tony, as he called himself, claimed to have attended the same university as Kendra, graduating a few years previous. She signed his book, and his hand lingered on hers as she handed over the novel. The guy made her skin crawl, but she was in public, and the circumstances of the chance meeting assured her that she had no worries. The Chicago event, Printers Row, was one of the largest book events in the country with thousands in attendance. Silly worries, Joe assured her, which amounted to nothing.

A month later, Tony sent an email, which started with a rave review of the book. But soon, the message turned dark and sexual in nature. He said in quite specific terms how Kendra could have spiced up the novel. She consulted author friends, who warned of readers with strange obsessions. As a minor celebrity, Kendra now had to exercise caution. Crazies didn't just hit the streets in the dark of night; they strutted around during the day too.

Kendra didn't respond to the email, but when she attended the same book festival with Joe a year later, Tony showed up.

Kendra hated relying on Joe for protection, but she did. "I'd like you to meet my husband, Joe."

Unabashed, Tony asked, "Are you an author too?"

"Just a man supporting his wife's success." Joe leaned forward and gave Tony's hand a death-grip squeeze.

"So, there's no real reason for you to be here," Tony responded.

"Back up, man. She's with me," Joe said.

"But she wants me. Just look at her. She's practically salivating." Tony reached out to grab her arm.

Joe stepped in. "Get lost, buddy."

"So, you're one of those jealous husbands."

Joe took three steps forward, now nose to nose with the guy. "Maybe you and I should take this somewhere else."

Kendra felt like she was in the Wild West and that a gunfight might break out at any moment. As Tony lifted a fist, a younger man—Tony's spitting image—pulled down Tony's hand.

"Dad, what are you doing?" The younger man mumbled an apology and led Tony away.

The hair on Kendra's arms stood at attention, but Joe soothed her. "He shouldn't bother you again."

Anger rose in Kendra's chest as she recalled the incident. A woman still needed a man to ward off predators. She ground her teeth. The stark reality: Tony never bothered her again.

Kendra no longer had a burly guy for protection. She'd have to arm herself.

A call from Molly interrupted her thoughts. "I'm heading over. I need to spend some time on the lake and have a drink. Correcting papers will be the death of me."

"You're the fool who decided to teach writing to special education students," Kendra joked. "See you soon."

Kendra hoisted the kayaks off the corral and set two bottles of cold water inside the boats. By the time Molly showed up, clouds had vanished from the sky, showering blue on the lake and hot white sunshine onto their shoulders. They climbed into the boats and began to paddle.

"You've reinforced your doors. This brother-in-law of yours has you creeped out."

"He's living here," Kendra shouted over her shoulder. "Catch up with me. Voices carry on the lake."

Molly paddled hard and fast. "What do you mean, living here?" she whispered.

Kendra recounted her conversation with Russ Jameson.

"That's the pretty yellow house, right? Let's paddle by and see if we spot him."

"Discreetly."

The friends stayed close to shore, paddled in silence, and listened as the cackling geese provided background music. Kendra clenched her jaw as she lifted her eyes toward the Jameson place. The unattached garage, which Russ had fashioned into an apartment, stood about fifteen yards from the main house. Two small windows from above peeped out over the lake.

Through gritted teeth, Kendra asked, "See anything?"

As a teacher, Molly had a reputation for X-ray vision.

"Don't think so," she murmured.

Only when they reached the far end of the lake did Kendra let out a breath. She paddled next to Molly as trepidation tightened her expression.

Molly burst into laughter. "I'm sorry to laugh, but you're strung like my spinster aunt, Mirabelle. I have a good feeling about this. Relax."

"*Relax* isn't a word in my vocabulary. I thought you knew that."

"I'm just saying. You've been through more in the last almost seven months than most people endure in a lifetime. It's easy to see problems where there are none. Easy to imagine a life of tragedy from now on. But I promise, things will get better. They already are. You held Emma the other day, and you're joining us for girls' night out. Just breathe, kiddo."

While Molly hadn't been at the coffee shop, Kendra knew the speed at which news traveled among the group. It still irked her how her childhood friends made it their business to share the simplest move Kendra had made. Then again, Molly had made a valid point. Kendra had been planning for the bottom to continue to fall out of her life since she'd lost her family. Worries about the next novel kept her nerves on edge. Avoiding sorrow kept a wall in front of her. Fear of rejection kept her from spending time with those who could offer her support.

"This is great fodder for your book," Molly added. "You always say you disguise your life as fiction."

"Right."

As they rowed back over the glassy water, Kendra couldn't help but scour Russ's property. She tried averting her gaze but spotted a male figure moving through the trees in front of the garage. Sure enough, she saw Jake.

"Psst," she whispered.

Molly sculled up next to Kendra's boat.

"That's him."

Molly glanced over her shoulder in the opposite direction and then flashed a glimpse at the Jameson house, gleaning what she could from a three-second stare at Jake.

"He does look like Joe. No wonder you're freaked out."

Kendra's gut filled with satisfaction but only for a millisecond. He locked eyes with Kendra next, and his gaze bored through her.

By the time they reached Kendra's lakefront, fog covered the lake. She grabbed Molly's arm. Abandoned the kayaks. Dashed inside. Every strand of hair on her neck and limbs stood on end. Molly stayed close. Silent.

Kendra raced to each entry door. Unlocked and then relocked it. Double-checked the lock. When she made it to the front door—her last stop—she peered out the sidelight window. On the rocking chair. On the porch. A box.

Kendra viewed the box as she would a stray backpack at the airport. Small, compact. Not a pressure cooker with an explosive inside. So, why was every nerve in her body prickling? She told herself to chill. But as she viewed the address, her throat closed. Her name was written in large lettering across the top. With a Sharpie. No address. Just her name. She wished for a drug dog, some harbinger of safety.

She brought the package inside, dropped it on the table as if it were ticking, and shook her hands.

Molly's mouth gaped as she locked eyes with Kendra. "What is it? What's wrong?"

"Look at the box. Just my name? It has to be from him. What if he gets in the house? What if he blames me for Joe's death?"

"I have no idea. He definitely seems to have a thing for you."

"A thing? I told you months ago that I felt like someone was following me, and you blew me off. Said I was grieving and the mind could twist and turn when a person suffered the devastation I had. And now, you believe me?"

"Let's sit down. I feel like I might pass out." Molly headed into the family room, pulled down the blinds, and sank back onto the couch. Her face went parchment white and her breath shallow.

Kendra couldn't stop her limbs from clattering and tried to take a breath. If Molly was this freaked out, it meant that a sane person had reason for concern. So, Kendra wasn't crazy, and she should be shaking.

"The box hasn't exploded yet, so I'm guessing it isn't a bomb, but I'm positive Jake put it there."

Molly nodded. "I have a feeling you're right. Should we call the police?"

"And tell them what? A strange package arrived on the porch, and we'd like the bomb squad to examine it before we open it?"

Molly chuckled maniacally. She was losing it.

"The tables have turned," Kendra said, frowning at Molly.

"We need to move the box to a secure place. Outside. Away from the house."

"How do you propose we do that safely?" Kendra paced the room, searching for answers. A chill passed through her and held on tight. "I don't have anyone to call. Do you? Know anyone with a bomb dog?"

"We both need to calm down. Maybe it was the fog on the lake, the discussion about Jake and then seeing him. Add the package, and it's a recipe for two sane women to lose their shit. Stop pacing. You're making it worse."

"Oh, now, you're Miss Calm."

"No, I feel like my body temp has dropped a full ten degrees. I'm trying to calm down. Want some wine?"

"If we drink, he could show up, kill us, and leave our dead bodies to rot. No one would find us for weeks."

Molly outright laughed. "That's a little farfetched. One glass might clear our minds."

"Or muddy them."

Molly headed to the kitchen and poured two glasses. Kendra hated that they were trapped inside. The early evening fog was a fluke, and she was sure it'd created the perfect setting for them to flip out. More than anything, she was itching to examine the box. Small, discreet, not even large enough for a book, she realized.

She sipped her wine and pondered options. How could they securely open the box and remain safe? She could grab it with a pair of tongs and turn away as she lifted it. Surely, Jake wouldn't have put a bomb on her porch. Her mind started to settle.

She heard her phone ping. A text message.

No one texted her but Molly, and Molly was sitting smack in front of her. She retrieved her phone and peered at the message.

Dropped off a box of photos on your porch. Thought you might like them.

She handed the phone to Molly.

"Who is this from?" Molly asked.

"We were right on that account. It's from Jake. Should we believe him?"

"Maybe he's trying to prove he's who he says he is. Could be an innocent gesture. Not emotionally easy to hear, but informative. What do you want to do?"

"Sit on the deck and look inside. My curiosity is getting the best of me. What if he's watching us?"

Molly grimaced. "You can't live in fear of him. And then there's your burning desire to know what went on with Joe. What do you think?"

"Let's go for it."

Kendra marched to the table, picked up the box, and inhaled sharply as she waited for it to explode into smithereens. When that didn't happen, she carried it outside. "Bring the wine. I'll meet you on the deck."

Kendra grabbed a pair of scissors on her way outside. She set everything on the patio table and locked eyes with Molly. "Here we go."

As she sliced the box top, she struggled to calm her racing heart. Inside, Styrofoam peanuts protected the contents. She fingered her way to an envelope of photographs. A young Joe and Jake fishing. Joe and Jake skiing. Joe and Jake posed under a Christmas tree with Tonka trucks and action figures. A family photo—Joe and Jake posed in front of their parents, dressed for the holidays in their best outfits, little suit coats and bow ties. From toddlers to teens, they appeared to be the perfect family. At least fifty photos filled the manila wrapper.

A gut feeling confirmed the photographs matched the likeness of Jake, who'd unexpectedly appeared in her life. One after the other, she passed them to Molly, puffing on a cigarette and sipping wine between photos. Molly frowned, clearly disapproving of Kendra's smoking, but for once, she kept her mouth shut.

Kendra softened while holding Joe's memories. The piece of him she had never known offered insight into his childhood, into the man he had become and the husband who had left her behind. Sadness flooded her.

Kendra stepped inside, found the soft baby blanket, and held it under her nose. She inhaled deeply and forced out a ragged breath.

CHAPTER TEN

*D*ON'T LET *JAKE* IN. DON'T LET HIM OCCUPY THE EMPTY *place Joe left behind—even in your mind. He's a loose thread. Leave the madness behind. Focus on the future.* Those were the last words Kendra uttered before she fell asleep.

But once she awakened, her hands were drawn to the photographs like iron to magnet. Maybe if she searched hard enough—narrowed her eyes and read between the images—she could discover the parts of Joe's past that had led him to suicide.

She needed coffee before she could trust the discerning center of her brain—and a few deep breaths to ground herself. As a mystery author, Kendra knew well the value of research, of stepping back from the story and allowing distance. After downing a cup of high-test coffee in three gulps, she poured another tall serving and dived under the covers.

Kendra held one photo at a time, sipping and scrutinizing, scrutinizing and sipping. She came upon the photo of an infant—no label on the back to tell which boy, but she decided it didn't matter. Insight into the brothers would help unravel the mystery of Joe's death. On a second look, the resemblance to Joey plucked the saddest of heartstrings.

Sure, Joe had been distraught after Joey's sudden death, but she was too. She didn't take her life even though the thought had flitted through her head. Joe had been busy, shoring up his wife, but Kendra remembered the evening of Joey's death, how they'd held each other in bed, sobbing and drying their tears. Joe had been so happy—when they dated, throughout their engagement, on the honeymoon, and when Kendra became pregnant so soon after they married. He was so proud to have a son. His chest puffed out at Joey's baptism. Every evening upon his arrival home from work, he'd brushed a kiss against her cheek before he lifted his son in his arms and spent a solid hour delighting in every move, whimper, and expression Joey made.

In the photo of the infant, Kendra observed apprehension on the baby's face. Babies experienced stranger anxiety, and this child looked about nine months old, what Joey would have been now—the perfect age to struggle with that particular stage of development. She wouldn't read too much into this but would note the expression and compare it to later snapshots. If indeed this photo pictured a reportedly troubled Jake, she had even more reason to keep the information in the back of her mind. Clues to Jake might help her as much as clues to Joe.

Maybe she had overreacted to Jake's arrival on her stoop. Maybe he needed her since he had no one left. The seesaw game began. She'd been shocked and then scared when she discovered the article about the Kelly murders. But Jake had been acquitted. The fact that he'd suffered from emotional issues and possible drug addiction as a youth was no reason to assume he hadn't cleaned up his act or assume that he'd killed his parents and gotten off scot-free. Kendra had witnessed firsthand many teens who'd run off the tracks and then pulled their act together once they were old enough to realize the consequences of their decisions. Jill's husband had been alcohol-free for twenty years. Pot-smoking Erica had been a burnout in college but was now a workaholic CPA with a successful husband and two adorable kids.

She tamped out the spark in her brain. The one that had said, *Watch your back. Keep your distance. Look over your shoulder.*

Kendra decided she wouldn't go out of her way to get to know Jake better. It wasn't as if she planned to have him to Sunday dinner. She'd gratefully let him share this piece of Joe but not encourage him further.

Still, her heart softened.

If she took the time to ask Jean, she would tell her to research more, keep her eye on Jake, and use the anger to fuel her writing. Kendra walked into her office and blew a kiss at her agent's image before driving to the store for another pack of smokes.

CHAPTER ELEVEN

RUSS JAMESON PADDLED UP TO THE DOCK TWO MORN-
ings later as Kendra sipped her morning coffee on the deck.
"Howdy, Kendra."

"Hey, Russ." Kendra set down her coffee, rose from her chair, and strode down to the water's edge. "What brings you around this fine morning?"

"Don't want to alarm you, but I noticed some activity outside your house last night."

Kendra knitted her brows. "What kind of activity?"

"Just after dusk, I'd gone out for an evening cruise before the thick fog rolled in. The sunset promised to be a fine one before the haze, so I thought I'd catch one of the few ones left, but as I headed back, I noticed someone walking around the perimeter of your place. Too late for a repairman, I figured. Thought I should let you know."

"Man? Woman? Could you tell?"

"Appeared to be a man, but through the fog, it was hard to

tell. Maybe a friend dropped by and came round back to see if you were on the deck."

Kendra rubbed her thumbs over her fingernails and then shoved her fists into her jeans pockets. "Thanks for the info. Seems a little strange."

"Probably nothing to worry about, but a woman alone can't be too careful."

"I appreciate you letting me know. I'll keep an eye out."

Russ waved and paddled away, leaving Kendra to investigate her surroundings. She checked for signs of a visitor. Studied the deck from a distance and then moved closer to examine for footprints on the deck. Not that she expected to find evidence of an uninvited guest. Her best guess told her Jake had been back. Maybe he'd left something behind.

Backtracking through last night, she recalled leaving the house a few minutes before twilight. To her recollection, she hadn't noticed a car on the road or neighbors on an evening stroll. She had driven past the Jameson place, where Jake stayed now, but chosen not to study the house and refused to give Jake the satisfaction of her time and attention.

Even though she'd tempered her anger and mistrust of Jake and reconsidered her first impressions of him since he'd delivered the photos, she didn't need one more hiccup right now. Whatever Jake's agenda happened to be, if he didn't come straight out with it, she planned to ignore him.

Best sense she could make of Jake: he intended to stick around and wrangle some money out of Kendra. Probably felt entitled since he was Joe's brother. Maybe Joe had told him that he had made him the beneficiary on a life insurance policy—something along those lines. No, that didn't make sense. Local media had hushed Joe's suicide, but in a small town, gossip spread like California wildfires. The news had probably traveled over fences but hadn't made it to Pleasant Lake.

Confusion engulfed her. *Think. Be logical.*

If Jake had wanted to find out about Joe, he could have ordered a copy of the death certificate. A quick trip to the county clerk would have spelled out the ugly details.

All the more reason to tell her grief group. The sooner Kendra talked about Joe, the better. She hated when she ran into some virtual stranger or near acquaintance and was blindsided by words of condolence. Far easier to take charge and be the one to deliver the news. Control she desperately craved in life had been elusive since her loss. Now was as good a time as any to take back the reins.

Kendra's search of the outside of the house revealed nothing. Whoever had prowled around the place left no visible sign of their visit. It could have been Molly, for goodness' sake. Maybe she'd left something behind when they went kayaking two days ago. She wouldn't allow herself to envision a stranger on the property.

She gazed out at the lake and took in the reflection of leaves as their autumn colors played on the water. Sunshine cast easy shadows from the three stately white pines on the west end of her property. The water mirrored clouds and trees. Nothing bad could happen in such a peaceful paradise.

The sun disappeared behind a cloud, shrouding the house in shade as a stiff wind kicked up. Kendra turned her gaze to the lake as water chopped onto the shore. She grabbed her coffee and hurried inside. One thing she'd discovered about the lake: the weather changed in a moment's time. Too often, it matched her mood—or determined it.

She texted Molly. *Did you stop by last night?*

A ping sounded a second later.

No. Why? You were home, right?

Kendra checked herself, not wanting Molly to think she was losing her mind again.

Damn autocorrect. Meant to say, did you have a good night?

Yep. You?

Another dreamless sleep.

The hammer of clouts on the door frightened Kendra out of her skin.

Those two six-inch panel sidelights extending on either side of the entrance door allowed her to view visitors if they stood to the side of the entry. A blessing and a curse. She could hide in the office and pretend not to have heard the door. But a sudden inclination led her to answer the knock.

Jake stood, relaxed, as he peered through the side window. He greeted her with a friendly smile and wave. Kendra opened the heavy wooden door but stepped outside on the stoop rather than letting him in.

"Just wanted to be sure you found the package. You never texted me back."

"Yes." She kept her response brief and to the point.

In the scheme of the future, she had no desire to have a relationship with Joe's sibling. Although he'd tugged at her heartstrings earlier, other than discovering more about her dead husband, which in itself held a curious appeal, fostering a friendship would only drag her down in the long run.

"Any chance we could talk for a few minutes?"

"Listen, Jake, I know you're renting from Russ Jameson. I know someone roamed around my yard last night. If there's something you want, just say so. I don't have time or energy to play some long-drawn-out game with you."

"I have no idea what you're talking about. It wasn't me. You might not spend much time thinking about it, but I lost my brother. You're not the only one healing. I sent you the photos as an overture of friendship. I'd guess there are things about my brother you don't know, and I'm guessing your suppositions about me aren't true either. Better to listen to the living than the dead. You might surprise yourself."

A surge of sudden fury coursed through Kendra, making her

temples pound. An angry flush rose up her neck. "I knew my husband as well as anyone. We shared two years of the best love I've known in my entire life. I want to remember what we had, not have it tainted by some sick version of yours."

Jake took a quick step toward her. "What do you have against me?"

Kendra backed up, now wedged between the door and this six-two man with broad enough shoulders that no one could spot her from the street. He completely hid her behind his sheer mass.

"Step back. You're crowding me."

Jake stepped back an inch. "If you're uncomfortable, let's go someplace public. You want to hear what I have to say."

"Trust me when I say, I do not."

"Do you ever wonder why Joe killed himself? Do you ever think something outside of losing his son destroyed him?"

Kendra's mouth gaped. She didn't know how to respond. Her throat constricted, and she wanted to disappear. Furious, she lifted her arms and shoved Jake away. Caught off-balance, he stumbled off the porch.

Kendra lifted a finger and pointed at Jake. "Get away from me. And don't come back."

Jake backed up three feet and splayed his hands in front of his body. "I'm not trying to be the bad guy here. I get why you're upset. None of us wants to think the worst of those we love. But in my mind, you want answers, and I'm pretty sure I have them." He shook his head. "Take your time. Think about it. If you want to talk, I'm available. We got off on the wrong foot, for sure. I know I lack people skills. I'm working on it." He closed his eyes for a moment, and then he wheeled around and strode down the front walk.

Kendra slipped inside and flipped the dead bolt, drew the chain lock across the door, and slid down to the floor, holding her head in her hands. Jake had scared her. No, more than that. His message had scared her.

Yes, she had been a bundle of nerves since losing her family. Yes, she could barely keep her head straight. Yes, she could hardly trust herself, much less someone else.

But Jake's arrival was officially more than she could handle. He hadn't threatened her. He hadn't hurt her. But he creeped her out. Whether a good guy or a bad guy, he made her question her safety. Or worse, her sanity. She couldn't decide which. But did she want to hear Jake's version of the truth? No.

After squeezing her fists white, she let out a steady stream of air, marched to the office, and called Molly. As soon as the line connected, Kendra remembered Molly was back at school. All day. She had a brief planning period first thing in the morning, which had already passed, and twenty-five minutes of lunch, if all went according to plan, with barely a minute in between to hit the restroom.

Kendra ended the call and Googled Jake Kelly's trial, searching for information that might explain his behavior.

Because Jake had been only fifteen years old at the time of his parents' murders and because he hadn't been convicted of the crimes, the records had been sealed. Kendra printed a few articles from local gazettes, and the grizzly details set her feet afire. She lifted them off the carpet and huddled beneath crossed arms, hugging fear to her chest.

Joseph and Sarah Kelly had been discovered in their bedroom. Each had sustained knife wounds to their torso, neck, and face. Kendra did not need to research to understand the crimes had been personal. If the murders had occurred as part of a simple robbery, they might have been shot, not sliced to bits like soup vegetables.

All evidence had proven Joe had been away at college, attending a frat party at the time of the crimes. Witnesses came forward in droves, and Joe was cleared of any suspicion.

No murder weapon was found at the scene. The defense demonstrated there was no ill will between parents and son. Although the media reported Jake had a history of some minor drug use, he had no history of violence.

Money had never been an issue for the family. Dad was a successful plastic surgeon, Mom his business manager. They'd worked long hours on occasion but made sure to have family dinners and attend all their children's sports games and school functions. The defense proposed a disgruntled patient as the killer, a thoughtful and realistic defense, which eventually won over the jury.

Even though the trial lasted two weeks, Jake had been acquitted within two hours. His hands were clean. He'd been home at the time of the murders, but he was listening to music when he fell asleep. Claim was, Jake's headphones blocked out any sound. His parents were killed in the master suite, a room on the first floor and on the opposite side of the house. Jake was upstairs.

He hadn't heard a sound.

Kendra raised an eyebrow at this detail. Two people killed in such a gruesome fashion must have fought off their attacker—unless two assailants had simultaneously killed his parents and they hadn't resisted. At all? Didn't make one iota of sense. Not to her. A layperson. The Kellys hadn't been bound or gagged, nor had they been drugged.

Holy fuck! Could this really be true? Joe had lied about his childhood, hidden the brutal murder of his parents? His own mother? His own father? He left that out? What you leave out is what you've forgotten, the time mom served chicken two days in a row. The time dad couldn't start the grill.

Kendra took a breath. Back to research. Emotion later. She recognized she was out of touch with headphone abilities. When she Googled, she found out that even then you could purchase noise-blocking earmuffs. They resembled muffs from her mother's childhood, and the reviews suggested they were quite effective, even in those days.

Kendra Googled Joe and Jake's maternal grandmother, Marcy Walker, and learned the elderly woman had passed away two short years ago. Her obituary detailed a brave yearlong battle with pancreatic cancer. At the time of her death, Jake had been twenty-nine years old, if she did the math correctly. That made him thirty-one years of age now. It seemed to fit.

As far as Kendra's research revealed, Jake had led a news-free, criminal-free life since being the lone suspect in his parents' murders.

Kendra began to second-guess her reaction to Jake. She'd been unkind, cruel even, to push Jake away. She'd been through the worst months of her life—she'd overreacted because of the impossible pain she'd suffered since losing her family.

Maybe it was time to rethink her reactions. Maybe it was time to offer kindness to a young man who had been left alone without a single family member to support and console him.

Maybe Kendra had more in common with Jake than she cared to admit. But if she acknowledged that, she also had to admit that Joe had left out the most important part of his life. His parents were brutally murdered!

CHAPTER TWELVE

AKE'S WORDS PLAYED IN HER HEAD LIKE A SONG THAT wouldn't let go. *"Better to listen to the living than the dead. You might surprise yourself. There's a lot to learn.... I'm not the bad guy here."*

Not for the first or even the second time, Kendra questioned how well she had known Joe.

She checked her watch and did the math. It was before sunrise in San Diego, but Jean was an early riser, and if Kendra called right now, she might catch Jean before she dived into work for the day.

She considered a plain old phone call but opted to FaceTime instead. She needed to see Jean's face.

Seconds later, the call connected.

"You sure know how to wake a gal up, don't you?" Jean's face appeared on the screen, her short gray hair standing on end as she smoothed a hand over her head.

"Sorry to call so early, but I wanted to catch you before you started working for the day."

"Hold on while I grab some coffee."

Kendra walked into the kitchen and made a cup of tea while Jean went to fetch her drink.

When she came back into the office, she sat down and waited for Jean.

"What's up?" Jean's face filled the monitor, still disheveled but smiling.

"I want to run something by you." Kendra explained in detail every step of Jake's arrival in her life and the message he'd relayed.

Jean listened thoughtfully and without interruption. After Kendra finished, she asked, "What's your gut telling you?"

"My gut hasn't been all that reliable lately, but part of me believes him, and of course, I'm dying of curiosity. It's not like I'm anxious to hear anything bad about Joe—the guy was my husband, for God's sake. But I'll never find peace if I don't uncover all the facts. It seems as if Joe painted a rather rosy picture of his life, and while I understand his hesitation in sharing the truth with me, I have to know what happened."

"Let's decide how you can do that safely. In my mind, Jake might have some valuable information. But your mental health and physical safety are paramount. The scene you described at the front door is somewhat alarming, but you're on high alert right now anyway, so that's a factor you can't ignore. Let's think about a couple of things." Jean furrowed her brow and sipped her coffee. "What's his motivation?"

"He seems somehow infatuated with the fact that I'm family. Or he's faking that. Other than that, I don't really know. Money maybe? He hasn't mentioned money, but maybe that's a reason. He's working his way up to asking for money."

"But you don't feel like he wants to kill you. He doesn't appear vindictive?"

"Mostly, it seems as if he wants to get some things off his chest."

"Step back and think about all the possible motivations. Write them down. If you truly feel like you can be safe around him, I would suggest planning things. You be the instigator. You set the agenda and the tone. Be sure he knows who's boss and who's running the show. If things get uncomfortable, you end the meeting. Maybe a neutral place. Somewhere public. Safer all around."

"That makes sense, but I wonder if I had him here, if he might be more forthcoming."

"Maybe, but that's riskier too. Could you let someone know what you're arranging and have them close at hand if need be?"

"I'm not sure that would work. I don't think any of my friends would support me. They already think I've lost my mind. On the other hand, my friend Molly knows I'm afraid of him. She'd never agree to me meeting him privately. Realistically, I'm fearful of everything right now, so I'm not a good judge."

"Daylight hours work best. Can you meet outside? You can always put me on speed dial, and if things go awry, call me. If you call, I can alert 911 that you need help. Granted, I'm across the country, so it's less than an ideal solution, but it's something."

"The weather is cooling off a bit, but I have a deck heater. I could have him come during the afternoon. It might work."

"Or think about other options. Maybe tell a friend you're meeting with him and that you want to be able to check in with them, or just ask someone to call you when you know he'll be there, and then you'll be able to connect with someone."

"All good ideas." Kendra felt the knot in her stomach loosen. "I'll feel better once I talk to him. Even if he relays upsetting news, I can vet that after our meeting and decide whether he's full of shit or not."

"Good idea."

"I can't tell you how much better I feel. You're a good friend. Thank you."

"Stand up," Jean ordered.

Kendra obeyed, the routine a habit now. She spun on her heel.

"You look good, but I want you to eat more. Have you had any treats lately? I remember what a sweet tooth you had when we first met at the conference. Seemed like every time I turned around, you were sitting down with a cupcake or a pastry from the coffee shop."

"I actually haven't had much, but I'm thinking about making cookies today."

Jean nodded and smiled. "Air-express some this way. As I recall, you're an expert at finding the best recipes."

They touched on the weather, Jean's current project, Kendra's writing, and a few other items before air-kissing and signing off. Despite Kendra's earlier misgivings, she had a plan.

Minutes later, the phone rang.

Molly was on her lunch hour. "Hey, just calling to remind you about tomorrow."

"Got it."

"Wow, your voice sounds different. You're happy."

"Ouch. You sure know how to hurt a girl. I just Face-Timed with JJ. She's medicine for my soul."

"Maybe you should plan to talk to her daily."

Kendra's blood pressure spiked. She hated it when Molly was snarky. "She's a busy woman. And if I did that every day, I'd become accustomed to it and not appreciate it as much."

"And I suppose you schemed about Jake."

"What are you talking about?" How Molly inhabited Kendra's head remained a mystery.

"You're a sucker. Even more so since you lost your family. I'm not trying to be harsh, but I know you, and this is about Jake, that fake brother-in-law of yours. Don't fall for him. Do you hear me? Do not."

"Fall for him? Nothing could be further from my mind. You're off track. Way off track."

"He looks like Joe, acts like Joe, triggers memories for you. He's dangerous. And I'm not just talking about your physical welfare. I'm talking about your emotional health, which, in my humble opinion, is hanging by a thread. Turns out, Joe was poison for you."

Heat rose up Kendra's neck and settled on her cheeks. "Why don't you tell me how you really feel?"

"I never liked him. And guess what? I was right."

Silence weighed on the line.

After a few delayed heartbeats, Molly continued. "I'm saying this because I love you. I don't want you to get hurt. You've suffered enough already."

Kendra scraped the edge of her desk with a fingernail. "So, what's the plan for tomorrow night? Where are we having dinner?"

"Don't shut me out, Kendra. Please. I want the very best for you."

"Yeah, sure. So, what time and where?"

"Detroit Street Filling Station. It's new. Vegan. Six o'clock."

"Sounds good. Listen, I've gotta go." Kendra ended the call and stared at her phone for a solid minute before dialing Jake's number.

"Hi," she said when he picked up the call. "Kendra here. Since you're my new neighbor, how about coming over for pot roast tonight, say about six o'clock? A good hearty meal, a decent bottle of wine, and some simple conversation."

Jake sounded thrilled, and for a moment, Kendra worried she had just invited a poisonous snake into her home. She'd be careful.

CHAPTER THIRTEEN

JAKE KNOCKED ON THE DOOR PRECISELY AT SIX. LIKE HIS brother, he appeared to have a penchant for promptness. Kendra had loved that about Joe. Impatient as she was, waiting chewed at her gut.

She opened the door to a lovely man, holding a bouquet of flowers.

"It's impolite to show up without a gift for the hostess."

Kendra intuited he was letting her know not to overreact to his gesture. He was being courteous, nothing more, but also presenting her with a peace offering.

"Thanks," she said as she took the flowers from him. She walked into the kitchen and reached above the refrigerator for a vase, filled it with water, and arranged the flowers inside—a beautiful display of mini sunflowers, burgundy carnations, a spray of orange blossoms, and red hypericum berries, accented with lush greens. The arrangement brought autumn indoors.

"They are beautiful."

"Joe told me you love flowers."

As if a knife had sliced her spine, Kendra realized Joe had talked with Jake since he'd known her. How was this happening? Joe had carried on a relationship with his brother. Never shared a word about Jake being alive and well, but rather, he'd told her bald-faced lies about him. Why? How could she possibly make sense of this? Or convince herself Joe wasn't a liar? Her train of thought spiked a white-hot fury.

She'd been smart, unlocked all four doors for an easy getaway should the need occur. She led the way into the family room and gestured to the chair that faced the lake, too pissed off at Molly to care a lick about safety. Her anger had fueled her afternoon, and she was sure she could kick Jake's ass before he had a clue what was happening.

Kendra offered Jake a simple nod. "Wine?"

"I'm more of a beer guy, but if you don't have beer, sure."

"I have some Oktoberfest."

Jake stood with hands shoved in his pockets, looking a bit awkward and unsure. "That's great."

Kendra pulled a bottle from the fridge and lifted off the cap with an opener. "Glass?"

"No need." The same expression Joe had used.

Kendra's heart skipped a beat or three. She lifted the top off the roast pan and checked on dinner. "Should be ready in thirty minutes. Let's sit and chat for a bit."

Kendra always offered company the lake view. She had the pleasure of looking at the lake all day. They did not.

Jake took a seat and rested his arms on the sides of the over-stuffed furniture. "I don't want you to be uncomfortable. I understand none of this is easy."

Kendra sat down and pondered her laced fingers. "I'm sorry I reacted so strongly. It's just that I have to protect myself right now. My shield is feeble. Seems to have lost some strength in the past months." *Control the evening. Only your agenda. Not Jake's.*

Jake's eyes radiated compassion. "I'm not sure what Joe told you about me, but it's quite possible he felt a need to cover the truth. You see, we led a troubled childhood."

Kendra's gaze narrowed on Jake as she leaned forward. Often, people told her their life stories. She felt as if a sign on her forehead read, *Tell me everything. I have a good ear.* Some days, it seemed a burden, others a gift. Today was a gift.

"My parents had a very successful business and lots of money. But they didn't know how to fit kids into their lives. I'm not sure why they had us. They were driven, both of them. My dad was a plastic surgeon in La Jolla, a popular place to be unhappy with your appearance. Mom was his nurse and eventually went on to become his office manager. Joe and I both felt like we were the two prescribed kids, assigned to the ideal nuclear family, but nothing more than that. I don't remember either of my parents ever being happy to see us, proud of us, or excited about what we were doing.

"Joe had massive engineering skills. He could take anything apart and put it back together. He did that instead of playing with toys. Me, I spent my waking hours trying to get their attention. Guess I wasn't as smart as Joe. He'd figured out early on that they were unavailable. I wouldn't give up. I even did some pretty crazy stuff when I was a kid. Once, I refused to eat for several days. They didn't even notice. I stayed in my room for the entire weekend sometimes. Joe was the only one who commented."

Kendra's stomach twisted into knots. *Who was lying? Joe? Jake?* Yes, she knew Joe had lied about Jake. Clearly, he was alive. The resemblance was uncanny, but these two versions of the Kelly boys' childhoods were diametrically opposed. Joe had described an idyllic childhood with caring parents. What Jake had described was anything but. She shook with anger. In her gut, she guessed

Joe was the liar, but it was almost too much to take in. And how should she handle Jake?

Caution lights flashed around her.

"Why should I believe you? This is not what I heard from Joe."

"Joe was a pathological liar. He was so dishonest, I suspect he could no longer tell truth from fiction. He had a habit of painting life with a wide brush—with a tendency to use fiction to match the life he wanted to portray. He believed himself after a while."

"I need something more factual, not psychobabble nonsense."

Jake narrowed his eyes. "Fine. When we were little, we used to spend time at friends of our parents. He'd steal from them, and once, when he got caught, he actually suggested that my mom's friend had told him he could have a model airplane kit from their basement.

"He hadn't fully zipped his backpack, so the corner of the box was peeking out from his bag. When Mr. O'Connor confronted him, Joe said, 'Oh, Mrs. O'Connor gave it to me.' Mrs. O'Connor stood behind Joe, shaking her head, but Joe kept insisting. Mr. O'Connor gave him every chance to tell the truth, and when Mrs. O'Connor stepped in, Joe swore she was lying. He wouldn't stop shouting about it. He was brazen when backed into a corner. When we got home and Mom asked him where the kit had come from, he said, 'None of your business,' and stormed off to his room."

"How did your parents handle it?"

Jake's stare bored into Kendra's skull. "How do you think? They bought another airplane kit—the same one, of course—to replace the one Joe had stolen. There were never any real consequences. He grew up thinking he was immune to rules and laws."

Kendra couldn't picture Joe doing this. This wasn't the Joe she had known. It didn't fit. Not really. "I need more."

Jake shook his head. "Did Joe ever show you his knife?"

Kendra's breath caught in her throat. "What knife?"

"Dad was supposed to take us on a fishing trip. One of those trips he always said he'd take us on but put off for years. He was famous for promising a guys' trip and then bailing out at the last minute—work took precedence over everything else in life. He planned to take us to McCloud River for a week of camping and fishing. The day before, he canceled and gave us the gifts he had gotten us for the trip—a lantern for me and a fishing knife for Joe. I think he hoped the gifts would serve as proof he'd intended to take us, but he never did. Joe was pissed, but boy, he loved that knife. It became one of his prized possessions, yet he never had the chance to use it."

Joe had a knife. Despite the fact that Kendra's hairs stood on end and her jaw bunched with tension, she evened out her voice. "What does a knife have to do with anything?"

"I thought you knew. My parents were murdered in 2006. I was just a kid, but I was even considered a suspect. Makes perfect sense when I think about it now. I was home. Mom and Dad were sleeping. We all were. When I woke up in the morning, I was in the kitchen, grabbing breakfast before school. Something felt wrong. You know, that feeling you have when the hair on your neck stands on end and there's an odd chill to the air you can't shake." Jake shivered. "Just thinking about it brings it all back." His face twisted in pain.

For a moment, he seemed to become a teen again. Innocence had most likely been stripped from him on that day, and his eyes glazed over.

"I'm not sure why I went into their bedroom. I never went in there. It was their space, you know? We weren't the family that spent Sunday mornings cuddled up in bed with Mom and Dad, if you get my drift. Plus, I was a teenager then. Old enough to realize private stuff went on in parents' bedrooms."

"I'm not sure I follow. What does any of this have to do with Joe having a knife?"

"My parents were stabbed to death."

A chill snaked down Kendra's spine.

"Are you trying to pin your parents' murders on Joe?"

"No. Well, maybe. I'm don't know. The thing is, Joe was away at college, quickly ruled out as a suspect, and he sure didn't jump in with help or even words of support when I was headed for trial. He pretty much abandoned me."

"Did the knife come up as the murder weapon?"

"The weapon was never found."

"Did you tell the police that Joe had a knife, that you suspected him? It sounds like you believe Joe was responsible for their deaths."

"I would never have told the cops. Joe was my brother, for God's sake. We didn't rat on each other. At least I wouldn't have ratted on him. Fuck, he didn't even show up for the trial." Jake's faced tensed with anger.

Kendra's heart twisted as she tried to quell her nerves. "I'm not sure what you want or what you hope to gain by sharing this with me. I loved Joe. I believed in him. Joe was not a killer."

Jake scrubbed his face with a hand. "I'm not so different from you. I'd like closure." Jake seemed to shrink back into his seat.

Kendra's nerves raced. What she wanted more than anything was to dart to the closet and find Joe's knife. She remembered saving it. Somewhere in the closet. *Where the hell had she put it? He had made a point of telling her it was one of his prized possessions, a gift from his dad.*

"Can we back up?"

Jake looked as if she'd woken him from a trance. "What? You think my brother was a saint. You're wrong." His mood went dark. He clenched his fists then opened them as if ready to attack, as if her words had sent him somewhere he didn't want to go. She'd cornered him, and he came out clawing. "There are some things I can't talk about. You get that, right?"

Kendra blinked, fearful but unsure how she had provoked him. Maybe Molly had been right. Maybe this guy was a loose cannon. In reality, what proof did she have, other than his striking resemblance to her husband, that he was indeed Joe's brother? She hadn't ID'd him. He could be a charlatan. Why he would pretend to be anyone but who he said he was, she couldn't imagine, except for the fact that her life had become a full-time *Dateline* episode.

She steadied herself and chose her next words carefully.

"I'm so sorry. I've overstepped my bounds. Maybe this is a good time for a break. Dinner?"

He stared at her but looked through her. Kendra waited a heartbeat and then stood and strode past Jake. As she walked by him, he grabbed her arm. His grasp was tight, powerful.

She locked eyes with him and offered him a half-grin, struggling to hide her panic and calm her racing heart. "You remind me so much of Joe. Talking about tough memories was something he avoided like the plague. Let's eat. I don't want you to tell me anything that doesn't feel right."

Jake hung his head, and his shoulders slumped. Still gripping her arm, he seemed at war with himself.

She patted his shoulder with her free hand. "Please let go of my arm. You're hurting me. I'd hate to have to ask you to leave."

Jake released her from his grip, gazing at his hand as if he had no consciousness of grabbing her. Confusion etched his brow. "I'm really sorry. I never should have touched you."

She continued into the kitchen. "I don't know what's troubling you, but it will be okay."

Kendra caught herself calming her breath, struggling to voluntarily slow her hammering heart.

He laughed wryly. "Don't you hate it when people say that?"

She laughed back. "I really do."

She handed him plates, napkins, and silverware and gestured to the table. "Can you set the table?"

"There are a lot of things I can't do, but that's something I can."

Kendra had wrinkled a nerve, but through the grace of the universe, she had been able to smooth it out. She set the roast and vegetables on a serving platter and carried it to the table.

"Let's talk about simple things. I'm an author. I'm interested in what people read. What's your favorite book?"

"*The Silence of the Lambs*. Hands down."

A spear straightened Kendra's spine. She hadn't expected that. This man was a mystery. Maybe worse. What if he'd killed Joe and made it look like a suicide? She shivered and fought to maintain a cool demeanor.

"Russ mentioned you're an author too. What do you write?"

"Travelogues. Not near what you've accomplished."

"Favorite vegetable?" Kendra tried to lighten the mood.

"Spinach. Makes you strong."

Kendra chuckled. "I do love the taste, and *Popeye* reruns are delightful."

"I know we decided to stick with easy conversation, but can I ask you something?"

Kendra hesitated, mid-bite, bringing her napkin up and covering her mouth. She peeked out at him with a questioning look.

"Would you mind showing me a photo of your baby?"

Kendra choked and coughed. "Let's stick with easier conversation."

CHAPTER FOURTEEN

T HE FOLLOWING MORNING, KENDRA SPENT A GOOD twenty minutes searching for Joe's knife. She remembered the box she'd stored it in. It had always amazed her how much Joe treasured the knife, and how he always kept it snugly placed within its leather sheath and in the top drawer of his dresser, to keep it close and protect it, he had said. She'd placed it in an athletic shoe box which contained some of Joe's prized childhood paraphernalia—his slingshot, a boomerang, a few Teenage Mutant Ninja Turtles, a guitar pic, and a Power Ranger. Things he truly got excited about. Finally, after pulling out a stepstool and holding onto the closet shelves as she hoisted herself up, she found the container at the back of the top shelf, tucked behind other boxes of assorted shoes and boots. While even after his death, it had been a huge decision to keep any of his belongings, she was glad she had. She wanted to hold onto his memory at the time, and though she had no one to pass his memories on to, she couldn't bear to part with that piece of him. She pulled the knife out and examined it, but not without trepidation. Could Joe have killed his parents with this very knife? She couldn't imagine. Her hand quivered as she ran the side of the blade across her finger. Still sharp. Still in perfect condition, etched with an ornate pattern of soothing swirls. She mused about that. Having a knife that was both artistic and lethal seemed such a contradiction. Beautiful, yet deadly. Kendra held the smooth walnut handle and slid the 6" blade back inside the scabbard, noting the snap fastener which conveniently attached to a belt, and shuddered. After her nerves quieted to a tolerable level, she climbed the three steps of the stool, steadying herself as she replaced the box back on the shelf, hiding it behind other boxes. The less she reminded herself of its existence, the better.

Kendra fought to push thoughts away. Her husband a killer? She shook like a skeleton blowing in the stiff October wind. *Enough. Write.*

That she did. That afternoon, she pondered Jake's visit as she readied herself for the night out with the girls. As she stood under the hot spray of the shower and scrubbed her head, she considered what a puzzle Jake seemed. On the surface, he appeared to be an average guy. But just beneath the skin, complications reigned.

Jake had scared her silly when he grabbed her arm last night, and thoughts of him being a murderer both petrified her and induced a serious case of denial. She'd done a masterful job of defusing his sudden spike of aggression, but sheer luck had averted a possible catastrophe. He'd liked hearing she thought of him fondly as she connected his likeness to Joe. But for an entire two hours after his departure, she had been unable to take a breath without it catching on her ribs.

Kendra hated that she questioned herself when another person's behavior upset her. But that was exactly what she had done. Had she overreacted to Jake's grip on her arm? Had she provoked him in some way?

The Silence of the Lambs? That revelation had scared her bones cold. She swore they'd rattled inside her for weeks after she finished the book. Was there any darker novel? *Rosemary's Baby* perhaps. That, coupled with the realization that the knife Jake mentioned was under her roof. Maybe she should lose it in the lake the next time she kayaked. If it was the murder weapon, she didn't want it anywhere near her, but on the other hand, if it was used in Joe's parents' murders, shouldn't someone of authority have it? *Enough. You're going out tonight.*

Kendra dried her hair and checked her phone.

Molly had texted. *Come early, and we'll have a quick drink at the bar and catch up.*

Kendra guessed Molly wanted a follow-up on yesterday's conversation. Molly's notions about Kendra being vulnerable weren't wrong, and in the case of last night, her overprotectiveness had been appropriate, but Kendra couldn't let an opportunity to know more about Joe pass. And she still frowned whenever the conversation replayed in her head. She wasn't sharing any information about Jake with Molly.

Kendra texted back. *K.*

Yet Kendra wanted to run a few things by Molly. She'd filter her words, make up a fake scenario, and claim it was going into the current manuscript. While certain events were better left out of the conversation—if she told Molly about Jake's aggressive behavior and his choice of reading material, she'd lock Kendra up for spending even a minute with him—she was curious about Molly's take on emotionally disturbed kids.

Kendra retrieved her favorite jeans and a cozy cowl-neck sweater from the closet. Molly always dressed like she was on the hunt when the girls went out. Her married friends did the same. But Kendra was happiest in the background. Even before meeting Joe.

She donned a light wool coat and headed into the brisk night air. Since the days were getting shorter, the sun set about six p.m. Far too early. As Kendra eased down the gravel road—tunneled by elms, oaks, and sycamore trees, which still held tightly on to their changing leaves—she felt a stir of excitement. Going out with friends seemed normal. One more baby step in the great scheme of the future.

But as soon as she approached the car, she felt like turning around, going inside and holing up. When Kendra considered the future, her heart sank. *Who am I kidding?* She had no future. Maybe as an author but not personally.

The negative thoughts sucked her in like a Dyson. She hated how she reminded herself of one of the fish in the lake. Flip-flopping on dry land. Not fitting in, no matter how much she tried. She couldn't imagine carrying on, moving past the losses. She'd wind up alone, childless, and unhappy. And she wasn't just moping.

When reality slaps you in the face, you have to accept it.

When she ducked inside the restaurant and spotted Molly, she relaxed. Already sitting at the bar, Molly drank some froufrou beverage from a fancy glass.

She gathered Kendra in an extended hug. "I'm so proud of you. You did it. You came out!"

"Trust me, I almost didn't."

"What do you want to drink? I'm having a Vootbeer."

"I *have* been out of circulation for a while. What the hell is that?"

Molly studied her drink. "Root beer, whipped cream, and … vodka. A big-girl root beer float." She made a contented sound as she sipped through her straw.

Kendra glanced from Molly's drink to the bartender. "Give

me something trendy but not too sweet." She slid onto the swivel seat next to Molly.

Molly sucked on a maraschino cherry. "So, tell me about Jake."

"What?"

Molly shot a knowing look at Kendra.

Did she drive by and see Jake's car?

Damn, maybe it was Molly who'd been following her all this time. Kendra could compare her to a helicopter mom. Despite the warnings she'd previously given herself, she spilled everything—even the firm grasp Jake had gripped her arm with and his favorite novel. Kendra couldn't keep a secret from Molly for ten seconds. It was one of her greatest weaknesses. *Not entirely true. I didn't tell her about the knife.*

"Promise me you will distance yourself from this guy. Do you hear me? He's creepy, Kendra. There was a reason—a very good reason—Joe didn't talk about his family. Sure, you feel like he withheld important background info from you, but he did so with intention. Some things are better left unknown."

"Honestly? I can't let go. Why Joe left me matters. I don't know if I'll ever be able to move past this. My life is essentially over. I'm not catastrophizing. I'm not just grieving. And besides, grief isn't a passing thing. It takes time. A long time. There's no magic switch I can toggle to turn it off."

"Just relax tonight. Be in the moment."

Kendra fought to remember. "Do you ever wonder what we did before we had to label everything and everyone?"

"What do you mean?"

"Mindfulness. Fully attending to what's happening. Like you're sipping your drink right now. You taste it, swirl it around in your mouth, say *mmm*, and swallow with total focus."

In spite of admonitions, Kendra deliberated over her blue martini. The blue reminded her of the ocean. It made her feel a bit wavy too. It tasted citrusy. Healthy. Like when you bit into a slice of orange or pineapple and felt like you'd just done something right for yourself.

"I'm doing it. Being mindful." She laughed.

Molly patted Kendra's thigh. "Good girl." She glanced toward the door. "There's Jill and Amy. Let's grab our table. And no more wallowing. I don't mean ever, just not tonight. If you want normal, you have to practice normal."

Kendra followed her friend's advice. Or tried to anyway. Come to think of it, Jean and Moderator Mary had suggested the same thing.

But the girls ripped on their husbands for a while, and Kendra had to bite her tongue. At least they had husbands to complain about. She tried to conjure up some memory of something Joe had done to drive her crazy.

"Joe used to make the strongest coffee," Kendra offered, trying to fit in.

Molly looked at her as if she had a third eye. "But you like strong coffee."

Kendra shrugged. She didn't want to commandeer the conversation to the real crises going on in her life …

They switched topics, which served all of them well in Kendra's mind. They discussed vegan options—pan-roasted Brussel sprouts, baby kale Caesar salad, candy cane beets, and roasted squash. Then, they talked about Botox and fillers. All appropriate and current subject matters.

Kendra lost track of time, savoring her sprouts and second blueberry martini when she felt a tap on her shoulder. Jake. She blinked, hoping she'd clear her vision and recognize she was on edge and simply imagining his presence. But, no, he was there. Directly behind him stood Russ Jameson. For some reason, she couldn't imagine these two guys going out to dinner at a vegan restaurant. Especially on a Friday. Far as she knew—not that she knew much—Russ spent most of his life on the lake or in his home. She had no idea what Jake did, but here they were, standing in front of her.

Kendra remained speechless, but Jake did not.

He introduced himself all around. "Hi, I'm Jake, Kendra's brother-in-law. And this here is my landlord, Russ. We live on Pleasant Lake. Neighbors of Kendra's." He sounded like a frigging cowboy.

Eyes widened. Mouths gaped.

Molly came to the rescue. She stood and shook hands with Jake. "My, you're the spitting image of your brother. Nice to meet you." She waved them away. "You guys enjoy this place." Molly then twisted a shoulder and returned to her seat.

Stunned, Jake narrowed his eyes but took the hint.

As soon as the men were out of earshot, Jill started. "Joe has a brother? Why didn't you say something? I thought he didn't have family. I mean, no living family."

"Don't fall in love with him," Erica piped in as Kendra shuddered.

Molly took charge. "It's a bit complicated, and we're here to have fun." She basically said, *Nothing's happening here. Move on,* but the suspense was tangible.

Her friends wanted to know every detail even though they slowly realized they had to leave this discussion for another time. One where Kendra wasn't in attendance.

Kendra knew the too-huge elephant wouldn't leave the room on its own. "Jake showed up a week or so ago. He's probably a money-grubber. I'm doing my best to ignore him. You know how family appears from out of the woodwork when someone dies. I'm sure he'll lose interest and move on. But don't encourage him, okay? Don't look at him, talk about him, or any such thing." She pulled Amy's hand toward her to avert Amy's attention from Jake.

Jill rested a hand on Kendra's arm. "He looks just like Joe. That's unnerving. Are you okay?"

Again, Kendra donned her *just fine* mask. "Me? Of course."

Erica shivered in her seat. "My nerves are prickly, and he's not my relative."

Kendra loathed the sympathetic gazes that flooded her.

"Let it go," Molly ordered.

And they did.

Molly stood. "Let's go to Vinology next. I'm in the mood for a nice glass of wine and some dessert. We can all Uber home if we have too much to drink."

Kendra tried the mindfulness shit the rest of the night, but frankly, mindfulness sucked when your life was already down the drain. She drank a little too much, laughed a little too loud, and prayed the Uber driver would find her house without taking a detour and cutting her heart out. On the other hand, her heart had already been mutilated. What remained was the involuntary beating. Kept her alive, but just barely.

CHAPTER FIFTEEN

KENDRA WOKE UP EARLY, SURPRISINGLY NOT HUNGOVER and full of energy. Sunshine flooded the back deck, and she stuck her head outside to check the temperature. Brisk fall air but not unmanageable. She started coffee, layered on sweats, and shoved her feet inside a pair of shoes before grabbing a fresh-brewed cup and heading outside.

She still had to deal with retrieving her car, but there was no rush. What meant the most now was seizing a bit of peace. Restoring order to her life. She sank into a deck chair—her favorite red Adirondack—and considered her options. When she peeled away the drama of the last week—primarily Jake—she gained some much-needed distance. Writing sustained her, centered her. Grief group helped. The time with JJ had renewed her. She vowed to focus on writing and grief group and nothing more. Distance would take a front seat. Discovering who Joe had been, his secrets, and his hidden motivation for taking his life could wait.

Molly's voice interrupted her reverie. "I thought I might find you out here."

Kendra snapped her head around, fearful for a moment that she hadn't locked the doors. "Did you come in the front?"

Molly's confusion was evident. "You were lost in thought. I just walked around back when I found the door locked and you didn't answer my knock. Relax. It's just me."

"Sorry. I thought I'd let my paranoia go, but you startled me."

"No worries." Molly pulled up a chair beside her and gazed out at the lake. "It's sure peaceful here. I went and got my car and thought I'd drive out and take you to town, so you don't have to call for a ride."

"You're a good friend. Thanks for taking over with the girls last night. I bet they were tittering behind my back."

"For sure, but I think I shut them down. I downplayed Jake's arrival and told them not to worry. I've got your back."

"I need a break from drama."

Molly patted Kendra's arm. "That's my girl. Now, get me a traveler"—she pointed at Kendra's mug—"and we'll go. I've got lots of papers to correct, and time's a-wasting."

Kendra hurried inside and filled a steaming travel mug with black coffee, just the way Molly liked it, and then met her friend out front. Once she settled in the passenger seat, she shared her decision to focus on writing and grief group.

"Perfect. Now that the weather's turning, it's a great time to hole up inside and write. How's the book coming?"

"Good. Great in fact. I'll have the first draft done soon, off to Jean, and then rewrites. I'm thinking this one will be better than the last." Lies came easy today.

Molly gripped her friend's hand. "I'm so proud of you."

After they retrieved Kendra's SUV, they gathered each other in a lingering hug.

"I'll be in touch," Kendra said.

"Text me."

Kendra drove home, thinking about her story and grief group. She needed to think about what she'd talk about in group this week. But first, writing.

Kendra spent the next four days doing just that. She exhausted hours at the keyboard, totally immersed in her story of a woman who had married a man she didn't know. Yes, she had somewhat turned her life into fiction but not in any recognizable way. *Write what you know.*

On Wednesday morning, she pondered grief. A mix of emotions percolated. She ping-ponged like a casualty of bipolar disorder. One minute, on top of the world, delighting in birdsong and a day full of opportunity. The next minute, in a deep, hollow cavern, the depth of emptiness and the absence of hope threatening to swallow her whole. Might be a topic worth exploring. What she'd learned: there was no checklist for grief. You couldn't just tick off the steps. Yet what the experts said held some merit. The stages all existed—shock, denial, bargaining, guilt, anger, depression, and acceptance. Kendra disagreed with the acceptance stage. In her mind, she might adjust to life without Joey and Joe, but she'd be damned if she ever accepted it. And the stages didn't follow any order; they came and went like an unexpected storm—fierce, then suddenly languid.

The permanent fog that had overshadowed her life the past six months lifted a bit—the out-of-body actions that had occupied her days were replaced by productive pages on her desktop, little moments of enjoyment. True laughter and pleasure began to seep back into her life. In tiny smidgens.

Kendra dressed in jeans and layered a blouse with a thick sweater. She also donned knee-high boots before heading into the evening cold. Temperatures had dropped considerably the past few days, and the damp chill that accompanied the falling thermometer put her in a constant state of shivers. She drove toward the church with an ounce of pleasure and looked forward to an opportunity to talk about whatever came to mind.

Was there a term for that now too? Or was talking off the cuff still considered a stream of consciousness? Group might be a good place to try that.

When she entered the basement, she spotted Nathan and offered him a hello nod and an easy smile.

"I brought a chair over for you."

Kendra thanked him and plopped in the chair, greeting the others as they took their seats.

Mary started the group. "We've come a long way," she said. "We've become a place of safety and trust."

Kendra's gaze circled the faces of agreement and felt the same.

"Who would like to start?"

"I spend days watching videos of my partner," Josh said. "He was just plain silly sometimes. He danced like no one was watching, but he shouldn't have. No sense of rhythm whatsoever." Josh chuckled. "I tried watching the videos with my mom, but she thinks it's a bad idea. She says I'm dwelling too much on the past. If we don't deal with the past, how do we face the future?"

"You have every right to do what you need to do to process your loss," Gary said.

Trevor began next. "I feel guilty to be alive. My sister and I led different lifestyles. I'm the one who overeats and drinks too much. I smoke. I don't take care of myself. But Kate ran marathons. She put only natural foods in her mouth. She never smoked. She barely let a drop of alcohol pass her lips. She has kids—a two-year-old and a four-year-old. Her husband is a saint. Invested and determined to give his children the best possible life. It should have been me."

"You don't look overweight," the words popped out of Gary's mouth.

At first, Kendra didn't know how to take his words. It seemed like an inappropriate comment, yet she guessed all the group members were sharing similar thoughts. She squelched a giggle.

"I figured the least I could do was get my act together after Kate died. At first, it was just fallout from her death. I couldn't eat, didn't want a drink, although if there's ever a time to crave alcohol …"

A chorus of soft laughter echoed from the group.

"Now, I'm focused on a healthy lifestyle for my niece and nephew. They need good role models."

"Good for you," Gary added.

"I miss her so much. Some days, I can't stand the pain. I'll pick up the phone just to hear her voice mails. I saved some messages she'd left me. Not purposefully, mind you, but just because they were special at the time. And some because I was too lazy to delete them. I treasure them now."

"Like Gary said. We're entitled to do what we need to do. If you want to spend a day listening to your sister's voice, good for you," Josh said.

A chill raced down Kendra's spine. Josh's words ran true. Next in the circle, eyes landed on Kendra. Listen to Joe's voice again? Just the thought made her sad.

Kendra offered a slight wave of her hand. "First, I want to thank you all for allowing me this safety. Life's gotten better this past week. I'm more functional, and I even allowed myself to cry, not those heartbreaking sobs, just gloomy tears. You guys made that possible."

Smiles met her words.

"I make these agreements with myself. I'll come to group and talk about this. I set up these self-defined boundaries. I'm realizing how futile that is—or maybe just foolish. The thing is, my husband hanged himself. He committed suicide. I struggle with this. I was aching, too, but I would never have deserted him when he needed me."

Mary sat forward and locked eyes with Kendra. "Maybe you're angry with him for leaving you when you needed him most. You hinted at that in our last meeting."

"I am." Kendra knotted her fingers. "But I feel like I'm betraying him by saying it aloud. He was in pain. Horrible pain. My pain shouldn't have taken precedence over his, but then again, why didn't he talk to me? I could have helped him. Held him. Told him we'd get through Joey's death together."

"You're allowed to be angry."

"It's like he wanted me to suffer more. Like it wasn't enough that we'd lost Joey—he had to punish me. Blame me. I was home alone with Joey when he died. I already felt at fault, but then when I walked into the garage and saw Joe hanging from the rafters, it was as if he were saying, *Fuck you. You don't deserve one iota of happiness. You took my son from me.*"

"Seems natural that you would feel that way," Nathan offered.

Kendra thinned her lips and squeezed her eyes shut tight. "He hurt me. He abandoned me. He had to have been furious with me to take his own life and plan it so that I would find him like that."

"I know it seems that way now," Mary said.

"So, you think, in time, I'll come to make sense of it in a different way? Because I'll tell you something else since this is my safe place." Kendra proceeded to tell the members about Jake, Joe's troubled past, his parents' murders, the fact that Joe hadn't shared a word of any of this with her.

Cathy—who'd lost her best friend, Nicole, to drowning—offered her sympathy and some advice. "You feel what you feel. There are no rules about that. You're entitled to be angry. You're entitled to question Joe's decision. It sounds like he had a tough childhood and suffered his fair share of trauma. I don't know what to say about his brother showing up, but I do sometimes think about suicide. What stops most of us from taking our lives is that we don't want to hurt those we love. I considered checking out after Nicole died, but it would have killed my parents and my siblings, to say nothing of Nicole's family. I couldn't do that to them. Depression is a bitch though. I finally saw my doctor."

Kendra cocked her head. "I haven't given a lot of thought about what stops us from doing ourselves in," she said, "but you're right. I'd never hurt my friends, but I think it's because I know how it feels to be left behind. The guilt I feel, the shame at admitting my husband—the love of my life—chose death over me, it eats me up. He chose to wrap a belt around his neck, secure it, and hang himself in our home—the place I worked and slept. My safe haven. I had to move. I had to pack up all our shit, all the pieces of our life together, tuck them away in boxes, and be alone. Utterly alone.

"I'm taking up too much of our time. Someone else go."

"We can move on if you want, Kendra, but thank you for trusting us with your story," Mary said.

The group continued for the next ninety minutes. As it did, a weight lifted from Kendra's shoulders. Whatever she needed to do to put Joe to rest, she would do it even if it meant time with Jake. To hell with the naysayers.

Nathan and Kendra had established a pattern the past few weeks, and as Mary ended the group, he grabbed her chair while Kendra dived into the restroom.

She met Cathy in the ladies' room and gathered her in a giant hug. "Your friend is looking down on you. She's so proud of you. You're a wise young woman, destined to do great things."

Cathy's eyes lit up. "You really think so?"

"I might be overstepping my bounds, but I do believe in an afterlife. I can't imagine your friend not watching over you."

"Thanks," the young girl said. "That means so much." She left Kendra alone at the sink.

Kendra left the restroom and found the room empty and Nathan waiting near the staircase. He shut off the lights after they climbed the stairs and guided her out of the building. A stiff wind met them, and Kendra knotted a scarf tight around her neck.

"Beer?" Nathan offered.

Kendra nodded and smiled. "Beer. Meet you there."

Nathan followed her to the neighborhood beer joint and laced his arm through hers as they waltzed down the street.

"You seem happy tonight."

Kendra couldn't contain her giddiness. "I never put much credence in talking about my grief, but that was one hell of a session."

"I'm surprised."

Kendra glanced at him, puzzled. "Why?"

"I would have guessed an author gets to the heart of her characters. When you do that on paper, doesn't it ring true?"

Kendra couldn't help but chuckle. "Just because we're authors doesn't mean we're astute about our own shit. Just sayin.'"

"True." Nathan squeezed her hand, and then he opened the door and allowed her to pass in front of him.

They assumed a spot, just a few seats down from their usual stools, and Nathan continued. "Human nature is a funny thing. We see others' conflicts so clearly, how people sabotage themselves and what stands in their way, but we're blind to our own frailties."

"Maybe you should be an author."

"Tried to write a poem once. I was about sixteen, a junior in high school, had a crazy crush on this senior girl. I figured if I wrote a poem—you know, all sentimental and romantic—she'd have to accept my invitation to prom."

"And?"

"She turned me down flat. Last time I picked up a pen to write anything personal."

"Rejection stinks."

"Hey, just so you know, that husband of yours made a huge mistake. He couldn't have been in his right mind to leave you behind. That's the God's truth."

Kendra blushed, a pink sheen suffusing her neck and cheeks. "Thanks," she said. "I'm not sure I believe you, but I appreciate the sentiment."

By the time Kendra glanced at her watch, she realized time had flown. "I have to go."

Nathan paid the tab and walked her to her SUV. "Any chance we could do dinner sometime? Not a date—I heard you loud and clear the first night we got together—but just as friends? I enjoy your company."

"Friday?" Kendra asked. "What's your number?"

Nathan recited his number, and Kendra filed it in her phone.

"Friday it is," he said before he gave her a brief hug and watched her drive away.

CHAPTER SIXTEEN

KENDRA HAD PREPARED FOR AN EMOTIONAL CRASH THE next morning. Before falling asleep the night before, she had actually warned herself that when she experienced a high like tonight, a low was soon to follow.

She woke with a piercing headache and a deep well of sadness in her gut. She missed Joe. She had actually absently reached for him this morning before coming to full wakefulness, patted his side of the bed, and wondered if he'd gone to the bathroom.

All these months, she'd fiercely denied feelings of loneliness and misery. Told herself that she'd lived alone the first thirty-eight years of her life—the adult years anyway—and she was accustomed to loneliness. No need to panic about sleeping alone. But she admitted now how much she missed resting her head in the crook of Joe's shoulder before she fell asleep at night and then again first thing in the morning. She missed his kisses, how he'd cupped her breast with his hand when they slept, how they'd spooned up with each other like socks and shoes, all nestled where they belonged.

Tears streaked her cheeks as she entered the kitchen. She swiped her face with the back of her pajama sleeve, drying the tears and snot dripped off her nose as she pulled out the coffee beans and filled the grinder. While the coffee brewed, she flicked on the gas fireplace and huddled in front of it, unable to abate the chill that started at her core and worked its way to her nose, fingers, and toes.

Warming her hands around a mug of hot coffee, she sat on the sofa and filed through the pictures of Joe and Jake for the umpteenth time, hoping for some clue of Joe's past, some logical explanation of his suicide. She rolled her eyes. Suicide wasn't a logical step. It wasn't simple cause and effect—if this, then that.

Sometimes, she couldn't believe her thoughts. How little they made sense. And it wasn't like anyone lived to explain the whys after they took their own life. Sure, there were those trite explanations—depression, despair, defeat, desolation, decline, demographics—but when Kendra recalled Jake's words, he'd intimated that Joe had a reason to take his own life. And the most recent studies about suicide suggested a far more complicated explanation—that those who took their own lives truly believed they were doing the world a favor.

She toyed with possible answers for Joe's choice. Money—they'd had plenty. Work—Joe had loved his job. Marriage—she thought he'd loved her. Joey—his death had left both her and Joe desolate, but was that enough of a reason? If, as Jake had suggested, there was more to Joe's past that had led to his suicide, what would it have been?

C'mon, Kendra. You play what-if all the time as an author. You can do this.

What if Joe had had something to do with his parents' murders? What if he had known something about Jake's involvement but protected his brother? What if Jake had known what Joe had done? He'd said he felt Joe had abandoned him. Had he threatened Joe? Had he scared Joe into killing himself? What if Jake hadn't been responsible, but Joe had known who was and kept that from the authorities, letting Jake go to trial when Joe could have prevented it?

Kendra reminded herself of her most recent promise to focus on her writing and her grief. *Why is life so damn complicated? Why do smart people do stupid things, like choose a rabbit hole over filling a blank page?*

Kendra tossed the photos into a wicker basket in the middle of the coffee table. She poured another cup of coffee and traipsed into her office, where she fired up her computer. An email notification flashed on the screen. Jake.

Why the hell did I include my email address on my website? You'd think I would have learned.

She pushed her hair off her forehead and raked her fingers through the tangles. She closed her eyes, asking, *Should I, or shouldn't I?* The tug was too great. She opened her email, clicking on Jake's message.

I don't want to bother you, and I'm embarrassed about my behavior when you had me for dinner, but I also think there are some things you're entitled to know.

Our family belonged to the Catholic church. One of the few things we did together, I guess you'd say. I'm sharing my opinion, which is probably biased, but our parents were more concerned about appearance than substance. They were religious about religion, if that makes sense.

We had to attend Mass every Sunday as well as Catholic school. Joe was an altar boy, and I followed in his footsteps years later. He told me to stay away from Father Warren, but I never thought much of his warning. He said the guy was creepy, but he was a priest. Kind of like how we think of cops when we're kids, priests are supposed to be the good guys. This guy wasn't. The parish priest had raped Joe. He never told me. Not until after it happened to me. He thought it was his fault. Both his rape and mine. That he wasn't strong enough. That he hadn't protected me. I reacted with lots of emotional issues. Joe, I guess, looking back on it, was busy keeping it a secret. We decided to tell our parents. Together. They told us we were making up stories. That's one of the reasons Joe never came home after he left for college.

Sorry to lay this on you in an email. I didn't mean to infer that Joe did anything wrong. When I thought about it later, maybe you thought I was making him out to be a bad guy. I wasn't. But you need to know he had demons.

Overtaken by shock, Kendra wrapped a blanket around her shoulders and reread Jake's message four times, committing every word to memory. Jake's message explained a lot. She wasn't sure how the timing worked. If somehow Joey's death had thrown Joe back into the dark place that must have occupied years of his life. Years when he'd felt trapped with a secret. Ashamed and guilty of who he was. No wonder he hadn't shared any of this with Kendra. She wished he had, but it made sense that he had been afraid and ashamed.

Kendra composed a message.

Dear Jake,

Thank you for sharing something so personal with me. I can't imagine what Joe suffered. What you suffered. I'm angry about how your parents handled this—or rather, the fact that they didn't. I'm so sorry. You and Joe were entitled to protection and, even more, to justice.

I wonder if counseling could have helped Joe. I wonder if you've ever considered counseling.

What occurs to me is that your parents let you down in a way that no child deserves. A parent's first job is to protect their child, to provide for their safety and well-being. Their disbelief had to cause both of you a great deal of pain. You must have felt unworthy, like a castaway, like you didn't matter.

Joe mattered. I loved him more passionately than I'd thought possible. I miss him incredibly. He was an amazing husband—devoted, considerate, doting even. He was an even better father—invested, loving, proud, and attentive. You both deserved the father Joe turned out to be. I hope you find some peace in knowing Joe found a way to be a great dad in spite of his trauma.

All the best,

Kendra

Kendra's stomach tightened. She leaned back in the chair and studied her words. The more time she spent thinking of what Joe had endured, the more she understood.

The tiny insecurities now made sense. Joe had always worried if he'd made her happy in the bedroom, if his "performance" had been enough. Kendra told him not to worry. No performance necessary. Joe had always checked in with her about his appearance as well, and when she started shopping for him, he'd made sure to tell her to stay away from the pastel dress shirts that had become fashionable for men.

"I'm a man's man. Stick with the whites. Go with dark colors if you must, but if you buy me a pink shirt, I'll burn it."

Seemed a little over the top, but now, she understood. Holding on to his manhood must have been paramount after the horrors he'd endured as a young boy.

Kendra spun around in her chair, unable to find an outlet for her despair. She so wanted to talk to Joe. To tell him how sorry she was. Wanted to soothe him. Stroke his brow. Let him know that they could have built a life even though they had suffered the heartbreak of losing Joey. She wanted to fix it for him. Make him better.

Instead, Kendra went to the kitchen and brewed a cup of hot tea, carried it to the family room, and gazed out at the lake. The wind pushed waves onto the shore, capping white as they twirled over each other. Gray clouds settled low in the sky, making daytime disappear, taking all signs of light and hope with them.

It was sometimes impossible to make sense of life. To reason why things happened. If there was some ultimate purpose for the pain we suffered. If somehow, without that pain, we would be void of the human experience and less human as a result.

Kendra imagined her life differently. If Joe and Joey had lived, if she'd had the chance to do it all again. She hadn't needed to lose them to know how much she loved them. She hadn't needed to suffer such unimaginable pain to become a better person. There was no sense to be made of the past seven months, no great order she could envision being served by this immeasurable loss.

She wouldn't turn into some champion for suicide prevention or SIDS research because of her losses. Those roles were for someone else, not her. There wasn't one single positive thing to be gained by death. Just loneliness, heartache, desperation, and unending sadness. Nothing more.

CHAPTER SEVENTEEN

KENDRA'S ATTENTION WAS DRAWN TO A SOUND. ON HER front porch. Scraping. Metal grating concrete. She rose from the chair and walked gingerly toward the noise, taking care to peek out the window aside her front entrance door. She watched Molly, leaning over with a shovel, removing something from her front porch. As she narrowed her eyes, she saw a rabbit. Smashed and bloody, a mass of intestines and bones.

Molly's head lifted, and she gazed at Kendra through a tearful face. Kendra opened the door and stared.

"Stay inside. You don't need to see this."

"What's going on? What happened?"

Kendra watched Molly tremble, broken and devastated.

"Go inside," Molly repeated, a quiver to her voice Kendra seldom heard.

Kendra couldn't close the door. Her eyes rested on the dead bunny in the shovel's bowl. "I don't understand." She stepped outside and took the shovel handle from Molly's hands, carrying the shovel and its dead contents across the gravel road and dumping it in the brush.

After she strode back across the street, she rested the shovel against the garage and went to her friend. "Come inside." She led Molly indoors and sat her down at the dining room table, hurrying to the kitchen to brew a cup of tea, gathering tissues in her hand, and carting them to Molly.

Molly couldn't control the shaking of her limbs, nor stem the flood of tears. "I came over to surprise you. Oh, I left a container of cookies on the chair. On your porch. That poor little bunny was lying dead on your doorstep. Someone had killed him, and I don't think it was an animal. Someone had planted that little baby there. Someone is trying to scare you. What the hell is going on, Kendra?"

Kendra tried to soothe her friend. "I'm not sure. Blow your nose. Drink your tea. Take some breaths."

Molly fought to catch her breath between sobs. "I think … you should … call the police."

"Let's think this through."

Kendra knew what she had seen. Molly wasn't wrong. The animal had been desecrated. Its body didn't look like it had been mauled by a predator but rather like its head had been bashed in and its body gutted like a deer.

It couldn't have been Jake unless he'd planted the dead carcass at her door while she was asleep. His email message had suggested no hint of retaliation. He was polite and thoughtful in his words. He'd simply passed along information he felt would allow her to reach closure around Joe's suicide.

Who else would do this? Who did she know?

None of this made sense, but so little of her life did.

She grasped Molly's hand. "It could have been a coyote. Russ mentioned we have them here. I don't know what they do to their prey, but nature's pretty ugly. Living at the lake is like my little slice of heaven, but bad things happen in the wild. I don't want to make more of this than is warranted. Catch your breath, and we'll have some cookies. Then, we'll sort this out."

Molly slumped in her chair and continued to shake.

Kendra's mind ran a four-minute mile. Coyotes. Eagles. Facebook posts had warned neighbors to keep their small animals inside. But a coyote would eat its prey, not smash in its head and leave it for the vultures. And not on her front porch.

She put her hand beneath Molly's chin and turned her face, trying to make light of the situation. "So, what are you doing here anyway? Aren't you supposed to be teaching? Did you skip school?"

Molly blinked a few times and came back to the moment. "We had conferences last night. I'm off today. And I have something to share with you. I made cookies to celebrate."

Kendra's face lit up. "Then, let's celebrate! Just hold on a minute. I want to hose off the porch."

She hustled out the side door, unwound the hose from the reel, and turned on the water. Before she adjusted the nozzle to spray off the porch, she noticed a trail of blood along the wooden slats of the porch. She stood back for a minute and squinted. It almost looked like a word. Surely, she was imagining the worst again. Making up things that weren't there. But as she moved closer, she made out a word. *MURDERER*. Was she seeing correctly? Too often, she questioned her vision. While she could summon Molly for confirmation, Kendra decided to do something else. She removed her cell phone from her back pocket and snapped a photo. Molly had something to celebrate. She couldn't possibly ruin Molly's news with this.

Still, it required every ounce of strength Kendra possessed to crush her fear. Kendra fell to her knees and shook. *Someone is after me.* With trembling hands, Kendra crept to the side of the house, stood, and with the nozzle on a high-pressured spray, she turned away and squeezed her eyes shut while she washed away the sick message.

When she opened her eyes, the word had disappeared. Only a puddle of water remained. But she couldn't unsee what she had read. She couldn't calm her racing heart or cool her clammy palms. The hose, a slithering snake, lay on the ground where she'd dropped it. She wanted more than anything to pull it together for Molly. Molly deserved that. With every fiber of her being, Kendra attempted to stop the rattling and reduce it to jitters that trailed every inch of her skin. She'd deal with this incident later. Not a lot later, but some.

When she reentered the house, she found Molly in the kitchen, pulling a plate out of the cupboard and loading it with freshly baked chocolate chip cookies. She set the plate on the dining room table and returned to the kitchen, gathering two glasses and a half-gallon of milk.

Once she settled in the seat next to Kendra, she dropped her head. Confusion covered Kendra's face. But then she understood. The dead bunny had stolen Molly's joy.

"I hate that this bunny showed up on my porch," she said as she rubbed the gooseflesh along her arms. "You had good news, and now, you're sad."

"We should talk about this dead animal. This was planned and directed at you. On your fricking front porch of all things. First, Jake. Now, this. We need to do something. We can't just ignore this."

Kendra remained thoughtful for a moment, recognizing how relieved she was to have Molly in her camp. But whether they dealt with this right this minute or in a few hours would not matter in the long run. "First, tell me your news, and then we'll deal with what's going on in my life."

Sullen and seemingly ashamed, Molly spoke. "I've been

keeping something from you, and I feel horrible about it. You asked me not to treat you like glass, but I'm guilty of doing just that."

Kendra eyed her friend, unable to imagine what on earth Molly had hidden from her. "Would you just tell me?"

"I've been seeing someone. You remember Adam Mason, the guy who came to my class to do the STEM project? The engineer who built the gravity cruisers with the kids? They learned all about kinetic energy, friction, inertia, momentum …"

"Right, right. I got it. You thought the guy was cute. You liked that you'd met someone who didn't teach. But that was a long time ago, right? Last spring?"

"We've been seeing each other."

"That's great!"

Molly gazed at Kendra with a troubled expression. "I didn't want to tell you because I felt it would be like rubbing salt in a gaping wound. I didn't want to brag or hurt you."

Kendra locked gazes with Molly. "You have to stop this. I understand why you kept this from me, and I can't promise you that I don't miss Joe when I see couples. But I want you to be happy. You're the last of our group to find someone. Is it serious?"

Molly smiled, and her eyes sparkled. "Pretty. We're talking marriage."

"Whirlwind romance?"

"Yes, and no."

Kendra bit off half of a cookie. Over a filled mouth, she tried to talk. "When do I meet him?"

"I don't want you to feel like a third wheel." Molly frowned, as if she were disappointing Kendra.

"Let it go. I'm perfectly happy, being the tagalong. Better yet, I'll have you guys for dinner. Let's say, next Friday or Saturday night. Talk to Adam and see what works for him. Deal?"

Molly's eyes shone with excitement. "I can't wait for you to meet him. He's perfect."

Kendra narrowed her eyes. "You mean, as perfect as any man can be."

Molly laughed briefly, and then her gaze fixed back on the front door. "We can talk about Adam later. I can't stop thinking about that poor rabbit. Who would have left a dead bunny on your porch?"

Kendra bit her lip, needing to tamp down her fear. "I honestly have no idea. It could be a prank. Kids having their perverted fun."

"Or it could be serious. We could call that kooky Russ guy and see if he knows anything. He's the neighborhood watch guy, right?"

"He is, but I like my privacy. I don't want unwarranted attention. The guy's well meaning, but I've been able to maintain a certain amount of distance, and I like it that way."

"Still ..."

"I have something to show you. It's upsetting, but we've been through worse, and I need your level head." Kendra stood and popped the last of the cookie into her mouth.

She trailed into her office. Molly followed, brushing her hands on her jeans.

Kendra sat Molly down in front of the desktop, pulled up the email from Jake, and waited while Molly devoured the message. She sat back in the chair when she finished, staring at the screen and cupping her chin with her hand.

"What's he after? He's playing on your sympathy here. The way I see it, there are three possibilities: he's crazy, he's lying, and/ or he wants something. If he has your sympathy, he has you where he wants you. Vulnerable. Connected to him. Worse, needing him."

Kendra plopped down on the floor, crossed her ankles, and gazed up at her friend. "Why do you always look for the worst in people? This explains so much. If Joe and Jake were abused by a priest and nothing was done to prevent it, no wonder Joe ..."

"What? Decided to off himself? I don't mean to be cruel,

but lots of people are abused and survive to live happy, productive lives."

"Yeah, but some people struggle with shame, guilt, and insecurity. When Joey died, Joe probably felt like he was a bad father, like he wasn't able to do what he wanted most—raise a boy to adulthood with his innocence intact."

"I hear you, but you're such a softy. You can't always take people at face value. They'll take advantage of you. Think about it. You do author events for free. You fall for every person with his hand out. Tell me you didn't buy popcorn from the Boy Scouts this year."

Kendra looked sheepish. "I like caramel corn."

"And buy magazines from Jill's kids' fundraisers."

"They had a couple I read anyway."

Molly locked eyes with her friend. "Not everyone is true blue like you. Please, if Jake tries to get in touch with you again, tell him you're busy, meeting a deadline. You do have a deadline, right?"

"Yep. And I'm close to meeting it. You know me though. I like to edit before I turn in a draft. I want it to be as perfect as possible. Jean appreciates that."

Molly twisted around in the chair and gazed out at the lake. "Wish my students cared about that." Spinning to face Kendra, she continued. "One more thing. Someone is trying to scare you. Leaving a dead animal on your porch is meant to intimidate you, weaken your resolve. It could be Jake."

"I hear you. I'll check with Russ. But it's not an emergency, and I don't need him lurking. The more I think about it, it was probably kids."

"If kids are bashing in little bunny heads and slicing them open, they are sick individuals who might turn into serial killers."

"You watch too many homicide shows." Kendra stretched out her neck, not wanting to take Molly's words to heart. "I want another cookie."

Autumn sun shimmered on the water. Kendra pulled Molly

to the window and pointed at the reflection of the fall trees directly across the lake. They'd begun to paint a rainbow of golds, oranges, and reds on the water's surface.

"Okay, mistress of distraction. Promise me you will tell Jake you're busy. Hole up in the house and write. You're only allowed out to grocery shop and attend grief group."

"I hear you, but that's ridiculous. I don't do well as a hostage. I'm finally getting out and enjoying it. I'll write. I'll be careful. Now, get outta here and go call your beau. Text me later and let me know which night works for dinner."

Molly tipped her head at the plate of cookies as they strode back into the dining room. "Eat the rest of those. You're still too thin."

Kendra ushered her to the door. "Go. Have fun. Stop worrying about me."

CHAPTER EIGHTEEN

HY ON EARTH WOULD SOMEONE WANT TO FRIGHTEN me, a quiet, lonely widow who craves privacy above all else? The thought ran through the back of Kendra's mind all day. Even though she successfully reached her word count and accomplished much of the editing and rewriting, she couldn't ignore the overriding question.

Jake was the most logical culprit. He'd surprised, alarmed, and shocked her on more than one occasion. But just because he seemed a likely suspect didn't mean he was responsible.

After perusing for boats and finding the lake empty, she picked up the phone and dialed Russ Jameson.

"Kendra, what can I do for you?"

"Got a question for you. Any chance you've heard about dead animals being left on porches? I realize most everyone is gone for the winter, but I found a dead bunny on my front stoop, and it didn't look like the work of a coyote."

"Can't say I've heard anything, but I can come down and check it out for you. Too cold to fish today."

"I don't want to trouble you, just being careful. I already took care of the poor little fella. I buried him in the brush across from the house."

"Darn good idea. A hawk will find him and have a fine meal."

"Okay then." Kendra cringed.

"Tell you what. I'll check around and let you know if I hear anything. Meantime, lock your doors. Kids get bored in the country. Pranksters. Halloween isn't that far off."

"Pretty gross prank."

"Agreed, young lady. Anyhoo, I'll let you know if I find out anything. Oh, by the way, seems your author friend took a day job."

"Jake? What do you mean?"

"He cut his stay short. Thought he'd be here all winter, but he decided to take a job in Chicago. The guy's young and needs to make money, right?"

"Sure. Makes sense. I'll let you know if I hear of anyone looking for a winter retreat."

"Talk later."

Kendra bundled up. The shrubs needed trimming, and time was running short. She'd spotted a stray snowflake yesterday, and the idea of hauling out the hedge trimmer in a snowstorm held no appeal. She pulled on her gloves and stepped outside. The sight of a dead snake stopped her cold. Her body shrank back against the entry door, and she slid to the ground.

Why? Why me? Haven't I been through enough?

Movement from the road drew her attention. Russ Jameson was scrounging through the brush, searching for the dead bunny, no doubt. Unsure whether or not to call out to him, to become a frantic woman in need of a man's assistance, she stayed rooted to the concrete pad.

A truck rumbled down the road. UPS. For reasons she didn't

understand, Kendra let out a long breath, and her shoulders relaxed. Isaac had served as savior more than once.

She stood, ran inside, shut the back door, locked it, and hurried to the front.

As she opened the door, Isaac strode down her walkway, a bright smile lighting up his face. "Howdy, Kendra. How goes the battle?"

"You have a package for me? I don't recall ordering anything."

Goose bumps popped out on her arms. Her legs suddenly went boneless.

"Not sure where it's from. Maybe someone sent you a gift."

Kendra's heart sank. She'd had more than her fair share of gifts lately.

"Thanks, Isaac." Kendra reached out and took the package from Isaac—a smaller-sized cardboard box, nondescript, and weighing just a pound or so. "Got a minute?" she asked.

Isaac stood tall in his uniform, the picture of pride. "For you, I have all the time in the world."

Kendra ushered him inside, rushed to the kitchen, and loaded a half-dozen cookies into a storage bag. "I have a treat for you."

"You don't need to do that. I swear, you're the sweetest person on my route. You know, half the folks I see don't even speak to me."

"How is that possible?" In Kendra's mind, Isaac was an asset to the neighborhood, a credit to delivery services, and a friend.

"Folks don't like Black men out here in the boonies. Not unless we're working on their roads or picking up their garbage."

"I'm sorry to hear that. That's just not right."

Kendra wrapped her arms around Isaac's middle. His height challenged her to reach his neck. He hugged her back and thanked her for the cookies.

"Anything I can do for you while I'm here?"

"Um …"

"Just say the word." Isaac's face radiated kindness. "Don't be shy. Tell me what you need."

"There's this snake."

"Oh, I don't like snakes."

"Me neither. But this one's dead. By the back door."

"Sure enough. I noticed the shovel by the garage. Hey, what's Mr. Jameson doing across the street?"

"We seem to have some pranksters around. They think it's fun to leave dead animals on people's porches."

Russ tramped around the tall brown truck as soon as Kendra and Isaac stepped outside. "That's no coyote's work," he said. "I'd better keep a closer eye on your place."

Kendra cringed at the idea of anyone keeping an eye on her or her place, but there seemed little choice. She hesitated to tell Russ about the snake. She hated each and every moment having to do with dead animals, protection, and concern.

She exchanged a private look with Isaac. One that said, *Stay quiet.*

"Thanks, Russ. Now, if you'll excuse me, Isaac offered to get my hedger out for me."

"I'm happy to help you anytime. You don't need to bother this fine young man."

Isaac was far from a young man. He had to be pushing sixty even though his trim physique tended to disagree. His chest puffed out, as if Russ had proposed a challenge.

"I've got this," he said, stepping in front of Kendra.

Men and their jockeying for position. Then again, she had to admit, she'd rather have Isaac in her garage than Russ. Russ was the neighbor who was too much in your business. She'd been careful not to share an overabundance of personal information, and now that Jake had left, life would definitely improve. Keeping Russ at bay afforded Kendra the privacy she so craved—a simple life at the lake, no neighbors, and quiet, serene days.

Kendra offered Russ an apologetic smile. "Isaac is the UPS man who takes the extra measure to serve his customers."

Russ mumbled under his breath, "If you like that kind of thing."

"Thanks for stopping by, Russ. I'll be in touch if I see anything else suspicious."

Isaac asked no questions after Russ took his leave. She liked that about Isaac. He had the ability and wisdom to keep his nose where it belonged.

After he deposited the dead garter snake across the street with the bunny carcass, he leaned the shovel against the garage. "I'm gonna say a prayer that this shovel stays right where I left it. You need me, you call me." He reached inside his shirt pocket and handed her a card with his name and phone number.

"Thanks, Isaac. You're a true friend."

Isaac smiled and spun around to leave, but Kendra stopped him. "Didn't you used to work for an alarm company?"

"Sure did."

"I'm a single woman, living alone in the country. I have an alarm system, but I might need to have the system upgraded. It was here when I moved in, but I don't know a heck of a lot about these contraptions. Maybe you could recommend a reliable company that could check it out and suggest some additional measures I could take to feel more secure."

Isaac's face mirrored her concern. "I'll do it. I'm off Sundays and Mondays. If someone is trying to scare you by leaving dead animals on your stoop, I could install cameras, and we could catch the son of a gun."

"I hate to take up your days off. You have a family."

"My wife enjoys it when I leave the house." He chuckled. "We see too much of each other, and the thrill turns to irritation."

Kendra couldn't help but laugh along with him, but the thought of cameras outside her little slice of heaven put her in a bind. She didn't want to adjust her view of this little haven. If she had cameras, she'd really feel watched. Not that it made sense. She'd be the watchful one, not the other way around. Still, the idea of having to monitor the activity in and around her home spiked her anxiety rather than helped it subside.

"Can I think about it? Not you helping, but I can't say I like the idea of having cameras around my house."

Kendra pulled out her cell and photographed Isaac's contact information for safekeeping, and then she tucked his card into her pocket. "Thanks, Isaac. You're the best."

Isaac offered her a wide smile and moseyed back to his truck, his confident, long strides bringing a grin to Kendra's face. He left her standing in the front yard, surveying the fallen leaves, the gray pallor of the sky, the shriveling hosta leaves, and the brown grass. Michigan fall could be a depressing time of year.

When she strolled back inside, she brewed a cup of tea and curled up on the couch. Jake had disappeared into thin air. He'd come from nowhere and left for nowhere. Puzzling, to say the least. Molly would be thrilled though. And on the bright side, Kendra had more answers than ever before.

She rested her head against the back of the couch and mused about how she could weave the last few days into her current work in progress. Then again, reality was far less believable than fiction. She'd better stick to pulling ideas out of thin air for a bit.

CHAPTER NINETEEN

THE IDEA OF A DATE WITH NATHAN MADE HER STOMACH twirl. Scratch that. A casual dinner with a friend. She straightened her hair and debated on outfits. Nothing fancy, but nothing too relaxed either. Kendra settled on a dressy pair of leggings and a sweater with a colorful scarf, fall hues of rust and gold, and a pair of ankle boots. She and Nathan had texted this morning. They'd agreed on West End Grill, a fairly upscale establishment in Ann Arbor, where being a college town, all modes of dress were acceptable.

Nathan would pick her up at the house. She knew she'd been manipulative in allowing him to come to get her. In the back of her mind, Kendra hoped Russ would be out and about and see that Kendra had friends other than him to keep a watch over her. Ridiculous testiness on her part, but it was the truth.

The knock on the door sounded precisely at six p.m. She gave a slight nod. On time was good. She opened the door, and a smile crept across her face. Friend or not, Nathan looked dashing. Nice khakis with a button-down shirt underneath a polished brown leather jacket.

"Ready?" she asked.

Offering a wide smile, Nathan held Kendra's coat for her and then waited while she checked the back and side doors and turned on two lights—one in the kitchen and one in the family room. She locked the dead bolt on the front door, and they hurried down the front walk, Kendra feeling like a starry-eyed teenager again.

Nathan drove a truck. An F-150. Kendra liked the powerful feeling of sitting high in the seat, being able to see traffic better from the heightened vantage point.

They chatted about the cold temperatures and the snow flurries. It was only October! The weather occupied much Michiganian discussion, bringing to mind the state saying—*If you don't like the weather, stick around for five minutes. It'll change.*

Kendra's stomach flipped near the end of the ride. *Dinner at West End Grill is certainly a date. What will we talk about?*

Panic took over when Nathan parked, exited the truck, came around to the passenger side of the vehicle, opened the door, and extended his hand. She stared at him, her mouth gaping.

"I don't think I can do this."

Nathan nodded sympathetically. "I had a feeling you might get nervous. We have seats at the bar. Less like a date. More like a comfortable meetup."

Kendra scraped teeth over her bottom lip and studied the stars as they blanketed the sky.

When her eyes found Nathan again, his hand remained outstretched. "C'mon. We're doing this."

Kendra swallowed over the swelling lump in her throat. "Right."

She climbed down from the truck, and Nathan extended his arm. Kendra gripped it, her frayed nerves taking their toll on her legs and turning them to dough.

They strolled down the street, a fierce wind whipping through her hair and straight down the collar of her coat. Kendra picked up the pace, and soon, they were jogging down the street. They chuckled as they reached the steps of the restaurant and ducked inside, shaking the cold from their limbs at the same time.

Nathan strode over to the bar, grasping Kendra's hand and leading the way. Sure enough, two seats were reserved.

"What would you like to drink?" Nathan asked as he helped Kendra out of her coat and then held a chair for her.

She relaxed enough to give him a smile. "I'd love a glass of cabernet."

The bartender proved delightful and presented a wide range of choices. After they chose a bottle of wine, he filled two goblets with extra-large pours and then left them alone.

"Friends, remember? Just relax. What should we talk about?"

Kendra gazed at Nathan. His kind face radiated warmth, sympathy, and understanding—not in a way that made her cringe like her girlfriends' expressions, which always left her feeling small and inadequate, but in a connected way. In a *we're in this together* way.

She'd wondered what they'd discuss for a solid hour this afternoon, musing over the possibilities. He could tell her a funny story about work. She could tell him about writing. But before she knew it, she blurted out all the complications since Jake's arrival. His visits, the photos, the dead animals, the email, and then Jake's abrupt departure. Nathan listened thoughtfully.

"I'm pretty good at seeing the big picture," he said. "Do you want me to give you feedback or just be a sounding board?"

"Tell me what to do."

"I don't want to give you unsolicited advice, but since you're asking, let's take this one step at a time. As far as Jake, the brother-in-law, like it or not, everyone has their own motivation. He might, as he said, want closure."

Kendra spun her chair, so she and Nathan were nestled in their own little world.

"Closure is a reasonable request after a death, even more so after a suicide. But you can't ignore the other possibilities. He might want cash, or he might want to insert himself into your life and call you his new family. I've seen stranger things …"

Nathan went on to explain a situation in which a man his dad had known had a second family in secret, and then, near his death, he wanted the two families, who had never met, to become one. Introducing family members and stepsiblings after twenty years of having no idea the others existed—it sounded bizarre.

"But this Jake guy's sudden departure suggests otherwise. He might have needed to get his secret off his chest. Abuse screws people up. If they are kids when it happens, they're most likely threatened not to tell, and the fear runs deep. Also, the shame. In the case of my work, we've had occasion to respond to rapes, and often, the victim is too afraid to file a police report. Jake might have found telling you about the abuse cathartic in some way. Part of his process, not yours. See what I mean? He has his motivation, not your best interest at heart. Keep your eye out. My guess is, he'll be back."

"Interestingly though, the story helped me understand my husband better. Not that I'm suddenly okay with the decision Joe made to take his own life, but I do have some insight into his past."

"I'd say, Jake has issues, but then again, we all do. Your friend Molly is wise to advise you to maintain some distance, and the supposed information that Jake has moved should help provide that."

"What do you mean, supposed information?"

"I investigate fires; I don't just fight them. You can't assume you have the correct information. You need evidence too."

Kendra studied Nathan. The guy possessed not only intelligence, but wisdom as well. She liked him. As a friend, for sure, and she definitely felt a tug toward him for more. Not soon, but maybe someday. He didn't seem ashamed to be with her or fearful that he'd be doomed in her company.

"As far as the dead animals, that's just plain wrong. Of course, you're talking to the guy who rescues birds from trees. Every living thing is important to me. I'm the guy who puts a spider on a sheet of paper and delivers him back outside. So … I don't get it.

"Makes sense to check and be sure you're not the only one being targeted. If you are, then you start worrying."

They went on to order several shareable appetizers and mused about the incredible taste of the food. They finished the bottle of cabernet before venturing back outside into a brutal wind, which had picked up strength during the time they spent huddled inside.

Nathan drove her home, but as they rode down the gravel road to Kendra's home, she noticed they were being followed. Despite the wine, her paranoia was at an all-time high, given the dead carcasses on her entranceways. Yes, she'd been freaked out by Jake and the absence of familiar, trusted faces in her life.

Nathan noticed her checking over her shoulder every ten seconds. "What's wrong?"

"I've just been a nervous wreck lately. Imagining things. It's so dark out here. It's so isolated. I guess I'm on high alert. Is that truck following us?"

"Probably a neighbor." As he pulled into Kendra's drive just off the road, he turned off the truck but kept the headlights fixed on her home. "I'll walk you inside, make sure you're safe."

"Thanks," she said.

As they stepped out of the truck, Kendra detected the truck slowing after it passed her home. Russ Jameson. She cautioned herself. Indeed, she was overreacting. Russ had said he'd keep an eye on her place, and he was just delivering on his promise.

Nathan walked her to the door, waited while she unlocked the dead bolt, and joined her inside, locking the door behind him. "I can stay for a bit until you feel more settled."

"Coffee? Tea? I might have some wine. I've certainly had plenty, but if you'd like some, I'll see what I have."

"I've got it. You don't need to wait on me." Nathan located a beer in the back of the fridge.

Kendra flicked on a few more lights, flipped the switch on the gas fireplace, and stood in front of the fire, warming her frozen limbs. She watched as Nathan perused the place, popping his head in each room, as if checking for visitors.

"Nice view," he said before striding to the windows that faced the lake. He lifted a blind and peered out at the water. "Great place to write, I'd imagine."

"Want to see where the magic happens?" Kendra waltzed into her office and turned on the light.

Nathan followed on her heels. Kendra watched as his gaze panned the room—the desk unit with a laptop and desktop; the myriad of notebooks, where she jotted down research, story ideas, and notes to remind her of timelines and character details; piles of receipts; three containers of pencils and other writing implements; boxes of index cards; a stray coffee cup; and a half-empty water bottle.

"Guess I need to take a day and reorganize."

"Might disrupt your creative flow. I'm in awe of writers. I can't imagine coming up with stories."

"But you're a great storyteller."

Nathan flung his head back and laughed as he removed his coat. "I'll leave the writing to you."

Before they turned to leave the room, Kendra noticed the box Isaac had delivered yesterday. She'd completely forgotten about the package in the midst of yesterday's craziness. Now, it sat like Pandora's box. What was it with her and strange boxes? She could ignore it and toss it in the trash, but she knew her curiosity couldn't be contained. Even as a kid, she'd snuck into her parents' bedroom and unwrapped Christmas gifts before the big day, spoiling the surprise but loving knowing ahead of time.

After Nathan left or, considering her jumpy nerves, maybe in the morning, she'd be better able to decide.

Her phone pinged in her purse, and she went to the sofa to retrieve it. Two messages.

One was from Molly and read: *Next Saturday works. Adam can't wait to meet you.*

The second from Russ: *Everything all right? Saw a strange vehicle at your place.*

Russ's message gave her the willies, like fire ants covered her limbs. He was keeping too close an eye.

She responded quickly. *Not a stranger. A friend.*

Take that, you nosy neighbor.

"Everything all right?"

Kendra jerked her head around, stepped over to the couch, and plopped down next to Nathan, curling her legs up on the sofa. "Oh, sure. Hey, I have a question. I know we're just friends, but would you consider coming over for dinner next Saturday? My friend Molly is bringing her new beau over. It would be fun if you could join us. On the other hand, if I'm monopolizing your time …"

"Relax." His eyes softened, and he reached out and ran a finger down her arm.

The resulting tingles panicked and thrilled Kendra at the same time. She liked having Nathan around. She could say things to him that she couldn't to anyone else. He got her. He made her feel safe. But she wasn't ready for more than friendship.

"I'd love to come to dinner. What can I bring?"

"You cook?"

"I'm a firefighter. I cook for a crowd—and a discerning one at that."

"I haven't decided on a menu yet, but I can let you know Wednesday when I see you for grief group."

"Perfect." Nathan glanced down at his watch. "I'd better go. Twelve-hour shift tomorrow."

Kendra hopped up from her seat, a bundle of conflicting emotions. He should leave, or she might show him the bedroom. Up close and personal.

Nathan stood, donned his leather jacket, and paced to the front door, resting his large hand on the doorknob. "Thanks for a great evening. I really enjoy our … friendship." He leaned down and placed a gentle peck on Kendra's cheek.

She couldn't take her eyes off the soft blond hairs covering the back of his hand, the strength and security of his touch. His lips on her cheek dazed her.

After she watched him stride down the walkway and hop into his truck, she realized her hand still rested on her cheek, where he had kissed her.

CHAPTER TWENTY

KENDRA LEANED OVER THE SINK, BRUSHING HER TEETH. She flipped her hair back from her face and rose to look in the mirror. She shook her head and chastised herself for acting like a schoolgirl. Stupid, silly kid stuff. Crushes, superficial physical attractions. She was grieving. She shouldn't be fantasizing about another man. She'd felt different tonight though. Better. More normal. So what if she had a little crush on a fireman? He was becoming a good friend, and if Kendra needed anything right now, it was a good friend, one who was honest and on her side. Someone who understood her and didn't treat her like she'd lost her mind.

She headed into her office and gathered a pair of scissors before sitting down on the floor in front of the box. There was no decipherable address on the package. No recognizable one anyway. A part of her was intrigued, another anxious. Life had dealt her one too many strange surprises lately, none of them welcome. Chills crept up her spine as she sliced open the box, and she chastised herself for her overreaction. As she slid fingers beneath the taped edge, she held her breath and then let out a tremendous yowl as she perused the contents. Four containers of deodorant. She'd really outdone herself this time, ordering a subscribe-and-save supply. But as she checked the account, she realized she'd signed up for the family pack. That would teach her. At least she could sleep soundly and sweat-free tonight.

Kendra moseyed into the bedroom, climbed under the covers, and pulled them up to her chin. Her thoughts went back to the evening. There was no denying how calm she'd felt in Nathan's company, how settled, how sane. He'd left her feeling happy and normal. But how could she feel so good about him when she was still wrestling with the secrets about Joe? Shouldn't there be some kind of transition or page break, defining one from the other?

A flash of light interrupted Kendra's spinning thoughts. She rose from her bed, crept around to the window, and wriggled to peek between the one-inch gap between the blinds. If she pulled back the shade, whoever was outside would certainly spot her. She stayed low. Peered out between the shade to her left and then the one to her right. She'd been unrealistic to imagine she could see anything or anyone from that vantage point.

Thinking for a heartbeat, she hurried to the closet and removed the step stool, unfolding the tiny ladder near the window. She stood on tiptoe, hooding her eyes to see out the transom frame, nine feet up and directly over the bedroom door that led to the deck. She lacked height. Climbing down from the stool, she slid books out from under her bed. Her bookshelves were full to the brim, and beneath her bed had become the new storage place for the latest reads. After carefully stacking them on the stool, she climbed again, cautiously teetering on the pile.

With hands continuing to shield her eyes, she scrutinized the yard, scoping the fifty-yard expanse that led from her deck to the yard and finally down to the lake. She spotted a black form in shadow, the full moon lighting up the shape of … a sapling, bent over like one of those detectives on the front of a mystery book from way back when. She inched forward, pressing her face to the glass, cursing under her breath.

As soon as her nose met the glass, she toppled backward and grazed her forehead on the corner of the weighty mahogany dresser, sending books flying across the room. She lay on her back, stunned.

After several minutes, when the shock began to wane, Kendra reached up and ran her fingers along her temple. Bleeding. Disoriented. *Shit.*

She rolled onto her stomach, dreading the thought of stain-streaking drips of blood nestling into her white carpet, and inched toward the bathroom, clutching her bloodied fist to her chest.

Kendra knocked her head on the doorjamb, further proof of Murphy's Law taking a front seat in life. Once she reached the bathroom counter, she stood upright and leaned against the sink. She reached around the wall and turned on the light inside the water closet, attempting to avoid the harsh glare of the bulbs shrouding the bathroom mirror. What she saw in the reflection alarmed her.

Blood ran from her temple to her chin. She turned on the tap and ran a washcloth under cool water, wrung out the cloth, and dabbed her face, surveying the damage after she cleared away the blood. A two-inch gash from her forehead to the side of her left eye. Deep. Unsightly. Definitely in need of stitches.

Kendra pondered her options. She'd been drinking. She wasn't drunk, but she didn't feel safe enough to drive. Just what she needed—a DUI along with a gaping wound.

In the linen closet, she foraged and came up with a box of bandages. Kendra used one hand to clot the bleeding with the washcloth and the other to open the bandage. She needed to make a butterfly or two, just enough of a covering to seal the edges of the slice, and then cover the cut with an additional rectangle of gauze and tape. She'd get some much-needed rest and drive to the ER in the morning. The last thing she wanted was to run into the creep roaming around her yard in the night.

The head gash continued to bleed through the makeshift first aid she'd applied to the wound. She lay in bed and held the side of her head, praying for sleep and sunshine. She could use a little more light in her life.

৽

A throbbing headache met Kendra's wakefulness. She pressed a finger to her temple and yelped.

Darkness filled the room. Kendra rose gingerly from bed, shuffled over to the windows, and lifted the six blinds that covered her bedroom windows. She examined the outside, unable to see past the dock. Fog blanketed the lake in a shroud. Kendra gazed at a fire bush close to the deck, its leaves now crimson, and listened as rain pattered on the fallen leaves that covered her deck. More peaceful than the recent events of life suggested.

She headed to the bathroom, uncovering her wound and examining it in the magnifying mirror. Stitches still required. No luck with instant overnight healing.

Kendra changed into sweats, gently pulled her hair back in a ponytail, and grabbed her purse. Before heading to the garage, she turned on the back light to check for dead critters.

This is what my life has become.

Fifteen minutes later, she signed in at Chelsea Hospital's Emergency Room and reported the injury as the result of a fall. The intake nurse scrunched up her face when Kendra explained that she'd decided to wait until morning for treatment and immediately led her back to an exam room, instructing her to sit on the gurney and wait for the doctor.

Thankfully, Kendra had arrived early enough that the department was virtually empty. She listened as clanging carts rolled by, heavy footsteps wandered past the closed curtain of the cubicle, and voices chattered about Friday night happenings.

An elderly gentleman strode in a few seconds later, tall and a bit stooped, his white jacket bearing a name tag—Dr. Martin. With a friendly smile, he outstretched a hand to Kendra. "Tell me what happened, miss."

Kendra spilled the story, tears streaking her cheeks, a heaping mess—not from the injury, but from months of twisted sorrow that wouldn't let go.

The doctor assumed a seat next to her on the gurney and wrapped an age-spotted hand around her shoulder. "There, there now. Let me look."

The nurse had removed Kendra's self-administered bandage, and the doctor pushed back Kendra's bangs to investigate. "Yes, well, you did knock yourself up," he joked, "but it's a clean cut, nothing that won't heal well. And it's in a good spot. You won't need plastic surgery. I'm an expert."

Kendra sniffled and nodded. She felt like a fool, falling apart about something seemingly so inconsequential.

The doctor left her alone while he went to gather his supplies, and Kendra leaned back on the gurney, folding her knees up to her chest. The weight of grief devoured her. How much could one person endure? She wanted more than anything to curl up in a fetal position, shrink down to fun-size insignificance, and climb in a safe, sound-free womb. Fetuses didn't know how good they had it in there. They had no worries. No strife.

Maybe she should head out of town. Take a break. A writing retreat. Go somewhere nobody knew her. Incognito for a few days or even weeks. She only needed her laptop to do her job.

When the doctor returned, he stopped dead in his tracks. Again, Kendra saw the reflected sympathy in his eyes. While she hated that look from her friends, she welcomed it now. Maybe his fatherly demeanor drew her in; the profound need for comfort outweighed her desire to appear as a superhero.

He patted her shoulder. "There's more, isn't there?"

Kendra had experienced astute medical professionals in her past. The hospice nurse when her dad had died—the understanding hugs and the expert way of delivering bad news. Dr. Martin's manner meant more than all of those past experiences. He was here. Now.

Kendra sobbed as the words poured out of her. She told the doctor about her baby, her husband, the arrival of her estranged brother-in-law … everything.

"You're having a rough go. I'm sorry to hear that. Youth should be carefree, but life isn't like that. Take it from an old man who's seen and lived through a lot in this lifetime. There are times when there doesn't seem to be one single reason to wake up tomorrow. Depression can last for days, months, or unfortunately, stretch into years. But how you face these horrific obstacles matters. One of the best bits of advice I've had over the years is this: start over."

Kendra wrinkled her forehead, causing searing pain to pierce her skull. She lifted her hand and cupped her temple, determined to hold on to this message she'd so desperately needed to hear.

"You can mourn the past, and you should, but there comes a time when you must move forward. You're young. You have your whole life ahead of you. You can wallow in sorrow and grief, or you can be a survivor. Some counselors would probably say I'm unrealistic, but I've seen lots of patients in my years of practice. Humans are resilient. Don't fret when you feel energetic. Don't beat yourself up when you treasure holding a baby or kissing a new man. Let life in again. Celebrate the sunshine, the song of the birds, a good meal, a decent glass of wine."

Kendra closed her eyes and nodded. If only she could record his words. She needed to recite this message every morning. *Grieve but move forward. Be a survivor, not a victim.*

"I'm going to numb your head before I stitch you up. Lie back. Good. You're fine right there. Just close your eyes, and you'll be good as new in no time." He held a cotton ball dabbed with lidocaine against her cut.

Kendra shut her eyes and inhaled fully, as she had during labor, to release pain rather than hold on to it. Dr. Martin's touch, gentle and efficient, put her at ease. Her mind drifted to the lake, soft waves lapping on the sand, a mild breeze clearing the air. She sank into the pillow, letting the weight of her head rest, the heaviness of her body meet the gurney.

When the doctor patted her arm, she startled.

"All done," he said. "Not too bad, right?"

Kendra lightly touched her temple. A bandage covered the wound. "I didn't feel a thing."

"Seemed like you relaxed and caught your breath for a minute. I'm glad."

The doctor placed a strong hand behind her and helped Kendra sit up. She smiled and thanked him.

"Try to keep the area dry for the next week. You can come back, and we'll remove the stitches, or go to your primary and let her do it."

Kendra pushed up from the gurney and wobbled on weak legs.

"Hold steady," Doc Martin said. "Let's get you some juice before you drive. You came in by yourself, I take it?"

"Yes."

"I'll send someone in. You take care of yourself, all right?" He offered Kendra a look of encouragement, raising his brows like little tents over pale blue windows.

"Will do."

Kendra drank a container of juice and sat for a few minutes

before heading out of the ER. When she reached the parking lot, she surveyed the cars, trying to remember where she'd parked.

A truck pulled up under the entrance overhang, the passenger window lowering. Russ Jameson.

"You all right? Need a ride?"

Kendra, struck by confusion, gasped. "What?"

"I saw you head this way early this morning. Thought I'd better follow and make sure all was okeydokey. What happened? You okay to drive?"

"I'm fine."

Russ put his vehicle in park and strolled around the truck, putting a firm hand under Kendra's elbow. She stood dumbstruck and frightened. She pulled back.

"Jake told me all about your suffering," he said. "I'm just trying to help. You don't have to be afraid. Why, I've been a neighbor to folks at the lake for over fifty years."

Kendra tried not to feel creeped out, but she did. She struggled to make sense of Russ following her. Her head swam. Maybe as a result of the stitches, maybe as a result of the outpouring of emotion she'd allowed with the doctor. She fought to keep her legs rigid and remain standing.

"I'm fine," she whispered. "I just need some time alone."

Kendra locked eyes with Russ, daring him to make another move.

"There's a bench right over there," he said, pointing to a seating area outside the ER. He paused a respectful moment until Kendra spotted the bench and headed over to sit down. He followed at a distance and waited.

She sank down on the hard wood and held her head. Closed her eyes and asked for the umpteenth time, *Why me?*

CHAPTER TWENTY-ONE

WHEN KENDRA PULLED INTO HER DRIVEWAY, SHE spotted a mom van out front. Jill's. Since Kendra had moved to the lake, none of her friends, other than Molly, had bothered to come and visit. It wasn't like Kendra wanted company or had the energy for it, but when she saw the car, the absence of her other friends hit her square in the chest.

Jill's eyes narrowed on Kendra's bandage as she waved and stepped out on the pavement. "What the heck happened? You all right?"

"Fine. Just a couple of stitches. I was measuring for curtains and took a spill off the step stool."

"Sounds like something I'd do. Here, help me get this food out of the car."

Jill traipsed around to the back and opened the rear lift gate. She had a box loaded with a pot, bread, two containers, and a bottle of wine.

"Oh my! You didn't have to do all this!"

"Sure I did. I've been a bad friend these past few months. Molly told all of us to leave you alone, and I was lying in bed the other night after we all went out, thinking about you. I can't imagine why we went along with Molly. It's not like she's more of a friend to you than the rest of us. I'm worried about you, and I want to know how you're doing." She placed the box in Kendra's arms and closed the rear gate.

"Let's go inside." Kendra led the way up the winding walk to the front door, set the box down on the porch, and unlocked the door, letting Jill lead the way.

Once settled inside, she made a pot of tea. "We should sit on the deck. It's a beautiful morning, and you haven't been over to enjoy the view yet."

They sat next to each other, mugs of tea in hand, both gazing out at the lake for a long moment.

"I was thoughtless the other night, complaining about my life when you've lost so much."

Kendra had wondered if any of them were cognizant of her status while they moaned about the craziness of their lives. Kendra remembered well the demands of motherhood and the strain of being home with a baby with twenty-four/seven parenting responsibilities when Joe worked late or had business out of town. But she had been in the honeymoon phase, still enraptured by the miracle of baby Joey. Even though she'd been exhausted, she'd do it all again in a heartbeat, especially if it meant holding on to her baby one minute longer.

"No, you weren't. I'm in a different place right now, is all."

"I disagree. We all go on about our lives without asking you about yours because we don't know how to ask without worrying we'll say the wrong thing or send you into a deeper depression by bringing up Joe or Joey. It's not fair. I don't want to do that anymore. The thing is, you always depicted your life with Joe as such a fairy tale. Nobody's life is that perfect."

Kendra gazed at the lake. "It sure seemed perfect, and now that they're both gone, it hurts to think of it any other way. Then again," she said in a pensive moment, "if my life were paradise, why did my husband hang himself in our garage? Why did my baby die?"

Jill shook her head. "Molly said you found Joey in his crib. And then found Joe in the garage. I can't imagine." She cringed.

Kendra revisited the scene full force but different this time too. "We had the best morning together. He laughed aloud for the first time. I grabbed my phone and tried to make him laugh again, but you know how that goes—babies never cooperate for the camera. At least, not my little guy. Bath time came next. Joey loved the water. When we bathed him over the weekend, Joe had turned the sink sprayer on him. I was so upset with him. But Joey had loved it—his little cooing noises never stopped. So, I sprayed him with water, and he slapped his arms up and down and kicked his little feet. After that, he was all tuckered out, so I sat in the rocking chair in the family room and nursed him. The view was gorgeous out the family room window. All those trees—it was like living in my own Sherwood Forest. I laid him down for a nap after that …"

"I'm so sorry, Kendra. I should have been there for you."

"You were there. At the funeral. And honestly, it was all a blur for me. I have no idea who was there, who I spoke to, if I spoke at all. If not for Molly and Valium, I don't know if I'd have even shown up. And then with Joe …"

She stopped and inhaled a ragged breath. Even though she closed her eyes to block the memory, she could only envision Joe's lifeless body hanging from the garage rafters.

In that moment, she'd done a double take, the sight of him halting her like the abrupt appearance of a cliff's edge. Thick fog blanketed conscious thought, a virtual shade pulled over the scene. Kendra snapped her head around, at once backing away but feeling she had to take action. She fought the image. Tried to erase reality. But the scene was real. Joe, her husband and best friend, had dangled from a belt, in his freshly pressed gray suit, starched white dress shirt, and polished oxfords. The stark vision replayed a horror movie from her teenage years.

Kendra shook with cold.

Jill leaned forward and rested a hand on Kendra's knee. "You're reliving it, aren't you? Do you want to tell me?"

The nightmare interrupted, Kendra shook her head. "It feels so real. Still, after all this time. It's like my temperature drops twenty degrees, and I can't stop shaking from the chill, the shock, and the endlessness of those seconds, minutes, hours, and days. In some ways, it's an absolute haze, but at the same time, it's as vivid as if it were happening again right this moment. I want it to stop, but I'm powerless to control when and where it revisits me."

"I'm so sorry you had to go through that. So, so sorry. And I'm sorry I triggered the memory. That's exactly what I worried about."

"I often wonder," Kendra said, "if it's better to let it revisit when I'm awake. Maybe then I won't dream about it as much."

"Talking about it can take away the power of the memory."

"Someone else told me that. I can't recall who. Maybe the woman from the grief group. I really want to get better. Sometimes, I think all of you figure I've had enough time to recover, and you leave me out because I'm not 'getting over it' fast enough."

"We want you to get better, but it's not about our timetable. Although, there's a fine line between being a survivor and a victim. You know me, I'm pushy. And if you were to ask for my advice, I'd say, rejoin the universe whether you feel like it or not. *Fake it till you make it* attitude."

"I have so little energy some days."

"You have to push yourself. Years from now, when this isn't so fresh, you'll be glad you did. Think about it. Joe left you. He abandoned you after the worst moment of your life. Doesn't that piss you off?"

"Trust me, I'm pissed off plenty. And I sorta want to know why. People say, with suicide, you never know. Joe didn't leave a note, so I'm in the dark about that too."

Jill let out a disgusted growl. "Bastard."

"You're pissed at him."

"Damn right. We all are. He left you. Worse than that, he piled on when you needed him most. And in a very selfish way."

"There's so much research now that says people who take their own lives are in such desperate pain that they can't see beyond that. Joe must have thought I'd be better off without him."

"I call bullshit. He was hiding something."

Kendra narrowed her eyes.

"All these newfangled ideas about letting everyone go their own way, making choices about what gender they are and who they want to love, how addiction is an illness—think about it, how did Joe's suicide help you? It's all selfish. Joe was selfish. I understand if you disagree, but you'll eventually see it the same way."

"I'm angry with him, if that's what you're getting at. But I miss him too. I want my life back."

"Then, reclaim it. Get a new life. As much as you want life to go back to the way it was, it'll never happen. Go for a walk with me. Come over for dinner. Get out of this goddamn house. I get it … this is a beautiful spot, but you're even more isolated here. I don't think it's healthy."

Kendra's stomach knotted. Heat rose up her neck. Who was Jill to show up at her home and tell her how to live her life? She'd disappeared for more than seven months, and then she'd had the nerve to show up and tell her how to heal.

"Thanks for bringing me food. I appreciate it. But I should get some things done. I've been writing …"

Jill stared at Kendra, boring a hole into her chest. "Another lonely activity." Disgusted, Jill rose from her seat. "If you want to sit in this beautiful, lonely spot and wallow, go ahead. But you're making a mistake. You can't stop living because Joe and Joey did. I get frustrated. I don't want you to waste your life. If you do, you'll regret it someday."

Kendra wanted to slap Jill. She had no idea what it was like to lose everything. She had no idea what it was like to be completely and utterly alone in the blink of an eye. She had no idea of the depth of sorrow Kendra carried with her every second of the day. How the nights were endless, how sleep wouldn't come, even when exhaustion overwhelmed her.

"Why are you doing this? I thought you came as a friend?"

"I know, and I'm sorry, but I feel strongly about this. You're letting Joe destroy you. In all the years we've been friends, you've never acted like a victim. I'm concerned. I only want the best for you."

She should have been glad Jill had dropped by, given her a hug, and walked her to the door, but she couldn't move. Paralyzed in her seat, she could barely breathe. As if from someplace in the sky, she watched as Jill deposited her mug on the kitchen counter and marched out of the house.

As if stuck in cement, Kendra felt hopelessness grip her like a vise—or maybe like that damn belt Joe had tightened around his neck.

CHAPTER TWENTY-TWO

ENDRA SHOOK OFF DIZZYING THOUGHTS. SHE CLIMBED into bed and cuddled up with Joey's blanket and a note-book, and jotted down ideas for the next scene in her novel, a feeble attempt at avoiding the threads of her conversation with Jill. Excitement hummed through her as she thought about the next steps her protagonist would take, confronting a fear head on with mixed results.

That was reality after all. People faced their fears for what-ever reason—whether forced into it, provoked by a visceral reac-tion, a planned attack, a chance encounter, or a sudden crisis. Just like when she had found Joe in the garage. Who knew why she'd jumped into action? Someone else might have called 911 before trying anything, or rushed down the street while screaming for help, or remained paralyzed or fainted with shock. No matter which, humans tapped into a piece of themselves that might have been hidden under mounds of childhood indoctrination they'd never signed up for. A fight-or-flight syndrome built on years of old patterns—some intentional, but most, not so much. Who showed up? When and why? Kendra imagined she could research this for years and still not understand. There were so many factors to think about and understand.

Kendra threw off Joey's blanket and marched to her computer. She'd never sleep until she figured out a piece of this business. How she reacted. How characters reacted. She Googled *fight or flight*.

An interesting question. Kendra mulled over who she wanted to be. Was there a choice? When she thought about her grief, could she choose to be one who took flight, or would she fight? As it was, she felt frozen, unable to move from grieving. She felt guilty just thinking about leaving grief behind her and living again. If, as Dr. Martin at the ER had advised, Kendra started over, how would that look? If, as Jill had insisted, she went about her life as if she had a life, how would that appear? The ideas made her already-aching head pound. Could she push past the guilt? Could she leave her family behind? Was there another alternative?

Knowing more about Joe had allowed Kendra further understanding of his choice to end his life. She didn't excuse Joe's actions. Rather, she had a way of explaining them now. Sure, those details were extreme and probably only a seed of his life, but the story had helped her to appreciate his possible line of thought. On a semi-rational level. A pierce of pain struck Kendra's side.

My husband killed himself. Headed into the garage, just outside the door. Wrapped a belt around his neck and hanged himself. He'd wanted me to find him. Not someone else. He was punishing me. Holding me hostage.

In his mind, I'd killed Joey. This is my sentence. To live a life of guilt and pain. To never forgive myself because he couldn't forgive me.

Fuck him.

While Kendra waited for the sluggish internet connection to load the page, she made a cup of tea, anger fueling her.

The information Kendra discovered fascinated her.

Sometimes, the fight-or-flight response was inaccurate. There were steps one could take to control it, such as triggering a relaxation response to deflect the racing heartbeat, the spike in blood pressure. Research suggested one could explore new ways to deal with stress.

Kendra's biggest fear was that she'd freeze when faced with a personal crisis. Become immobile and, as a result, be gobbled up by the monster under her bed. She reviewed the physical changes that occurred in the body as a result of an acute threat. The nervous and endocrine systems going into overdrive. The fact that it took twenty to sixty minutes for the body to come down after a perceived threat. Not so good.

On the other hand, increased pulse and rapid respiration provided greater oxygen intake. The rise in blood pressure increased oxygen to the brain, raising alertness. The extra blood sugar released added energy.

Lots of pros and cons. Kendra recognized she had fought for Joe and Joey at the time of their deaths. But her fight was out of shock and disbelief. She'd refused to believe they were gone. But as she mused over the multiple reactions people had in times of crisis, she couldn't help think of her own reactions to losing her boys. She had neither flown nor fought. In her opinion, she'd turned to ice. Paralyzed by her grief, she chose to hide away for as long as possible. If it weren't for Molly, she'd never have gone out again. If it weren't for Jake showing up, she'd never have questioned Joe's motivations but rather mourned him benignly and endlessly. If she hadn't been forced to attend a grief group, she'd never have met Nathan, and he'd turned out in many ways to be a savior of sorts.

Kendra wished she had more of a scientific mind. As much as this data fascinated her, trying the techniques required to change an instinctual reaction would demand thought in the middle of a crisis. She doubted she was astute enough to signal herself should she find herself in that position again. She might be able to use the information for a scene in one of her books, but the reality of being objective while in the midst of a predicament, much less a disaster, well, she might need years of training before she could achieve that kind of focus.

Like it or not, Kendra had a grief group to attend and then a dinner party to plan for Saturday. She'd been feverishly writing for days, thanks to the research she'd been enthralled with. By four o'clock, she'd written a slew of words, but now, it was time to shower, or her group members would want her to sit near the door. She reeked.

Kendra pulled into the church parking lot right on time and smiled to herself. This group had become a lifeline, a place where she could rediscover her existence and maybe, one of these days, a bit of happiness and serenity.

Kendra scanned the lot—looking for Nathan's truck, she realized. A flush covered her cheeks. She didn't have a crush on him or anything silly like that, just looked forward to his company. His companionship settled her. It was just that. Probably.

His truck wasn't in the lot, and Kendra's heart sank. Maybe he was ill or had to work an extra shift. In any case, the idea of heading inside without Nathan to lean on left her a bit unsteady. Once she spotted Gary's car, she relaxed. They were all here for each other.

Kendra listened the best she could and offered support in the ways she wanted to be supported. When Cathy spoke about losing Nicole and how her rescue efforts had proven futile, everyone in the group wept with her. In an involuntary and instinctual instant of support, the group joined hands and stayed silent for a long moment.

Brendan shared photos of his brother, Matthew—his

kindergarten snapshot, his high school graduation, his wedding, his widow, his children. Living his pain seemed to plummet all of them into a contemplative trance. Each lived their own private agony, knowing and understanding Brendan's loss in a way the average person could not.

Kendra's gaze drifted to the narrow transom window, and her mind fell into a memory—Joey reaching for her as he nursed, his eyes so focused on hers that she could feel the connection. The life she passed on to him through her milk. She felt suddenly overcome by the boy he would have grown to be, the man she would never know. Chills exploded on her limbs, a treacherous cold that made her arms and legs tremble under the weight of her pain.

When Kendra's turn came, she shared the highs and lows of the past days, her recent fall, the overwhelming desire to fold into her pain, to let it pull her under, and then the tremendous urge to fight back. "I'm like a pogo stick, jumping way up and coming down rock hard, struggling to keep my balance."

Mary responded to her, "You're healing."

Kendra's face twisted, and she fingered the stitches on her forehead, confused for a minute. *This is healing?* She had offered the same brief explanation of her wound that she'd offered Jill. A simple lie and then added, "Really?"

"So many people fight the grief, but grief is not a passage traveled around, only through. It might not feel like it at the time, but it's actually good to have those spells."

Other members acknowledged the wisdom of Mary's words. Either they were further along in the process than Kendra or they recognized, like Kendra, how hard they fought to keep the pain at bay.

"The pain didn't devour you, did it?"

"Well," Kendra said, "I've had moments. If breathing wasn't involuntary, sometimes, I don't think I'd be here. Then again, I've been able to write again. That's a significant change."

As she gazed around the group, the members nodded. They didn't have opinions about the pace of her grief, like Jill. They didn't expect anything more of her than who she was today.

"Thank you," she murmured. "I don't know where I'd be without you guys."

Footsteps drew their attention to the staircase. Kendra couldn't hide her pleasure in seeing Nathan descend the stairs. She had set up a chair for him, just in case, and he smiled and nodded his appreciation as he took the seat beside her.

"Sorry to be late. Had a call that held me up."

"No worries," Mary said.

Nathan waited for other members to share tales of their week before sharing his progress. "Dad loved the park. Didn't matter which one, but he'd walk miles to be in nature. He'd spend hours on the trails at Gallup Park, trucking through the Arboretum every chance he had. I reached out to the Arboretum this week and asked if I could purchase a bench on his behalf. It's been satisfying for me, creating an opportunity for folks to stop and sit for a while, enjoying the beauty of the place in his memory."

"We often find fulfillment in leaving a legacy of our loved ones. Well done, Nathan."

Kendra knew they all sought approval. A voice that let them each know that the grieving process took many shapes and forms. What each person decided to do—or not do—was met with joint approval. Only those who had walked the same dreadful path truly understood. While grief was a universal experience, until you'd lost a loved one, you couldn't truly know what it was like.

Josh's head remained focused on the floor. "You guys are full of shit. Acting all Pollyanna. This isn't a party, dammit. I lost my best friend. He's never coming back. I don't care how many benches I put around town with his name on them. He's not coming back."

The group stilled but listened respectfully.

"Death isn't some neat little package we can gift back. What's wrong with you people?"

Gary stepped in. "You're in a great deal of pain. I'm sorry."

For all of them, Kendra realized, the loneliness—the inability to reach for the phone and hear the voices of loved ones—left them adrift, unbalanced, and ungrounded. Josh was a different personality. Or maybe he was one of those people who would wallow in his grief for a long time. Kendra felt sad for him, but she didn't want to go back there either. In that moment, she realized Jill had had a point. She had been wallowing.

She wouldn't have imagined that sharing her grief would actually lift her spirits, but that was exactly the result. She hoped that Josh would find the same peace.

At the end of the session, Kendra went up to each and every member and offered a hug. Josh turned his back to her, but verve still coursed through her veins.

Nathan replaced Kendra's folding chair and waited for her by the stairs. "I hate to assume, but beer? I need to hear how you hurt yourself."

Kendra's eyes sparkled. "Absolutely."

"I can drive and then drop you off back here if you'd like."

"People will start to talk," Kendra joked.

Nathan led her to his truck and opened the door. "Let's leave them to it."

He drove out of the lot and into Clinton with a smile on his face. "Sorry I missed the first part of the meeting."

"Don't apologize. You have an important job. People depend on you."

Nathan patted her thigh. "You're a great lady, Kendra Kelly. Has anyone ever told you that?"

Kendra dipped her head. "Not in a very long time."

"There you go."

"Thanks."

Kendra chose to share generalizations of the week, most of them positive. *Keep it light and friendly.*

Nathan stopped her mid-story. "Wait, you didn't tell me about your head."

Kendra glossed over the particulars. "What can I say? Clumsy is my middle name. I fell off a chair. Just a minor cut. Only required a few stitches."

When Nathan parked the truck, he turned and pushed back Kendra's hair. "Next time you decide to take a spill, call me. I'm a trained paramedic."

Kendra chuckled. "I'll do that." She briefly mentioned Russ showing up at the hospital.

They strolled down the street to the comfortable neighborhood dive, ducked inside the warm establishment, and took a few minutes, settling in at the bar and ordering drinks.

"Back to your neighbor."

"Russ. There's always something to report. He saw me drive by early in the morning and claimed to be worried. I blew him off. Then, he dropped by to check and see if I needed anything yesterday. I was in the middle of writing, so I didn't answer right away. The guy just kept laying on the bell. On top of that, he was irritated when I did finally answer. I explained I had pages to turn in to my agent and was working on a deadline."

Nathan tipped his head back and laughed. "Here's my take on guys like Russ. They don't have a clue about boundaries. On one hand, they try to get your attention by, well, being attentive. On the other hand, they lack finesse or social grace."

"I hadn't thought of that. In any case, he bugs me. I can't put a finger on it. He just gives me the willies."

They shared a good laugh about that.

"Just be smart," Nathan added. "I like that you told him you're working on a deadline. If he doesn't respect that, you should probably keep an eye out. Who knows who this guy is, right?"

Kendra agreed.

"What can I bring Saturday?"

Kendra's thoughts jumped to *a condom* before she had a chance to filter them. Thank God her mouth didn't fire prematurely. "Dessert?"

"I love to bake. I make this dark chocolate, salted caramel Oreo pie."

"You are a wonder," Kendra said.

This guy didn't just bake dessert. He might just be dessert.

CHAPTER TWENTY-THREE

FOR THE FIRST TIME IN A LONG WHILE, KENDRA LOOKED with pleasant anticipation to the weekend and the first dinner party in her new home. She'd told Molly not to bring a dish, and she spent the day cooking—lasagna, Caesar salad with homemade dressing, and several appetizers. She filled portabella mushrooms with cheese and dried tomatoes, baked spinach puffs in muffin tins, and wrapped bacon around plump dates.

The table decorations gave the place a homey feel. Kendra stood back and admired her work. The floors gleamed, the windows shone, and she could see her reflection in the kitchen appliances.

A knock on the door drew her out of the kitchen. A moment's hesitation caught in her throat until Kendra spotted Nathan, arms laden with bags and dishes. He was thirty minutes early. She had a habit of showing up early too.

"Hey," he said when she opened the door. "Thought I'd see if

I could give you a hand. I don't know about you, but I get a little harried, coordinating last-minute details. What can I do to help?"

Kendra lifted the pie from Nathan's palm and set it on the counter. He also brought a bottle of wine and a bundle of fall flowers.

"These are for you." He handed them to her as she spun around.

Her eyes settled on his, warmth filling her gut. "You're the best. Thank you."

Don't fall for him. He's a friend. Nothing more.

She put him to work, uncorking wine and arranging appetizers on a tray. They moved together easily in her cramped kitchen. Even the few times they bumped into each other seemed like a perfect dance.

Hell, who am I kidding? I'm falling for him.

Minutes after they finished final preparations and clinked glasses to celebrate their success, Molly and Adam appeared. Introductions were a bit awkward. Adam was hardly Molly's type. Socially inept, he blinked and looked off into space when asked a question while Molly hung on every word. Somehow, Kendra had pictured the evening as a gathering of four old friends seeing each other after a long absence. Hugs all around. It was nothing of the kind.

Has Molly lost her mind?

After dinner, Molly joined Kendra in the kitchen for dish duty. The men tucked into the family room with their drinks, talking football. Kendra marveled at Nathan's ability to see Adam as he was and find a way around his quirks.

Molly grabbed Kendra's arm. "What do you think? He's amazing, isn't he?"

Kendra shook her off and fumbled internally as she pretended to busy herself with silverware. "He's unexpected."

Molly beamed. "I'm not sure what I like best about him. He's brilliant."

"I always imagined you with someone … more mainstream, I guess."

"Mainstream and I haven't gotten along in the past, so why repeat the same mistake?"

Kendra turned on the water and rinsed plates as Molly filled leftover containers and delivered serving dishes to the sink.

"As long as you're happy. He's just a bit socially awkward. Not like it's a huge turnoff, but it's noticeable."

"What you're saying is, I've been teaching special ed so long that I don't know what normal is anymore."

Kendra turned and faced her. "It's not that—well, maybe it is. Who can say? I just want you to be happy, and traveling in social circles is a thing couples do. Just being protective."

"Don't cushion things. Just tell me what you think." Molly frowned and turned away.

"Jeez, this isn't going well at all. Adam is a nice guy, and clearly, he cares about you. This is probably my stuff, not yours. I'm reeling from a ton right now. I'm probably not the best judge of character. Let me get to know the guy better, and I'll get back to you."

Molly swallowed hard. "What's up with this Nathan guy?"

"He's just a friend. And tonight is about you. Not me."

"You've burst my bubble, so I'm not sure I want it to be about me anymore."

"Please give me another chance. I want to like him."

"Don't try to fake like him. I'll see through it."

Kendra slapped Molly's arm in an attempt to lighten the mood. "Time for Nathan's dessert."

Kendra pulled Nathan's creation from the fridge, and Molly marveled.

"He cooks?"

Kendra shrugged. "He's a fireman."

The women sliced the pie and put on a pot of coffee even though the air remained stale.

"Truce?" Kendra asked.

"I really want you to like him."

Kendra wrapped her arms around Molly. "He'll grow on me. I'm sure of it."

Molly remained quiet the rest of the evening.

When they said good night, Kendra made a point to talk to Adam. "It was so great to meet you. I hope you and Molly come back soon."

Adam actually smiled as he looked her in the eye. That final act seemed to please Molly.

Nathan stayed behind, puttering in the kitchen, washing the wine goblets by hand and cleaning the counters.

"Thank you for being so nice to my friends," she said.

"Thanks for including me. It's been a long time since I've hung out with anyone other than my crew. I enjoyed the company of women for a change."

"We smell better, and we're prettier."

Nathan turned to face Kendra and rested his hands on her shoulders. "Much," he said before leaning down to kiss her.

A tussle of emotions knotted her shoulders, but in the end, she shoved the conflicted ones to the rear. She let Nathan's lips touch hers and sank into his embrace. Fight as she might, this felt right.

Seconds stretched into what seemed like hours. Kendra floated in the contentment. She felt special, treasured.

When they broke apart, she gazed into Nathan's eyes, blue flecked with gold. She reached up and ran her fingers through his sandy-blond hair. "I like you," she said.

A V creased Nathan's forehead. "But …"

"Let's have a glass of wine and chat."

Kendra couldn't be sure what she wanted to say, where she

wanted this relationship to go, or how this man fit into her life. She didn't want him to leave, but she was scared silly about him staying. The last time she'd let a man into her heart turned out to be a disaster. The risk of losing another man she offered her heart and soul to was far too fearsome.

"How long have you been a firefighter?"

Nathan cocked his head. "Where did that come from?"

Kendra poured and handed him a glass of wine, then led him to the family room. They took seats next to each other on the couch, and Kendra crossed her legs beneath her and shifted to face him.

"Just curious."

"I've dated women before. This isn't an uncommon question. Yes, what I do is dangerous. But I'm extremely good at my job, and I don't take shortcuts."

"I'm not ready to date."

"Fine. We're friends. Getting to be better friends every day," he joked. "Want to go to the cider mill tomorrow? It's supposed to get up to sixty degrees, and the colors are gorgeous by the Huron River."

Kendra couldn't stop the smile that grew across her face. She'd been so busy, meting out feelings for so long, that it felt freeing just to be. "If I can have a caramel apple. Not that I need it after that dessert you made. Where did you learn to bake like that?"

An unexpected and immediate sheen covered Nathan's eyes. "My dad. He was a phenomenal cook. Baker too. I spent hours in the kitchen with him." He flushed. "I mean, we did guy stuff too—played football—but I love to eat, so I'd hang out near the fridge. He put me to work. Taught me everything I know."

"He'd be proud of your efforts tonight. That pie was incredible. When you retire from firefighting, you could open a bakery. Or a restaurant."

"You're already signing me up for a new career?"

"I didn't mean it like that. I'm sure I could do something other than write, choose a career that was steadier. Who knows if I can keep writing decent stories? In the meantime, I'm going to do what I love. I suck at it right now. Seems there are days I write a few thousand words, and they all wind up bland and muddy, but that's part of the process."

"I envy you. Time spent being creative and sharing your gift with others is meaningful."

"How could you ever think your job isn't meaningful?"

Nathan shrugged. A humble man who did what he thought was right.

"You're serving people. If I'm lucky, I entertain them."

"And touch their hearts."

Kendra shrugged. Her writing the past six months had become so guarded. The distance between writing and her characters had become more evident every day. She was sick of vacillating between fire and despair. She hoped, since allowing grief to be a part of her days, she could revise heart into the story. That remained to be seen. Kendra stood and paced the floor. "I'm not myself. Not in my writing. Not in anything."

"Come here." Nathan extended his arm and wrapped it around her shoulders. "You're going to be fine. Just fine."

She nestled into the crook of his neck and inhaled his spicy scent. He smelled like home, if she allowed her true feelings to surface.

"Thanks," she said. "It's been a long time since I've heard that. Now, you'd better go. We have plans tomorrow."

She could have made another decision. She could have taken him to her bed. In that moment, she was grateful Molly had insisted she move to the lake. If she'd still been in the home she'd made with Joe, she wouldn't have considered being with Nathan. Still, she needed more time. Kinda. Maybe.

Nathan hesitated and seemingly decided to leave rather than

push staying. "Tomorrow then," he said after setting his wineglass on the table. He donned his leather jacket and kissed Kendra again, letting his lips linger on hers.

"Tomorrow," she said. "Text me in the morning."

After Nathan left, Kendra locked the door behind him and watched him stride to the truck. She liked everything about this man but the timing. She was afraid to dive into a new relationship too soon. What if she was as clouded about Nathan as she was about Jake and Russ? Or more importantly, Joe? What if she'd misjudged him?

She could practically hear Jill's chastising voice. *"You have to trust again. If you don't, you'll be alone forever. What's the fun in that?"*

Kendra lay in bed and stared at the ceiling. Living at the lake provided her with a degree of quiet she had rarely known. She had grown up in the city, accustomed to the hum of traffic outside her window, the honk of horns, the occasional screech of brakes, sirens, construction equipment, and, well, noise.

Here, the only sound she heard was the intermittent boom of walnuts on the roof, the purr of the wind against the window, the patter of rain on the deck. All natural. An organic life.

At the mere thought of the nuts, Kendra listened to the subsequent pillage of walnuts, the howl of a gust of wind, and then the quiet. She smiled. Life was slowly seeping back. A little at a time but nonetheless.

She drifted off, her last image the anticipation of the cider mill, sitting at a table with Nathan, sipping cider and crunching on a crisp, gooey apple.

Minutes later, maybe longer, Kendra awoke to pounding. In the haze of a dream, she placed the sound as walnuts drumming the rooftop. But as she leaned on her arm and listened more closely, she recognized the sound as steady pounding. Knocking.

Someone was knocking on her door. She checked the time—three a.m. She froze.

No decent human being would hammer on her door in the middle of the night. She sniffed the air. If someone had spotted flames coming from her home, she could envision them alarming her. No smoke. No fire.

Kendra reached for her phone and dialed 911. After the call connected, she made her report to the operator. "I live on Pleasant Lake." She recited her address. "I hear knocking. There's someone pounding on my door. I don't smell fire. I'm worried. Can you send someone out?"

"Can you see who it is?"

Kendra couldn't hide her irritation. "If I go to the door, I might see who's there, but I'd also be putting myself at risk. Please. At least send a police officer. I need to feel safe in my home."

"Dispatching a vehicle now, ma'am. Stay on the line with me."

Kendra clenched her teeth. The beating became more insistent and moved from the front to the side door. From the side door to her bedroom door right off the deck. Her heart raced. Panic frayed her nerves. Goose bumps peppered her arms. She put the call on speaker as she raced to the closet and dressed, thinking of an out.

Which door would serve as the best escape?

"When will they be here? He's moving. I'm afraid he's going to break in."

"Two minutes away, ma'am. Stay on the line. As long as he's outside, you're safe. Do you have somewhere to hide? A basement? A closet?"

Kendra kept her voice hushed. Maybe the maniac outside would give up. Maybe he'd think she wasn't home and leave. "I live in a one-story home. I'm scared. I'm alone."

"The police are almost there. Stay calm."

Anything but relaxed, Kendra lifted a ten-pound dumbbell from her closet shelf. If this crazy broke in, she'd at least have a way to protect herself. In the next second, she heard the wail of sirens race down the street. With the sirens, the knocking ceased.

Kendra tiptoed to the front door in the dark, still afraid to turn on a light. Afraid to give this freak the satisfaction of knowing she was frightened out of her wits.

When the police cruiser parked in front of the house, she flipped on the porch light and gave the 911 operator an update. "Thank you. They're here." She ended the call and opened the door to the two uniformed officers.

She let them inside and hugged her arms around herself, quite unsuccessful at warming the chills that racked her body. "You scared him off. At least, I think you did. He stopped pounding when I heard the sirens."

The officers introduced themselves, and she gave them a short explanation.

"We'll check the perimeter." They both illuminated Maglites on their way out the door.

"I'll turn on all the outside lights." Kendra hurried to the back deck and then the side entrance, flicking all the switches as she went.

Several long minutes later, they returned to the door. Kendra unlocked it and allowed them inside. She paced and worried her fingers.

"Whoever was here seems to have gone."

"He could be anywhere. There are so many places to hide. There's the brush across the street. None of these houses are occupied. All of my immediate neighbors have left for the winter."

"Not much of a place for a single woman to live," one of the officers mumbled.

Kendra fought to maintain what little composure remained.

Officer Miller picked up on her irritation. "We're not just going to leave you. We'll do a thorough check of the area, the entire neighborhood, before we head out. Do you have any idea who would want to frighten you?"

Kendra forced her shoulders to loosen, stretched her fingers from fists. "I'm not sure." She mentally listed the possibilities. Jake, but he had disappeared. Russ, the meddlesome neighbor, or some kind of author stalker. She hated to accuse anyone without justification. "I really don't know. I mean, it's the middle of the night."

"We haven't had any other reports of mischief in the neighborhood. But we'll be sure to check around. Has anything else out of the ordinary happened as of late?"

Kendra's anxiety spiked even higher. "Yes." She told them about the dead animals and showed them the photograph she'd taken. *MURDERER.* "Maybe there's a connection between these events."

"Sounds like pranksters. Kids headed in the wrong direction. With the Halloween season and all …"

"Look," Kendra said. "I understand all that. But just because I'm a woman who chooses to live alone in a remote area doesn't mean I'm not entitled to the same protection as any other citizen."

"Yes, ma'am," Officer Miller said.

His partner's eyebrows arched. Kendra didn't like the guy. She suspected he thought of her as an overreacting female.

"We're making a report. If anything else untoward occurs, please call. We're here to protect and serve."

Kendra's anger forced fear to the background. She ushered the men out of her home and double-checked all the locks. At least they had scared off the intruder. Shit, she didn't even know what to call him. She had no real reason to assume it was a man and realized her stereotyping. She guessed this went both ways. The police had assumed she was a woman with an overactive imagination, just as she'd assumed the perpetrator was a male.

Horseshit. All horseshit.

She went back to bed, pulled the covers over her head, and prayed for sleep. For once, she had plans, and dammit, she had every intention of enjoying her time with Nathan. She considered calling him. Surely, he'd have a better bedside manner than those two jokers, but then she might have to wear the title of Crazy Female.

CHAPTER TWENTY-FOUR

KENDRA WOKE EARLY, EXCITED ABOUT HER DATE. She showered, slid into a pair of form-fitting jeans, and spent extra time on her hair and makeup even though her brain and heart played a rousing game of tug-of-war. Falling for Nathan seemed like a rebound from Joe. And Nathan did seem a little too good to be true. She might be looking for excuses to push him away. But the last guy who'd walked into her life like a white knight had left her totally alone and devastated. So, there was that.

After, Kendra poured another cup of coffee and gazed in the mirror, pleased with her reflection for the first time in a very long while. Her phone beeped. Nathan.

So sorry. Got called into work. Have to cancel today. Please forgive me.

Kendra's heart sank. She slammed her coffee mug on the bathroom counter. Sure, she was overreacting. But, dammit, she needed today.

No worries. It's your job.

And he'd canceled with a text rather than a phone call.

Serves me right. Putting all my eggs in Nathan's basket.

Her mind darted like a trapped animal. *The man has to work. Maybe he's letting me down gently. He's a firefighter—he can't take a day off. He hated dinner and never wants to see me again.*

What the hell would she do with the day? Wallow? Tempting.

Kendra tried to calm the negative thoughts. Nathan was probably in a rush, hence the quick text. She needed to be understanding.

She needed a day away from the computer. She needed time away from the house. The temps were mild today, a welcome period of Indian summer. Kendra was convinced not to let the beautiful weather go to waste. She'd go to the cider mill by herself, buy a caramel apple, sit by the Huron River, soak up some sunshine, and be … mindful. She chuckled.

Kendra sank into the couch, suddenly back in the throes of last night. She'd been distracted earlier, looking forward to some fun, but now that Nathan had canceled, she went back to the fear and anguish. Part of her thought she was losing her mind.

Did someone really show up in the middle of the night to frighten me to death? And who could it have been? Jake? Russ? Molly? Molly would have texted or called if she had some kind of emergency.

She'd made a mental note to tell Nathan about it, but that wasn't to be. She fought the urge to give in to her fear.

The doorbell rang, and she froze. Then, it rang again. Whoever was ringing was insistent.

She should have known better. Of course, it was Russ.

"I saw the police were here in the middle of the night. Everything all right?"

How Russ had gone all night without badgering Kendra was beyond her.

"Everything is fine, Russ."

"What happened?"

Kendra stepped outside. She had to come up with some excuse and fast, or Russ would see it as his duty to never let her out of his sight.

What was he doing up in the middle of the night? Does the man have no life? She couldn't come up with an answer.

"I have a police scanner, young lady. I know you reported someone at your door. If that ever happens again, you call me. I'm just down the road. I can be here faster than the police. And I have a gun. I can scare away an intruder in no time. You should have called me."

"I want to be sure the police have a record. Some strange things have happened around here lately. Just covering my tracks."

Russ shifted from foot to foot, as if he had something more to say. He scrubbed his face with his hand. "Keep me apprised as well. I've been in this neighborhood since I was a boy. I see it as my responsibility to keep everyone safe."

"Thanks for stopping by, Russ. I have to run." Kendra spun on her heel and went back inside, more determined than ever to leave the ever-present eye of the self-appointed neighborhood watch president.

A police scanner? Not that she should be surprised. Russ seemed to have eyes everywhere, but it still annoyed the snot out of her. In a way, she welcomed the anger. It provided the ideal diversion.

She raced to the front door and called out after him, "Hey, Russ."

He looked back like he'd won the lottery. "Yes?"

"How often have there been incidents of crime here over the years? Since you've been here all this time, you must have a pretty good handle on that."

Russ thrust out his chest and beamed. "Not much crime really. We had a time when we had some petty thefts if people left their garage doors open. A few mailbox thefts. Pretty much blew that off to prankster kids. Hooligans is what they are. Twenty years ago, there was a drowning in the lake, not a crime, but a tragic accident."

Kendra winced at the mention of a drowning. "Since I've been here, you think the incidents of disturbances have risen?"

Russ hesitated and pinched his brow. Kendra watched closely and decided he was trying to come up with a way to assuage her fears or dispel the fact that he thought she might be crazy.

"We just keep a watch out for each other here. We like to be good neighbors."

Kendra nodded, letting the unsaid lie go. "Thanks, Russ."

She waved at him, and he turned to leave.

For a moment, she thought about Russ's report of the drowning when she'd asked about crime but then blew it off as an aside he'd shared.

Time to get moving.

Kendra made sure she'd tucked her phone inside her purse, plucked her sunglasses from the counter, and checked to be sure all the doors were secure before she headed to the garage. As she dashed outside, she reconsidered the craziness of last night and almost ducked back inside. Then again, she'd be damned if she allowed some crazy teens to stop her from living her life.

As she entered the garage, she glanced over her shoulder, wondering if she'd ever leave her house without feeling like she was being watched. Determined to get away, she started up the SUV and headed through the country roads to the cider mill. It was packed, and she waited a good five minutes before securing a parking spot in the small lot south of the tiny mill.

Kendra grabbed her notebook, which she always kept in her glove compartment should a writing idea strike her away from home, and assumed a place in the long line, which wrapped around the mill. She shifted from foot to foot, dreaming about how incredible a caramel apple would taste. The pie Nathan had brought last night had seemed to reignite her sweet tooth.

Smells of cinnamon and apples wafted out of the establishment, and she listened as the old press moaned and groaned. By the time she purchased an apple, round and covered with caramel and nuts, she realized she was famished. Wanting nothing more than to park on the riverbank and enjoy her snack, she peered past the few picnic tables and families strewn on blankets to find a quiet spot on the river's edge.

She sat on a square of matted grass, mostly dirt, and took a big bite of her apple. It tasted like heaven, but within seconds, Kendra felt her stomach turn. Anger crept up her body in inches. From her toes to her knees and on up until it reached her head. The spread of fury settled in her head, which began to pound. She wrapped the apple in the piece of waxed paper it sat on, and she pulled out her notebook and a pen.

What was Joe thinking after we lost Joey?

Kendra set pen to paper and let her subconscious take over.

I can't stand to look at her.

How could she put Joey down for a nap and not keep an eye on him? How could she simply pick up the phone, call me at work, and ask me to come home in the middle of the day without a warning? She seemed so calm. So calm in fact that I thought there was a stupid issue with the sump pump alarm.

And then when I arrived, she delivered the news—Joey died?!—as if her world had ended, not mine. Joey was my son, my most treasured possession. She fell apart, clinging to me. Who was there to comfort me? No one. I was the one who had to call the funeral home and make arrangements—for them to pick up my baby's lifeless body from the hospital morgue.

She hadn't even given me the chance to hold my boy one last time in my own home. She allowed me no closure. Only a monster could do that.

I have to leave. I can't breathe the same air she does. And I can't face a home where my child no longer exists.

When Kendra came up for air, tears were streaming down her cheeks, deep sobs choked out of her throat—unfamiliar, strangled sounds. She ripped the page from her notebook, balled it up in her hand, stood, and raced to the nearest trash bin, where she pitched the words and her apple.

Scaling the hill in record time, Kendra darted to her car and started it up, putting it in reverse and nearly hitting a young family, she was in such a hurry to get out of the lot and back onto the road.

She drove aimlessly, her vision blurred by tears. Finally, she pulled over to the side of the road. A box of tissues sat in the passenger seat. Kendra blew her nose for the next few minutes, swiped her hair back from her face, and rubbed her arms to flatten the gooseflesh.

Without direction, she pulled back onto the road and drove—no idea where she was headed.

Thirty minutes later, she slowed by her old house, noticing the changes the new owners had made. They'd cut down trees galore, filled the front walk with bird feeders. Planted enough perennials to make the front yard look like a jungle. It was no longer her haven. No longer hers in any fashion.

Disgusted and lost, Kendra drove into Saline—the little burg she used to call home—and parked the car at Dan's, the dive bar on Main Street. It was only one o'clock in the afternoon. Should be quiet. She could sneak inside, grab a beer at the bar, and calm down.

The place was nearly empty and dark as a tomb inside, just as Kendra had hoped. She slid onto a barstool at the end of the counter and ordered a draft beer. The bartender recognized her, but as all good bartenders did, he sensed her need to be left alone and set her beer down along with a tall glass of water. He busied himself, wiping down the counter at the other end of the bar.

Kendra sipped her beer, letting the brew coat her tongue and throat and then take root in her belly. The hops helped.

After a large, long breath, Kendra's heart settled back in her chest. She glanced at the Lions game on the television, pretended to watch intently, and cleared her mind.

She sensed a group settle at a table behind her but didn't bother to turn around. What she craved was anonymity, not conversation. Female voices filled the air as they ordered drinks and food. Kendra ignored them. Minutes later though, she heard whispers.

"That's Kendra Kelly, the woman who lost her baby and husband last spring. I thought she moved to the lake. I haven't seen her around in ages. Can you imagine?"

"Her husband was a piece of work. I used to see him in here all the time. Juicing it up with a *friend*. I remember hearing how she thought she'd won the lottery, marrying that guy. Trolling is what he did. And then to hang himself? How selfish can a guy be?"

Kendra lost the ability to swallow and then to breathe. Part of her wanted to spin around and scream at them. The other part wanted to slither down the bar and out the door before anyone noticed her. Trolling? Joe? Heat licked her earlobes.

She slapped a twenty on the counter and slid off the barstool, ducking her head. Thankfully, there were two exits—one onto the main drag, the other into the back alleyway. A quick exit out the back, and Kendra leaned against the building, so light-headed that her body could barely stay upright.

A bench sat twenty feet away, and after taking a few deep breaths, Kendra made her way over and sank down. She rested her head between her knees for a minute or two before panic set in again. If those women came outside and found her sitting there, she'd really be exposed. It was more than she could bear.

She didn't want to go home, where she'd have to deal with the memories of last night. She required safety, not dread. More than anything, she needed to vent, scream, or hit something. Instead, she hurried to the car, locked herself inside, and texted Jill. Jill would be straight with her. Of that, she could be sure.

You busy?

John took the kids bowling. Just sitting here, reading. Why?

Can I stop by?

I'd love that!

Kendra headed the car in the direction of Jill's place, glad the house was close to town so she wouldn't have to drive past her former home again. Talk about over the top. Joe having an affair had never occurred to Kendra. Never. Not on the nights he'd worked late or had business trips out of town. She'd trusted him. Implicitly. Right up to the moment she found him hanging in the garage.

CHAPTER TWENTY-FIVE

ENDRA PULLED INTO JILL'S DRIVEWAY TEN MINUTES later, still fuming. She marched up the front walk and rang the bell, and Jill opened the door. Still stunned by what she'd overheard, Kendra walked inside.

"The kids aren't home? John's gone? You're alone?" She peered over her shoulder as Jill closed the entry door.

"What on earth? What's wrong?"

As Jill led her into the kitchen, Kendra tossed her purse on the entry bench as she recited the events of the last twenty-four hours, leaving out the date with Nathan, but describing the scary night, her trip to the cider mill and the beer at Dan's, along with the eavesdropping on the conversation about Joe. Jill instructed her to sit down and made them each a cup of tea.

"Joe having an affair? Did you know? Did you suspect?"

Jill hesitated a second too long for Kendra's comfort and then wagged her head back and forth. "Joe was a little smarmy."

"Smarmy?" Kendra's voice rose. "If you thought that, why didn't you ever say anything?"

"It wasn't my place. You were head over heels. He was your answer to the universe."

"So, if I was running toward a cliff and you saw the edge before I did, you wouldn't warn me?"

Jill set a cup of tea in front of Kendra and sat down next to her. "Not the same thing. Not by a long shot. When it comes to friends' choices for a mate, it's personal. Not my business. And smarmy isn't a cliff. Let's put it this way. You were more enamored with Joe than any of us, but that was as it should be."

"You mean to tell me that Amy, Erica, Kathy, and Molly all felt the same way, but none of you told me?" Kendra kicked the table leg. "And I suppose you knew he was a ladies' man and never happened to mention that either?"

"Hold on a minute. I know nothing about Joe's indiscretions or if he had any. I did hear he was a regular at Dan's, so maybe the fact that you were there today is why those women mentioned him. If they saw him there a lot, they might have seen something."

Kendra stood and paced the room. "How could he do this to me? I trusted him. I … made him my knight in shining armor. Shit." After the words left her mouth, she replayed the feelings of being stalked since his death. Here, she'd been thinking a man was following her, but it could be Joe's jealous mistress.

"I have to go," she fired at Jill.

"Wait. Please sit down. I want to talk about last night. You're out in the country. Alone. I know it's only fifteen minutes away, but it's isolated at the lake. Maybe your mind is playing games with you."

"And now, you think I'm crazy, imagining someone banging on my door in the middle of the night?" Another flood of heat ran up Kendra's neck, and she glared at Jill.

"Sit down. Please."

Kendra remained standing and stared Jill down.

Jill stood and rested a hand on her arm. "You've been through more than most of us go through in a lifetime. It's normal for you to be rattled. You moved out of town fast, and although you're not far away, you've kept to yourself for too long. Molly said the grief group is helping, and for that, we're grateful, but if you want me to be honest and tell you when I see you nearing the edge of a cliff, I have to say, I'm concerned. I don't know if you're imagining things or not, but I know you're not yourself. Will you take a breath? Can you listen?"

"I just found out my husband, who I worshipped and adored, not only abandoned me when he hanged himself, but evidently before that as well. I'm not sure why you expect me to calm down."

"I love you. I want what's best for you. I'm glad you came by today, but you need to hear me out. There's a reason we're all concerned. This is not just me. It's your best friends. Sweetie, you used to be the one who made sure we all got together, even when we were all so busy with our lives that we could barely see straight. Other than Molly, you haven't seen any of us more than a handful of times since you lost your family. That's not normal. You're withdrawn, scared, skittish, and confused."

Kendra fought to even out her breathing. "We have to do this another time." She grabbed her purse, slung it over her shoulder, and marched outside, slamming Jill's door behind her.

Once she made it to the car, she pulled out of Jill's driveway like she was the one with a fire to extinguish. There was no safe place anymore. No haven. No supportive friend to lean on. She had no choice but to go home.

Scrutinizing the rearview mirror, Kendra made sure she wasn't being followed.

༄

Two glasses of wine and three cigarettes later, Kendra calmed down enough to think. Jill wasn't wrong. When she reexamined her life with Joe, she couldn't deny the late nights, the smell of alcohol on his breath. He'd had business dinners, true. Or at least, that was what he told her. He came home disheveled some nights too. She attributed that to his long days. Maybe she'd been a fool. So anxious to have the perfect life that she'd lied to herself.

Kendra had never suspected Joe of being anything other than a guy who worked too hard, was a tad too devoted to his career. But they were both older and settled into their lives when they married. They'd had their routines established.

Kendra recognized what needed to happen next. She needed to look for clues. How distasteful.

Thanks a bunch, Joe. Leave me with two horrible deaths to grieve and now with news that you were unfaithful.

Not gonna happen today. Life was already a shit sandwich. No need to add mayo.

Kendra's phone buzzed, and she glanced at the message. Molly.

You okay? Jill messaged me that you were having a rough day.

Can anything happen to me that doesn't travel through the grapevine like wildfire?

Sorry. We just care about you.

I'm fine.

Kendra lit another cigarette and then promptly stubbed it out. She couldn't stand sitting alone for another second. She snatched a sweatshirt from inside, locked the door behind her, and headed down the road at a steady clip. The leaves had turned brilliant colors of crimson and gold, and she finally took the first true cleansing breath of the day. The sun shone brightly, creating a peaceful path as she slowed to a meandering pace. As she crested the first hill on the road, she spotted Russ across the way, chatting with one of the few remaining residents—an elderly woman named Betsy—as she rototilled her garden.

"Kendra! Just the person I was hoping to see."

Kendra summoned a wan smile and said hello.

Russ excused himself from his conversation with Betsy and joined her as she walked. "I have some news for you."

Kendra brightened a little, thinking maybe he had a lead on the middle-of-the-night disturbance yesterday. "Oh?"

"Your friend Jake is moving back to the lake. Evidently, the new job wasn't what he'd hoped. He's going to try to find something in Michigan. Said he might as well be close to family."

"Thanks for letting me know." Kendra sped her pace in order to lose Russ.

He took the hint. "Have a good walk." Russ turned and went back to continue his conversation with Betsy.

This had been the day from hell.

The next morning, a chill woke Kendra. In defiance of her stalker, she'd left a transom window open overnight, and the temps had dipped significantly. After shutting and locking the window, Kendra pulled on some sweats and made a full pot of coffee, and then she headed to the computer.

She pulled up all the bank and credit card statements from the year prior to Joe's death. Nothing seemed amiss. No charges to lingerie stores, florists, or jewelers. As far as the business trips, nothing seemed out of place. Joe seemed to have gone on all the business trips he'd mentioned, nothing untoward there, but he easily could have brought a companion. There was no way to verify that.

Next, she checked phone records. No strange phone numbers leaped out.

If Joe had had an affair, he'd covered his tracks well.

Kendra had done enough research in her writing career to

know about burner phones and the extent to which people would go to hide their secrets. And when it came right down to it, the reason to investigate Joe's paramour was to challenge the stalker and be rid of her once and for all. She shamed herself for thinking a man was tracking her. She blamed the mistake on the fog of grief.

Another option existed though. Kendra spun her chair around to her desktop and sent a short email, secured a reservation, then quickly packed a backpack with essentials, and locked up the house.

Within thirty minutes, she parked at the mall, went inside, dived into a restroom, and changed. She shoved her hair up into a ball cap and exited on the other side of the shopping center, where she met her Uber driver and was off to the airport. If someone was following her, well, two could play this game.

CHAPTER TWENTY-SIX

AFTER DISEMBARKING THE PLANE, KENDRA STEPPED outside into gorgeous sunshine and unimaginable warmth. Thirty minutes later, she checked into the La Jolla Shores Hotel and gazed out the window at the welcome sight of the Pacific Ocean. Nothing relaxed Kendra more than the ocean—water of any kind for that matter. She inhaled a steady breath and gathered her purse and backpack.

Following directions from the navigation system of a rental car, Kendra drove for ten minutes, winding down Torrey Pines Road and perusing the exquisite beach homes along the coast. She had three potential addresses to search for answers. One for Purest Heart of Mary Catholic Church, one for the house where Joe and Jake had grown up, and one for Jake's supposed apartment as an adult. She drove past the church first, and then she decided to park.

Kendra had no idea what she was looking for or what she hoped to find. Answers, yes, but to what questions exactly?

The church was smaller than she'd anticipated, but several buildings occupied the grounds: two school buildings—both labeled the Mercy Academy—a pastoral center, and the church. Located along Girard Avenue and across the street from a few shops, Kendra sat behind the wheel for a few moments and tried to picture Joe as a little boy, walking to school. Even though she had no idea how he had gotten to and from school every day, she imagined him toting a backpack and dragging it along the ground, as little boys were apt to do, kicking rocks and lost in thoughts of recess and his favorite friends or classes. She pondered him during his teens, long and lanky, a basketball player with height but a lack of coordination, smarter than the devil though and determined. What was it like for him to come to this place, which, instead of a safe haven for a carefree childhood, had become a place of horrors and nightmares?

Kendra pondered going inside the church, but what would be accomplished? She'd lost her spirituality along with Joe and Joey, and she had no desire to retrieve it. Add that to the secrets she carried for Joe and Jake, and she fired up the engine and drove off. It was silly of her to come to La Jolla. A stupid, foolish impulse and an expensive trip if all it amounted to was an afternoon stroll on the beach.

Ten minutes later, she pulled into the drive of a stunning home right on the beach. Unclear of her intentions, her stomach flipping, she entered the open gates and parked in the driveway. The sheer size of the place was intimidating. She envisioned a butler answering the door. Clearly out of her element, she mustered courage from a secret place she'd had no idea still existed and paraded up a long walkway to the front door.

The exterior, largely glass, made her eyes saucer. The rough-hewn archway that led from the driveway to the door wound through the property for a stretch of at least fifty feet, and the steep bluff the house sat on caused her heartbeat to quicken with anxiety.

Indeed, she hadn't envisioned this as Joe's childhood home. Even if she didn't get answers from the current residents, the sight of the home allowed her into an unknown place in Joe's life and, more than that, one she could barely comprehend. How he'd wound up in a tiny Michigan town with a small-time girl like her, she hadn't a clue.

Kendra rang the bell and continued to examine the residence. Everywhere she looked, she was able to see inside through the walls of windows. On the right, she surveyed an office with a single mahogany table at least twelve feet in length. A lone Queen Anne chair stood statuesquely behind the table. Not one scrap of paper, flower arrangement, framed photo, or laptop was strewn on the desktop. It was ornate but devoid of a homey feel, and Kendra told herself she'd never want to live in such a cold environment or raise a child there. Then again, ocean waves lapped on the shore on the other side of the house, so she might want to rethink her initial judgment.

Kendra peered in the room to her left. A dining room of sorts, but why have a dining room that didn't face the water? Probably because you had more than one dining room.

The trip-trap of footsteps across the terra-cotta flooring caught Kendra's attention. When she focused on the figure advancing toward her, she eyed a teensy bit of a woman, quite determined in her gait. The woman was older, most likely in her late seventies, but spry and exquisitely dressed with short, curly white hair tucked politely behind her ears.

"Hello, dear," she said with a smile. "How may I help you?"

Kendra's words caught in her throat. She hadn't anticipated a friendly greeting but rather someone suspicious of her unexpected arrival. Her words came out with hesitation. "Sorry to trouble you. I'm Kendra Kelly. I believe my husband, Joe Kelly, grew up in this house, and I thought you might be able to provide me with some information."

"Joe Kelly. Really?" Her eyebrows lifted. "I'm Sylvia O'Connor. Please, come in."

Kendra blindly followed the petite woman down the hall and into a kitchen nook at the back of the house. Although Sylvia indicated Kendra take a seat, Kendra's feet carried her to the wall of glass overlooking the ocean. The sheer vastness of the view stole her breath, and her hand settled over her heart, as if to quiet its racing.

"How beautiful!" Kendra exclaimed. She stood stone still for a solid minute, mystified that Joe hadn't shared any details of his childhood home.

"Have a seat, dear. Tea? Wine? It's never too early for wine."

Still stunned by the sight, Kendra forcibly turned away from the magnificent view and answered the woman. "Tea would be wonderful."

Sylvia put the pot on to boil and stepped over to the table, where she pulled out a seat for Kendra. "Sit here. That way, you can enjoy the view."

"I've never seen anything so lovely. Have you lived here long?"

Sylvia stammered for a heartbeat before answering. "After Joe and Sarah … died …" She chose her words carefully. "We were neighbors and lived just down the way. We knew the history of the house and that it would be a hard sell under the, uh … circumstances. Purchasing the home, in our awkward way, was something we could do to honor the Kellys. Besides, we were dear friends and spent so much time at each other's homes that this was already home to us in a way. Does that make sense?"

Too stunned to absorb the story all at once, Kendra leaned back in her chair and sat quietly for several moments. "Of course."

Sylvia poured hot water into two china teacups and carried them over to the table before she returned to the kitchen and procured a box of tea bags from a drawer. She grabbed two teaspoons and trotted back to the table. Kendra randomly chose a flavor of tea and then steeped the bag in her cup, anxious to continue the conversation.

"My husband died in May."

"Then you were married to Joe Jr. We called him Junior when he was growing up. I bet he didn't let you refer to him that way, did he? He hated the nickname. Got to the point where he wouldn't answer Sarah unless she called him Joe. He was a feisty boy, that one. The Catholic school had a few issues with him too, as I recall. A few serious ones. Catholic school isn't equipped to handle students with learning problems like Joe had."

"You mean, Jacob, don't you? Joe mentioned Jake, or Jacob, struggled some as a child."

"Oh, yes. Jacob gave Sarah fits, but he was a dream compared to Joe. That boy struggled from the day of his birth. Colic first and then a case of the terrible twos that lasted at least five years." Sylvia tittered softly at the memory. "I watched him when Sarah had a bit of minor surgery. The boy would not sleep. He was a miserable human being. Nothing made him happy.

"I felt so bad for Sarah and Joe Sr. but more so for little Joe. It was as if the child had been born into the wrong world. Nothing felt right to him. He complained all the time. Rarely did I see the boy at peace. When he hit adolescence, he became even more sullen."

"What about Jacob though? I thought he was troubled."

"Not especially. He found a savior in music. Real talented youngster, that one."

Kendra recalled finding out through her research that Jake claimed he had headphones on at the time of his parents' murders. She guessed that could have been true. Surveying the house, Kendra pondered where the bedrooms were. The master suite, where she assumed the Kellys had been killed, was supposedly on the first floor and then Jake's room upstairs.

"Are you looking for something?" Sylvia asked in response to Kendra's wandering gaze.

Kendra offered her an excuse for her behavior. "Sorry, I'm picturing my husband living here and trying to sort out why things ended the way they did. I'm searching for a connection."

"How did things end, dear?"

Kendra dipped her head, unwilling to meet Sylvia's sympathetic gaze. "Joe hanged himself shortly after we lost our baby to SIDS. It probably sounds ridiculous, my endless search for answers, but I'd like to understand more in hopes of moving forward. Lots of strange things have been happening lately. I'm wondering why."

Sylvia leaned forward and placed a hand on Kendra's knee. "You poor thing. I'm so sorry. How can I help?"

Kendra locked eyes with the woman, feeling more forthright than she had in months. "Please tell me about the murders, the aftermath, anything you can. It helps me piece things together."

"After Sarah and Joe died, Joe sort of vanished. He was off at USC, probably busy being a college kid and doing college kid things. The family wasn't *close*. I suppose I wasn't too surprised he didn't rush back or stay for the trial. He and Jake might have been close growing up, but those relationships with siblings, in my experience, can change quite a bit when people leave home or go through a tragedy like those boys did. Maybe Joe believed Jake killed his parents." She stood and walked to the counter. "You know, there aren't many murders in La Jolla. We're a small community. A cozy, sleepy seaside town."

Kendra wrinkled her forehead. Such an opulent place being referred to as cozy and sleepy made her sit up straight. In Sylvia's eyes, Kendra guessed it was true. But Kendra knew about the Broderick murders in nearby Hillcrest in 1989 and, more recently, the brutal killing of surfer Emery Kauanui Jr. in 2007.

She surmised any small town with this much wealth served as the perfect breeding ground for scandal and intrigue.

Throw in the Kelly murders, and La Jolla's sleepy little seaside village reputation was up for grabs.

Kendra considered her options. Still in shock, she recognized this was a chance for serious answers.

"I read that Jacob was accused of the murders. I certainly don't want to pry, and if you'd rather not discuss the slayings, I completely understand. You lost dear friends, and although time has passed, I can't imagine the pain ever goes away."

"Oh, honey, I'm an old woman. I have a limited amount of time left. Most all my friends are gone at this stage of my life. I'm enjoying your company. You can ask me anything. I have age and the wisdom of many years of imperfect living to share." She chuckled softly and rose from the table.

Sylvia shuffled through the cupboards for a few minutes before returning with a plate of cookies. She nibbled on one as she waited for Kendra to speak.

Whatever hesitation Kendra initially had, she abandoned. "Did you have a personal opinion about the circumstances surrounding the murders?"

"You don't need to dance around. You want to know if I think Jacob killed his parents."

Kendra swallowed hard. "Yes," she admitted.

"The boys had a troubled childhood. It's only when you're old like me that you can reflect back on life and see things with clear lenses. Joe and Sarah were nice people. They tried their best. But they weren't particularly affectionate people, nor did they have a handle on child rearing, and with Junior's personality disorder, they had their work cut out for them. They didn't always discipline the boys but rather vacillated between harsh punishments and ignoring them. The boys didn't have clear boundaries. When you have children who constantly push the limits, it's imperative to be consistent."

"Can I ask your background?"

"I worked as a clinical psychologist for forty years. The money"—she paused and considered her surroundings—"came from my family and my husband's success. William is a real estate investor."

Kendra's eyes viewed the panorama. "Did Joe's parents get him help?"

Sylvia hesitated. "They were both in denial. They thought he was just an unruly child. A handful of a boy."

"So, what's your take on Jake's guilt or innocence?"

"The circumstances around the killings pointed to someone who knew the couple well. The crimes were personal. Both Joe and Sarah were stabbed. The murderer was angry. Certainly a crime of passion. I'd rule out an affair, just because I knew them both. Not that either of them was faithful for the duration of their marriage, but they had a comfortable arrangement. They liked the security of marriage but chose to dabble in lust."

"How did Joe come out of all this?"

"Let me warm your tea." Sylvia stood and flipped on the burner under the kettle.

As if Sylvia had read her thoughts, she spoke. "I've been witness to the darkest of the human psyche. Unimaginable pain and heartache inflicted on the wealthiest people on earth. This luxurious environment would seem to give way to the best in humanity. Somehow, the opposite occurs. That's not to say that good people don't inhabit our community. There are those of us, despite our financial riches, who aspire to live a decent, worthwhile life. Others mistake money for power and permission to act in any way they see fit.

"But I digress."

"Jacob confided in me. He said he and Joe were sexually

abused by a priest at their church. Do you know where they attended school?"

"Purest Heart of Mary. The Catholic church has suffered from predatorily disposed priests. We all know that. I'd guess Jacob was telling the truth. He wasn't the only one to accuse a priest from the school. My heart breaks for those children. Suffering that kind of abuse can seriously alter the course of one's life."

"So, you think Jacob killed his parents?"

"I'd tell you if I knew. But unless I was witness to the crime, I wouldn't ever pass judgment. As a psychologist, I'd be a bad jury member. I see both sides. I understand trauma and its repercussions."

"Can you tell me about Jacob's life after his parents' deaths?"

"He was raised by his grandmother. In town. In a smaller home, nothing of this nature. He dropped out of high school and had issues with petty crime but shy of your Joe's issues or their parents' demise. The boy was a lost soul. How did Joe fare? I lost contact with him after his parents died."

Kendra gazed out at the sea, lost in thought. Joe had told her virtually nothing of his past and chosen to share only the briefest snippets. "I thought I knew my husband. I guess, not so much. Joe had this charisma about him. At least with me, but it turns out, he told me lots of tall tales and was a completely different man than the one I knew. I don't know how to resolve that."

Sylvia laid a compassionate hand on Kendra's arm. "I'm sorry you had to learn about these sordid details in this way. People are complicated creatures. Who knows what happened to Joe as an adult? He might have tried to rewrite his past with you, but it maybe it caught up with him in the end."

"I'm trying to put a life together. I'm sure there's no way to tie up his death with a neat little bow, but in spite of that, I'm trying to find some closure. Why did Joe leave me? And why all the lies? Is there anything else you think I need to know?"

"We lost track of Joe. There were lots of crazy rumors, but I didn't pay too much attention. I sort of remember he was engaged to his college sweetheart, but she broke off the engagement at the last minute. Something about him sleeping with someone else, I think. You know how these things go. Sex can either make a relationship perfect or tear it apart. I have no idea where his demons led him."

Sylvia gazed out at the sea for a moment before continuing. "All of the traumas we suffer manifest themselves in some way throughout our lives. Most of us make the choice to survive the worst. We're resilient in the face of catastrophe." She patted Kendra's hand. "I wish I had an answer for you."

Kendra swallowed over the lump in her throat. "Thank you for your kindness. You've been quite helpful." A mixed bag, for sure, but probably more useful than anything, considering this new information.

Sylvia retraced her steps through the hallway, the kitchen, and toward the front door. When they reached the front door, Kendra thanked Sylvia again. The woman extended her arms, and Kendra returned the gesture with a hug.

Meeting Sylvia had been both a gift and a wound opener.

Bile rose in Kendra's throat, and her heart clenched in her chest. *My husband lied to me on a daily basis, cheated on me, and killed himself in order to punish me for losing our baby, and I'm the one picking up the pieces, feeling guilty, and questioning my sanity? How can I ever trust my judgment again? How can I find peace in this kind of devastation?*

CHAPTER TWENTY-SEVEN

A FTER KENDRA LEFT SYLVIA'S HOME, SHE CHECKED HER phone. A text from Nathan.

You available for a chat?

Out of town for a couple of days. See you at grief group?

Kendra had booked a flight for Wednesday. If she landed on time, she'd head directly to retrieve her car, go to group, and then make her way home afterward.

But in the meantime, she had time on her hands. She lifted her phone again and called Jean, who answered on the first ring.

"I was just thinking of you. Is this an ESP call?"

"I'm in Cali. You busy?"

Jean's voice tinkled with laughter. "When you decide to make a move, you don't waste any time, do you?"

"It's a long story. And I know how you love stories. Meet you for a drink?"

"I'm up to my eyeballs in pages from one of my authors who

decided to turn in a story that's missing significant chunks of plot, but for you? Absolutely. Name the spot."

JJ lived in an apartment complex in San Diego, just a short trip down I-5.

Kendra pulled up a map of places nearby. There was a beautiful restaurant right on the beach, but she craved anonymity today. Not that anyone she knew would be sitting at a restaurant on the beach in the middle of the afternoon, but still. "How about Rock Bottom? Beer and pretzels sound good. Tell you the truth, I need to drown my sorrows with food and beverage."

"Be there in thirty minutes."

At the restaurant, Kendra headed toward the restroom, pleased with herself for reaching out to Jean and thrilled at the prospect of putting the afternoon in order. Business done, she exited the restroom and found a seat at a bar table when Jean ambled into the place. Kendra wrapped her in a hug and held on tight. Jean tittered with laughter.

"Need a lifeline?"

"How'd you guess?" Kendra stepped back and held Jean at arm's length. "It's so good to see you. How laying eyes on you makes me feel totally whole, I'll never understand. In any case, I welcome it. And you. Thanks for coming on such short notice."

Jean eased her large frame into a booth, and Kendra assumed a seat across from her.

After they ordered beers and pretzels, Jean leaned forward and cupped her chin in her hands. "Spill it."

Kendra jabbered nonstop about her visit with Sylvia and the conversation she'd overheard at her old neighborhood bar about Joe, and she didn't stop for a breath until the pretzels showed up.

Jean sat back, hands around her head, and rocked. "Life is full of complications."

Kendra blew out a puff of air. "That's a nice way to put it."

"So, you fell for a guy who charmed the hell out of you."

"I feel like a damn fool."

"Ha. Now, that's funny. You're just a normal woman. I don't know if I've ever met a woman who hasn't done the same. It's sad and a shame but not the end of the world. Oh, I know you're dealing with a boatload, but being angry is so much easier than being sad. It's energizing. Hard to say if you'll ever know if your husband had affairs or who he was involved with, but the intel that he was a player gives you one more good reason to move forward with your life. Easier said than done, I realize, but seriously.

"What concerns me more at this juncture though are all these other things that have been happening since your move to the lake. You're learning more about Joe's past, but why were dead animals on your property? Who is trying to frighten you, and why? You have to be safe. That's a given. Tackle that first."

"Please," Kendra said, "tell me. I need information. I need to know what to do."

"There are lots of fascinating stalker cases. And trust me, a stalker is no joke. First, I'd firm up that alarm system of yours. And it seems like you have a few possible candidates already. This Russ guy and Jake, the brother. Now, who else?"

Kendra leaned back in her chair, thinking hard. "If Joe had an affair, a stilted lover? I've been thinking all along it's a man, but if Joe had an affair … a stilted lover … maybe it's a woman."

"What would her motivation be?"

"Um … maybe revenge. If she couldn't have him, no one should?"

"Seems like a stretch. Would he have promised her something? Money?"

"If it's money they're after, it's probably Jake. But why wouldn't he just come right out and tell me he wanted part of Joe's inheritance? And if Joe had killed his parents and let Jake take the fall, well, hell, I'd be pissed too."

"So, Jake is a definite suspect, and he's acted a little unstable around you. Let's get back to a woman. Have you searched records? Found anything?"

"Done, and no."

"There has to be something. Guys are buffoons at pulling off affairs. They tend to fumble."

"Or maybe I was just too gullible to notice. Maybe he destroyed evidence before he hanged himself."

Jean grabbed a pretzel, dipped it in melted cheese, and chewed thoughtfully for a good minute. "It could be that Joe promised her something. Maybe she demonstrated some stalking behavior, and Joe got nervous, tried to break things off. Maybe she threatened him, backed him into a corner when he was already feeling vulnerable. She could be harassing you as a way to get back at him. Stalkers don't tend to be rational, mainstream, upstanding citizens. Most of them are harmless, but you can't take that risk."

"Once I'm home, I'll work on the alarm system. Keep my eye out for a woman. Other than that, I'm hoping this person runs out of steam or gets hit by a truck."

Jean glanced at her watch. "Sorry, doll, but I have to go back to those pages."

Kendra rose from her chair as JJ did. "Thanks for taking time to see me. I feel tons better. The visit with Sylvia was a lot."

JJ wrapped her arms around Kendra. "You're doing great." She glanced at the empty plate on the table. "It's nice to see you eat. Keep it up and keep in touch."

Kendra held tight before letting Jeannie go.

A little sad and bereft, she watched her agent and friend leave the restaurant.

Before heading back to the hotel, Kendra drove by Jake's former apartment, a large complex with many buildings. She rolled her eyes. How she'd thought she'd find something of use here was beyond her. She wasn't a private investigator who could interview his neighbors with any authority. And what would her questions be? She'd leave that to a professional should the need arise.

Kendra touched down at five p.m. on Wednesday, met her Uber, hopped into her car at the mall, and drove to grief group. Not that she was in the mood. But it might be nice to see Nathan, lay eyes on him anyway. She was still struggling with being stiffed out of their date. But a distraction from the sadness of the anniversary of Joey's ten- month birthday would certainly help her get through this horrid day.

Memories had assaulted her from every angle on the flight. A stark realization came to her. When she'd written the piece from Joe's perspective at the cider mill, she understood she'd been blaming herself for Joey's death. Out of the blue, another memory came to her.

When Joey had been a week old, she'd been bathing him in the sink.

As she'd washed him, Joe had stood behind her and said, "I want him to stay little. That way, no one can ever hurt him."

It had seemed so odd to her at the time, the strength behind his words. Of course, every parent wanted to protect their child endlessly, but perhaps Joe's comment had related to his abuse.

Once Kendra reached the church, she went inside. Nathan had already arrived, and although there was an open seat next to him, she chose to sit next to Gary, afraid she might break down if she were in close proximity to Nathan and the comfort his presence provided.

During group, Kendra felt numb, fingering her bracelet and lost in thought about the day Joe had given it to her. A family heirloom, his mother's, he wanted Kendra to have it now that they were expecting. In a weird way, Kendra had felt Joe had presented her with a piece of his mother, a gift which spoke to his confidence in her ability to mother a child. But now that she knew more, she realized she'd misinterpreted the gesture.

Why did he give it to me?

She twisted the locket in her fingers. Knowing what she did, she didn't feel it was appropriate to wear it any longer. She released the clasp, removed it, and stuffed it inside her jeans pocket.

Mary interrupted Kendra's thoughts. "Kendra, you're miles away tonight. What's going on?"

"Today is Joey's ten-month birthday," she offered. "I have so many memories assaulting me from every direction. I don't want to cry, but I miss him so, and I can't help wondering where he would be right now, standing alone, taking his first steps around furniture, laughing aloud, saying his first …" Kendra choked on her words.

Gary offered his hand, and she took it.

Although every member of the group shared words of sympathy and support, Kendra couldn't take them in. Every muscle in her body tightened. She ached with fatigue, as if she were reliving Joey's death again.

When group ended, Kendra made her way outside. Hurried footsteps sounded behind her, and she startled, suddenly panic-stricken. She froze in place.

"Hey, it's just me." Nathan stopped at her side. "I know this is a tough time for you. Want to go for coffee?"

Kendra shook her head. "It's been a rough couple of days. I think I'd just like to go home and get some rest."

"I'm really sorry about canceling on you on Sunday. I ended up working a thirty-six-hour shift and then slept a ton once I made it home. Forgive me?"

"Sure," Kendra said.

"Where did you go? You didn't mention a trip?"

"In search of answers."

Nathan scrubbed his jaw. "Find any?"

"Nothing I'm happy about. Seems like my husband was a ladies' man. All evidence points that way anyhow. I don't have hard facts, just a strong hunch after eavesdropping on a conversation. And I also learned he had a probable history of unfaithfulness dating back to college."

"That's gotta add insult to injury."

Kendra gazed up at Nathan and smiled. "At least. How about I give you a call tomorrow?"

Nathan nodded. "I'll walk you to your car."

They trekked the twenty yards across the lot, and Kendra unlocked the car.

"Drive safely." Nathan offered her a brief hug and closed the door behind her.

Kendra drove cautiously down the narrow roads, on the lookout for deer darting out from the woods. This time of year, the herds were plentiful. Deer season hadn't yet started, so herds remained in what they thought were safe conditions. Kendra's foot hovered above the brake pedal as she coasted toward home. Her place was only a quarter mile away now, and she had a halfway decent view of her home from the road. Everything looked fine from this angle. She lifted the garage door and pulled inside to the familiar musty smell of aged wood planks.

CHAPTER TWENTY-EIGHT

GRABBING HER BAG FROM THE PASSENGER SEAT, KENDRA illuminated the garage light as she edged her way to the sidewalk from the garage to the house. She tensed at every sound—the creak of the garage door, the wind dropping a branch at her feet. She hesitated for a moment as she neared the back door, unequipped with the strength to weather unwanted gifts, and then scurried inside the screen door, keys at the ready. She unlocked the door and flipped on the light switch.

Kendra backed away, the hair on her neck standing at attention. A chill coursed through her body. Her home had been entirely ransacked. Kitchen drawers lay on the floor, their contents resembling the results of a hurricane—violently pitched debris.

Petrified yet with every nerve on fire, Kendra forced her feet to move. She stepped outside, unsure if she was alone or if whoever had wreaked havoc on her home was still inside. Once she entered the garage, she turned on every available light and went immediately to her car. She climbed in the vehicle and locked the SUV doors, pulled out her phone, and dialed 911.

She reported the break-in and told the operator what she'd discovered. The operator advised her to stay put as long as she felt safe, that the police were on their way. Kendra already had a plan. She fired up the ignition and cracked the garage door. If she needed to exit, she could. The operator stayed on the line with her, chatting about the weather.

Time passed in inches. Seconds dragged. Kendra turned up the car's heat, her mind a web of twisted thoughts. Sirens wailed in the distance. Kendra pressed the remote for the garage door, lifting it wide open. Flashing lights followed the sound, a police cruiser arriving in the driveway seconds later.

Once the police unit parked and the officers exited the vehicle, Kendra turned off the ignition and slid out of the car to meet them. Her legs had turned liquid. She leaned against the side of her vehicle for support.

"We have a report of a break-in. Are you the homeowner?"

"Yes, I'm Kendra Kelly. I was away for a couple of days, and I came home to a mess. I wasn't sure if there was still someone in the house, so I came outside and waited for you."

Officer Miller reintroduced himself along with his new partner, Officer Davis. She wasn't relieved to see them. Miller at least had treated her like a nutcase the last time he was here.

"We'll go inside and check out the scene. Stay in our vehicle while we clear the house."

Officer Davis led Kendra to the police car, opening the passenger door and waiting for her to climb inside. Kendra watched, her heart in her throat, as Officers Miller and Davis entered through the side door, guns drawn, shouting their arrival.

Panic consumed Kendra. Her entire life seemed surreal. She huddled on the car floor with hands covering her head, hoping to block out the sound of gunshots. An eternity seemed to pass. All quiet. In reality, only minutes had ticked by.

The officers tapped on the window to alert her. She pulled herself up, and Officer Davis opened the car door.

"We have a few questions. What time did you leave the house?"

Kendra stepped out of the vehicle. Her bones rattled in the chilly evening air. "I was out of town for a few days and then went to a meeting directly from the airport. I'm not crazy. You've been here before. Someone is trying to scare me. They're doing a bang-up job."

"Let's go inside and see if anything is missing."

Kendra could barely stand, much less walk. Her shoulders slumped, and her heart started pounding so loudly that she couldn't hear. She swallowed it down, the bitter taste lingering in her mouth.

Inside the house, Kendra surveyed the damage. Now that all the lights were on, she noticed muddy footprints on the floor. A shiver crept up her spine and caused her limbs to shake violently. Whoever it was had been in her home—her space, her haven. The violation felt personal. Her heart beat with the ferocity of a runaway train.

Officer Davis stepped into the kitchen. "You'll need to do a walk-through. Looks like the perpetrator entered through the door off your bedroom, which leads out to the deck. The lock has been tampered with."

The thought of someone entering the bedroom turned Kendra boneless. What if she'd been home? How would she have protected herself? She could have been harmed—or worse.

The officers accompanied Kendra as she examined each room. Every single drawer had been rummaged through, every cupboard emptied.

"It appears someone was looking for a particular item," Officer Davis said.

Kendra resisted taking in his words. She wanted the officers to leave. She needed time to absorb the defilement, but if the policemen left, she'd be alone. She couldn't stay here tonight. It wasn't safe. Would she ever be safe again?

Bile rose in Kendra's throat for the second time. She swallowed. Her head began to throb. She considered her options while she rubbed her arms, unsuccessful with the feeble attempt to calm her nerves. She could call Molly. She could try Nathan. She could say screw it and invite the burglar back.

Just tell me what you want and get it over with. Take me too. I don't care anymore. Just make it stop.

Who wanted to torment her? The only logical choice was Jake. He was back in town. But that was almost too easy. Or Russ, she guessed. But he didn't make sense as a threat. Not a legitimate threat. Would Joe's mistress have combed through the house? If so, what had she been looking for? Kendra had heard enough bizarre tales and watched enough crime TV to recognize strangers were capable of inexplicable behavior when motivated by greed or envy. She could no longer trust another living soul.

She glanced at the officers. "I can take it from here."

"Ma'am, I'd advise against staying here tonight. Call a friend or go to a hotel. Tomorrow, during daylight hours, you can clean up and get an alarm company out here to secure your home. You don't have any idea who's responsible?"

"Not really." Did she? None that made sense. And why hadn't the alarm system worked?

"We've had some home invasions in the area. Mostly equipment stolen from garages—snowblowers, garden edgers, lawn mowers, items of that nature."

"Do you think anything is missing?" Officer Davis added.

Kendra took in the remains of the tornado, and her eyebrows lifted. "I can't say for certain."

"We'll file a report. Take time tomorrow to do a full inventory and give us a call." Officer Miller handed Kendra his business card.

"Should I try to patch up the door before I leave? I hesitate to leave the house when it's unsecured."

"If you have a sheet of plywood, I'm happy to hammer it in place," Officer Davis offered. "Needless to say, staying here tonight isn't advisable. We'll certainly make a couple of passes by the house tonight. I can't imagine the perpetrator returning, but I can't guarantee that they won't."

Davis followed Kendra to the garage, where she found some plywood the previous owners had left behind, a hammer, and some nails. The officers patched up the door as Kendra hugged her arms tightly around her body, trying to shake off the unyielding chill of being violated.

When they finished the project and turned to leave through the front entrance, Kendra followed them, careful to lock up behind them, only realizing after she turned the dead bolt that no matter how many locks she buttoned up, her house was still vulnerable.

Regardless of the facts, Kendra had no intention of going anywhere. Other than a hotel, where she knew she wouldn't sleep, she had nowhere to go, no friends to turn to.

As she faced the wreckage, her eyes caught the footprints on the floor again. Whoever had been inside her home wore boots with heavy soles; the intricate pattern of the prints—the size of a man's foot—indicated more than a simple horizontal tread but included a cloverleaf oval in the middle. Kendra snapped a photo with her cell phone.

She slumped to the floor, held her head in her hands, and grappled for a clear and steady thought. Logic dictated someone was out to scare the living shit out of her. Logic dictated the same someone wanted something from her. Logic dictated Jake. He'd told her about the abuse Joe had suffered. His abuse. That didn't supply motivation though. Could another provocation exist?

Think, dammit.

With no other viable option but to clean up the mess, Kendra surveyed the damage. She used old coping skills—distance from emotion along with practical solutions. She could only determine if something had been stolen after she reorganized every living space.

After photographing further evidence of the break-in, she'd start work in the kitchen. For the life of her, she could not recall if the police had taken their own photos. She would be up all night, worried, but she thought the burglar revisiting the crime at this point seemed unlikely. Especially after she lit up the house like a fireball.

She sorted silverware, utensils, hand towels, measuring cups, and every other kitchen product known to man. While Kendra and Molly had donated or thrown out unnecessary items before moving, Kendra still discovered doubles of kitchen gadgets. How many wire whisks could a person need? She set a garbage bag next to her and discarded them.

Kendra tried telling herself she was imagining the worst. Her mind had played tricks on her before. Her friends were right. Kendra was defenseless. Perpetrators took advantage of susceptible, unarmed women. She'd be damned if she was that woman.

After two hours of righting the kitchen, she moved on to her office. The contents of two file drawers lay strewn on the floor. Thankfully, Kendra kept no valuable papers in her home. Her will, book contracts, and bank information were logged on her computer, but her computer was password-protected, and paper documents were stored in a safe deposit box at the bank. It didn't appear the computer had been tampered with. Her laptop was still in her backpack, and the desktop seemed untouched. At least there was that.

Kendra re-sorted papers, and discarded what she no longer needed. Chastised herself for not being more organized with paperwork. If ever she needed an assistant, it was now.

She managed to methodically replace the contents in the correct file folders. In the living, family, and dining rooms, there were few drawers to contend with, the damage to those rooms minimal. Kendra had only to place cushions back onto the sofas and chairs. She moved on.

Her bedroom had caught the worst of it. The personal assault felt most significant here. The notion of a stranger touching her lingerie creeped her out. The idea of an outsider going through her photographs, which lay in heaps on her bedroom carpet, felt like the nastiest assault of them all. By the time she finished reordering belongings and treasured personal mementos of her family, Kendra's head was ready to explode.

When Kendra opened the closet door, she could barely believe the mess. All of her clothing was on the floor in heaps. Shoe boxes lay askew, the contents of the most intimate parts of her life rummaged through like garbage, examined and touched by a stranger. Kendra realized she was in a state of shock. She sat down on the carpeted floor in the closet doorway and waited for her heart rate to calm. While waiting for her pulse to return to normal, she took deep breaths, remembering what she'd researched about the flight, fight, or freeze reaction. She told herself everything would be all right, and took stock, using her senses as it instructed in the article. She saw her toothbrush, her makeup on the counter, smelled the lemon candle on the nightstand, listened to the silence, and repeated the mantra, "No feeling is final."

She calmed after a bit, then methodically planned how she'd attack righting the walk-in closet. She removed all the items which lay atop her clothing—shoes, belts, boxes, linens, photos, socks, underwear, and placed them on the adjoining bathroom floor, Then, she hung items back on hangers and replaced them on the rod. The enormity of the disarray rocked her. *Just finish.* The act of matching pairs of shoes and finding the proper boxes calmed her. She climbed on the stepstool and put them back. The act of reorganizing allowed her a semblance of control. Kendra got down on her knees. The sweaters which had been neatly folded and placed on the built-in shelves were strewn beneath them. She folded and replaced them all.

By three a.m., Kendra had finished putting her home back together. Exhausted, she placed two ice cubes in a rock glass, filled it to the brim with bourbon, grabbed her smokes from her purse and a saucer from the cupboard for a makeshift ashtray. She planted herself on the living room sofa and lit a cigarette. *No smoking in the house, be damned.*

CHAPTER TWENTY-NINE

KENDRA AWOKE TO A HEAP OF DEFEAT. EVERYWHERE she looked were reminders—the disgusting, smelly ashtray on the coffee table, the empty rocks tumbler, the damn plywood over the back bedroom door, the stark neatness of her closet. She couldn't catch a break no matter how hard she tried. Still in yesterday's clothing, she pulled her hair back and into a ponytail. She started coffee, the tug to give in and give up as relentless as the pull of an undertow. Giving in to this recent battering would set her on a path of self-destruction if she let it. She couldn't afford that.

She filled a supersized mug with strong black coffee and texted Isaac. *This alarm system is giving me fits. Any chance you could stop by this week?*

Isaac answered within seconds. *On my way.*

When she spotted Isaac on the porch an hour later, she sighed in relief. She almost hadn't recognized him, dressed in a pair of jeans, a polo shirt, and a light jacket, accustomed as she was at seeing him in his brown uniform.

She invited him in, served him a cup of coffee, and joined him at the dining room table. "You didn't need to take the day off. I could have waited until the weekend."

"No worries. I love tinkering. Let me see if I can figure out why your system failed last night and what you need for added protection."

Isaac left his coffee cup on the kitchen counter and strode over to the alarm pad to investigate.

When he stood in front of her twenty minutes later, he wore a worried expression. "You hadn't armed the system. Here, I'll show you."

Isaac led her over to the alarm pad. Sure enough, Kendra had been disarming rather than arming the system. She'd been hitting the wrong damned button.

"Don't feel bad," Isaac said. "It's an easy mistake."

Kendra had never been good with technology, but she was downright embarrassed.

Isaac patted her shoulder and suggested a plan. "Your system is really outdated. One of the first models, and hardwired. If we put in a new system, everything will be foolproof and state of the art. I can probably finish it today … not so much work to install. Soon enough, this place will be as secure as Fort Knox. And the units are wireless now, so you can operate it from your phone or computer. Much easier to use. Pretty flawless, compared to this old dog." He tapped a finger on the current alarm pad. "I'm going to buy you a system, okay? A few hundred bucks, most likely, but your peace of mind is worth it. Be back in an hour or so."

"I don't care how much it costs. Should I come with you?"

"Sit tight. You can reimburse me later."

Kendra paced the entire time Isaac was away, chain-smoking, and overdosing on caffeine.

True to his word, Isaac returned shortly, loaded in boxes of supplies and tools, and went to work within the hour.

Kendra wore a path in the carpet for another solid fifteen minutes and watched him work as he moved through the house installing entry sensors. Meanwhile, she kicked bruises into her stupid skull for not understanding something as simple as an alarm system, and then decided to make Isaac some lunch. She had tuna and rye bread. Joe's favorite sandwich.

Kendra leaned outside the side door where Isaac now stood attaching a motion detector to the gutter. "Lunch is on the counter," she said.

Weird, but Joe's presence filled her, his solid, steadying manner. She felt close to him in a way she hadn't since his death, and a sudden urge to surround the space with his memories and put herself back in his company overcame her. It seemed odd after the upheaval of last night, but she decided to roll with it—probably part of the grieving process, and after all she'd been through, she needed some centering.

In the back of Kendra's closet, which she had just visited for hours last night, she had placed a box of her most treasured possessions inside a velvet bag and hung them on the same hanger as her wedding dress, which she had sealed away in a zip-up clothing bag when she moved. There were ticket stubs from the Lady Gaga concert they'd attended on their third date, the necklace her had given her after their first month of dating—a family heirloom, he had said, the cigar band Joe had placed on her finger when he first suggested marriage, photos of their wedding, her wedding ring. As she thought about it now, the wardrobe bag was an item that had remained untouched last night, and a sense of urgency plagued her. She hoped none of the items had been tampered with or removed.

While Kendra had fooled herself into thinking she'd made a significant effort toward recovery by tucking the items away after

Joe's suicide, she was now drawn to them, feeling that acknowledging Joe's presence in her life would help her move on, or forward, or whatever the hell terminology she was told to use. She
was beyond ready to be rid of the anger and emptiness.

As conflicted as Kendra was, she recognized this as part of
grieving. She recalled hearing brief conversations about secrets
last night at group but had been too intent on her own sadness
to pay much attention. Nevertheless, Mary had said grief was full
of peaks and valleys, so Kendra decided to embrace the moment.

Kendra left the kitchen and dived into the closet. She un-
zipped the bag, located the drawstring bag, lifted it from around
the hanger, clutched it to her chest, and released her breath. *Thank
God it's here.*

In the family room, she sank into her favorite chair—a dainty
upholstered seat with whitewashed wooden trim. Kendra untied
the delicate roping of the bag and emptied the contents of the
sack. Through a fog of tears, she opened a jewelry box and then
placed her wedding and engagement rings on her finger, held the
hand out in front of her, and blinked to clear her vision. The di-
amond was much murkier than the day Joe had first placed it on
her finger—whether from actual debris or the tainted end, she
couldn't be sure.

Kendra continued to delve into the contents—she fingered
the opal necklace adorned with diamonds in a delicate platinum
setting. The fiery rainbow of colors danced in the sunlight.

After undoing the clasp, Kendra placed the chain around her
neck and fastened it. It rested against her skin as if it belonged
there.

She chuckled as she gazed at the cigar band, and let tears
trail her cheeks as she regarded wedding photos, reciting their
self-written vows.

"*You are the best man to ever come into my life. I promise to love
you through thick and thin, through sleepless nights and unforeseen*

absences. Through illness and anger. I promise to always remember falling in love with you …"

As Kendra read the words, she realized how naive she had been. She and Joe hadn't lived through any hard times before their marriage. And after, when faced with an impossible challenge, albeit more serious than they ever could have predicted, he'd checked out.

Anger twisted her gut. Kendra couldn't decide whether she was justified in loving him or justified in her anger. Probably both. In any case, she refused to deny her feelings again.

While she'd thought she knew her husband better than he knew himself, she recognized she hadn't known him at all. Sure, she'd appreciated his day-to-day habits, his easygoing nature, his accomplishments, and his self-assurance, but she had known little of his insecurities, his flaws, or his struggles. Those frailties cemented a relationship. She wanted to be loved and treasured in spite of who she was at her core—a mix of poise and insecurity, a girl who desired acceptance and connection. She and Joe had shared few of those confidences. He'd neglected to tell her the truth about his parents, his childhood, his need for a mistress, and who knew what else?

Sadness weighed in her bones. While a part of her understood his shame, she wished they had had a trusting relationship. She wished Joe had felt safe with her. She could have prevented his suicide if he'd let her in. They could have still been together. He wouldn't have needed anyone but her. Joey might still have died, but in her wildest dreams, preventing that tragedy hadn't been within her control.

Kendra left her chair and headed into her office to dust. Accomplishing this small task after all the craziness of last night would help her gain control.

After Isaac finished his sandwich, she heard the back door

open and close but continued to clean. When he reentered the house, she heard voices.

Russ, nosy as an entertainment journalist.

Damn him.

But that was Russ. He hawked the neighborhood and clamored for some new incident to fuel his boredom.

He chatted with Isaac—which seemed odd, considering their somewhat-contentious relationship—asked him questions about what he was doing, how secure the place would be once the system was installed. When Kendra heard Russ ask Isaac what had precipitated the need for the alarm, her irritation rose to the surface, and she clenched her teeth. Of course, Russ already knew. His acting all innocent, as if he hadn't listened to the police scanner last night, irked her. On the other hand, it was unlike Russ to stay away for so long after knowing what had happened.

If Russ had had a single thing to do with the burglary … not that she suspected him, but still. Why wasn't she suspecting him?

Kendra shivered away a stiff wave of fear and continued with housework, relieved when she heard Isaac excuse himself to finish the job and encouraged Russ to leave the house.

The locksmith showed up around two p.m. Kendra left out the break-in scenario and just asked the guy to fix the door and install a new lock, one with a combination only she would know. The man completed his work in short order, and Isaac stayed on another hour, disarming her old system.

By the time dusk settled, Isaac walked Kendra through the logistics of arming the updated state-of-the-art system and showed her how the cameras and motion detectors worked, and she went online to connect the alarm through Wi-Fi and fill out the necessary alert forms. "It may take a few days for the company to implement the new account and records. Maybe not. Most likely, they'll send you an email when it's fully activated. In the meantime, it's active based on what I see here."

Kendra took copious notes and taped them to the cabinet above her desk. Even she had to admit—the new alarm was quite straightforward. After she used it a few times, she was sure it would become second-nature to operate it.

After demonstrating to Isaac that she had a handle on the system, he sat her down. "I'm not one to pry," he said. "But what happened to you last night is worrisome, to say the least. You should consider getting a dog too. Maybe go to the Humane Society and see if they have an older pup who likes to bark. You need to feel safe. We've had dogs for years. Even the most mild-mannered pup will go ballistic if their master is in danger."

"That's a really good idea. I'll look into it."

Isaac patted her shoulder. "You need anything, I'm a phone call away. And wow, that's a pretty necklace."

Kendra touched the choker and thanked him, then, after handing him a check to cover the cost of the system, walked him to the side door, gave him a long bear hug, and locked up as soon as he was outside. She loaded the lunch dishes in the dishwasher and barely made it into the living room when she heard a knock on the door. Isaac must have left something behind.

Kendra hurried to the front entry, unlocked the door, and flung it open. "What did you forget?"

It was Jake.

CHAPTER THIRTY

"**C**AN WE TALK?"

Kendra bit her cheek. Pondering on the spot didn't come easily since her recent trip to California. "I'm busy meeting a deadline." She shut the door and bolted it, leaning against the sturdy wood, feeling captive in the house once again.

Damn it, Joe. How dare you leave me with this mess!

Kendra had no way to move out of sight without Jake seeing which direction she took. From the side-view window, he could see if she went into the kitchen, the office, the guest room, the family room, the master suite.

Caged and cornered. Just how he wanted her.

She had no weapon. No way to defend herself. While she could set the alarm system from her phone, she faltered for a moment. She hadn't had time to arm it yet. Or had she? *Why can't I think straight? Will I ever have a clear thought again?*

Kendra stood, stone silent, and held her breath. Eventually,

Jake had to give up. She could sit in front of the door, curled up on the floor so he couldn't see her. Wait him out. The temperature was in the low thirties. He'd get cold, standing there. The wind continued to howl. Dark would settle soon. At least she was inside and warm. She rubbed her arms. She was anything but warm. She was icy scared. For some reason, Jake's appearance triggered all the wrong reactions.

Her cell phone was in the study. She could make a run for it. Call Nathan. Or the cops. Or she could call out to Jake and tell him to meet her at the police station tomorrow. Now, there—a reasonable solution.

Kendra peered around to view the sidelight windows. Sure enough, Jake's back or some part of his jacket was pressed against the window.

"I have to get back to work," she shouted. "I'll meet you in Saline tomorrow at ten o'clock at the police station on Harris Street."

Jake narrowed his eyes in confusion. "I have no idea why we'd need to meet at the police station. For the umpteenth time, you don't need to be afraid of me."

"Go home, Jake, wherever that is. I'll send you an email with my attorney's name and address. Better yet, I'll include his phone number. You can call him. Anything you have to say, he can let me know. From now on, we'll speak through him."

Reduced to yelling through the door. What a joke her life had become.

"Let me explain. I know you're upset."

Kendra's brain sped like a runaway train. Why was Jake badgering her like this? "Talk to my lawyer."

"You want me to stand out here and shout your personal business to the world? How my brother set me up to take the fall for our parents' murders when he was responsible? How Joe, your husband, brutally murdered our parents and let his baby brother go to jail?" His voice escalated with each spoken word.

"Oh, for God's sake," Kendra wailed as she opened the door. "Get in here and shut the fuck up before you get Russ down here."

Jake didn't come inside, as Kendra had expected. He lifted his hands, showing they were empty. "I'm not going to hurt you."

He stared at her neck.

Kendra reached up and fingered the choker. "What?"

His voice softened further. "Can I come in?"

Kendra gestured Jake inside.

He tramped inside, stamped his feet on the area rug, and strode over to the couch, where he took a seat. He pushed his hair off his forehead. Clearly rattled, he took a moment to regain his composure. "Will you sit down?"

"No. Tell me what you want."

He stared at the necklace, his eyes boring into the jewels. Seconds later, Jake's eyes welled with tears. "You've had the proof all along."

Kendra glanced at the necklace. "I don't have a clue what you're talking about."

"Please sit down."

Kendra stood, hands on hips, and challenged Jake.

"My mother wore that necklace every day of her life. She never took it off. Not to shower, not when she swam. Never took it off. Never."

"And your point is?"

"When I found my parents, murdered in their beds, I wondered if there had been a robbery. Everything happened in slow motion. My brain couldn't compute the scene. Blood was everywhere, dripping from their bodies, covering the sheets, the carpet—everything." He stopped for a moment as he relived the memory. "I've never seen so much blood."

"I remember it clearly. My mom's necklace was gone. I was

struck by the thought, *Mom never takes off her necklace.* But someone entering our home and taking that—only that—didn't make sense. I told the police about it when they came. They weren't interested. Sure, part of me gets that now. They had two brutal murders to deal with. My parents were loved and respected by the community. La Jolla didn't suffer the crime other communities endured. In San Diego, double murders might happen more frequently, considering the diverse population. But the dregs of society lived there, not in our precious little town. No one would have broken into our home, killed my parents, and only taken a single piece of jewelry. Don't you see?"

"I don't."

"Joe had to have been there. Joe killed them."

"You're jumping to conclusions."

"Maybe. Maybe not. This is the only explanation that makes sense. Joe had to have been home. He said he was away at school—and I don't know for sure—but he could have easily had friends lie for him. Joe was good at that. He was a charmer. I'm sure you're aware of that. You fell for him."

Jake had a point. She had fallen for Joe. Big time. Taken him at face value. Believed the stories of his youth, his described estrangement from his family, his lies about their deaths.

"Go on."

"He could have come home, killed them, and gone back to school. The police never found any sign of forced entry. That's why I became their chief suspect."

Kendra's legs no longer kept her upright. She sank to the floor and leaned her back against the wall.

"If Joe killed our parents—and I bet a winning Lotto ticket that he did—he let me go through a trial, but even more, he left me alone with my devastated grandmother to suffer through the shame of being named the one and only suspect."

Kendra held her head in her hands. Minutes later, she locked eyes with Jake. His eyes bored into her. She averted her gaze. She had no clue if Jake had an antisocial personality disorder, was a psychopath, or was just plain manipulative, but he was doing a damn good job of convincing her that Joe had had some involvement in their parents' murders. Maybe Jake spoke the truth.

"Jake, I'm tempted to believe you. All this has been overwhelming for me, and to be honest, I didn't know you were still alive …"

She clutched the necklace. A lodestone or a curse. She was tempted to give it to him. As evidence. As soon as the word "evidence" popped into her brain, it triggered thoughts of Joe's knife. In all her mop-up work and reordering efforts last night, she'd neglected to look for Joe's box of memorabilia. Was it still there? Had she overlooked it?

"Wait a minute … did you break in here last night? Were you looking for the knife?"

"I don't know what the hell you're talking about. What knife?"

"Joe's knife. The one your dad gave him. You mentioned it before and here you are looking for evidence."

"I didn't come looking for evidence. You just happened to be wearing it when I got here. Yes, I believe more than ever that my brother killed our parents, but I would never break into your home. Never."

Kendra closed her eyes and took a deep breath. *Calm down. Think.*

"Give me some time with this. If you'd like the necklace as evidence or want me to keep it and tell the police I've had it all along so it doesn't look like you're lying for your own gain, if you want to clear your name or something like that, let me know. I'll do whatever you want. I'm finally understanding your need for closure as well as my own. Joe lied to me about your entire family. As you can imagine, it's a boatload to deal with. I'm sorry I've been difficult."

Jake sighed. "Thank you." He stared at her with sad eyes. "You mentioned the knife. I don't know if you had it to begin with, but it sounds like you did and now you think I broke in and stole it from you? I swear on my parents' graves, I don't have it. I've never had it. You know what? When it comes right down to it, Joe took advantage of both of us. We're on the same side. I would be happy to help you in any way I can just as you are willing to help me … I can give you more details about Joe, whatever you need, and I appreciate your offer of support."

Kendra was tempted to hug him, but something kept her rooted to her spot. He was too much like Joe, and while she did finally feel she could trust Jake, she hesitated to get too close to him.

"Can I get back to you on that?"

Kendra nodded. "Of course."

Jake smiled. "I'm glad we're working things through."

"Me too."

Jake strode toward the door. "I'll be in touch."

"Just text or call first, please. I'm still a bit jumpy."

Jake offered a half-smile and stepped outside. Kendra closed the door behind him and let out a huge sigh.

CHAPTER THIRTY-ONE

KENDRA'S HEAD SPUN. SHE DIDN'T WANT TO FACE ANY of these facts, but it became more apparent to her by the second that Joe hadn't been close to the person she'd thought. How could she have been so naive? So blind. Jill was right. She and the girls had seen right through him. How she wished they'd told her. Would she have listened? Probably not.

Kendra craved company. In the aftermath of the break-in last night, she recognized the security Isaac had provided her by sticking around the house all day. True, he was busy with the alarm system, but he was company too. It had been forever since Kendra had had the company of someone she trusted implicitly.

She picked up the phone and texted Nathan.

You busy? Feel like coming over?

Thought you'd never ask. On my way.

Kendra took the fastest shower ever, donned a cozy sweater and her most flattering jeans, slapped on some blush and mascara, and wound her hair in a topknot.

When he arrived, Nathan took her in his arms and held her. "I've missed you."

They snuggled up on the couch after Kendra turned on the gas fireplace and set out a bottle of cabernet and glasses. The room warmed instantly, taking the chill off the air.

"Tell me what's been going on."

Kendra paused for a moment, pouring two glasses of wine and clinking glasses with Nathan before taking a fortifying sip. "You ready? There's a long list of things I want to tell you."

"Go," Nathan said as he turned to face her.

Kendra recited the events of the past few days. The revelations about Joe, the break-in, the visit from Jake, the knife, and the necklace. A full thirty minutes later, she came up for air.

Nathan patted her on the back. "Let's look for that knife." He jumped up from the couch and headed into her closet. "Where did you last see it?"

Kendra followed on his heels, then cut in front of him to pull out the stepstool from behind a rack of clothes. "On the top shelf, there, with the other boxes. The knife was in a man's shoebox with some of Joe's other memorabilia, you know, action figures, a boomerang, you know, kid stuff. I had tucked it way in the back after finding it. I guess I wanted to block out the idea of the knife. I don't recall seeing it last night, but I was in survival mode, just putting things back, not really thinking. You'd think I would have thought about it, but no." She shook her head in disgust.

"Stop being so hard on yourself." Nathan opened the stepstool and climbed up the few steps. He handed her one box after the other while she opened and examined the contents.

"None of these," she said after perusing a dozen boxes. "It was in a man's shoebox. Athletic shoes … a bigger box."

"Just a few more," Nathan said, handing her two at a time, then waiting for her to let him know if she spotted the knife.

"I went through all of these last night. They're as I left them."

"Reassuring, right?" Nathan joked.

Kendra laughed in spite of the panic seizing her chest. "I suppose."

"Well," Nathan said, "that's it. No more boxes."

Kendra hung her head, not wanting to deal with one more hard thing. She handed the boxes back to Nathan and watched as he replaced them on the shelf. When he finished, he dusted off his hands and then placed them on her cheeks. "I'm here now, and I can tell this is the last thing you need right now, but you need to call the police and report that the knife is missing. If this is all that's missing, the break-in seems to be about Joe, maybe not about you."

"How about I call in the morning? I don't want to think about any of this. I need a break."

Nathan nodded, took her hand and led her back to the sofa, where he sat down and drew her into his lap. He wrapped her in his arms and she took the first deep breath in what felt like hours. Her head rested on his chest, and she listened to his heartbeat. He was alive. He was here. He cared for her. They sat like that for a long time, just relaxing in the heat of each other's warmth.

Finally, Nathan lifted her head and brushed his lips on hers, starting with a gentle touch that became more fiery by the second. He kissed her cheeks, her eyelids, moaning with every new inch of skin he covered.

Kendra melted into him.

His fingers traveled beneath her sweater, snaking a curved line from her waist to her breast. Her breath came in short bursts as desire fought reason. She backed away, pushed against his chest, and gazed into his eyes. As much as Kendra wanted to resist, to save herself from another heartbreak, she couldn't squelch the yearning to be touched, to be connected, to feel alive.

She grasped Nathan's hand and led him into the bedroom. He closed the shades while she turned down the bed and stripped off her clothes. Once she lay down in bed, she reached out to him.

He shed his clothes and joined her, holding her close, letting his body meld with hers, slowly stroking her back.

Kendra rose above him and teased kisses along his face and neck. The urgency of the moment didn't escape her. If she allowed time for rational thought, she'd nix this idea, pronto.

A sudden realization hit her. Nathan was everything she'd always wanted. He was strong and open. He recognized her weaknesses and admitted his own. While she'd thought she had made love with Joe, she knew she hadn't.

Sex was about bodily pleasure. Making love was the joining of mind and heart, rolled into the meshing of flesh.

Easier said than done.

She rolled onto her back. "Wait," she said, wondering if she should stop him.

Nathan leaned on his elbow and gazed into her eyes. "Do I smell funny? Should I shower?"

She couldn't help but laugh. "Jitters."

"I'll stop if you want me to."

"No. Don't stop."

"Close your eyes," he said. "Take a breath."

Once she did, he continued. His kisses trailed her body—from her neck to her breasts, to her stomach, knees, and toes. His fingertips did the same, stuttering for the occasional squeeze, which made her moan. Kendra left her thoughts behind and went to a place of feeling, trusting, being totally with him.

She opened her eyes and took him in—his broad shoulders, the soft hairs of his chest tickling her breasts. Kendra wrapped her arms around him and held on to the rippled muscles extending the length of him. She closed her eyes again and joined him in sheer sensation. The tingles, the tautness of desire. She gave herself to him as he entered her. She wanted nothing more than to be as close to him as possible. She arched toward him, begging him to feel as one, for him to want her as much as she wanted him. Needed him. They came together in a cacophony of sound, howls and laughter, pleasure and release.

Nathan collapsed on top of her. His heart beat hard and fast against her chest.

Kendra nuzzled his neck. *Thank you* seemed weird, but she did want to thank him. For making her feel again. For bringing her back to life. "You just saved my life."

"It's what firefighters do."

Her eyes sparkled as she gazed at him.

"Years of training." He rolled over onto his back and slapped a hand across his chest. A heavy sigh escaped his lungs.

Kendra propped herself on an elbow, taking in the gold flecks in his pale blue eyes. "You're beautiful," she said as she ran her fingers through the soft fuzz on his chest.

He smiled at her, his eyes crinkling at the corners. "I'm the one who's supposed to say that."

"Beat you to it."

Kendra barely woke when Nathan kissed her good-bye. She heard him close the door and rose a few minutes later to activate the alarm and secure the dead bolt. The display on the nightstand read three a.m. As she tightened the belt of her robe, she peered outside and down the sidewalk, wistfully remembering the lovely evening with Nathan.

She shook her head in disbelief, blinking rapid-fire as she took in the scene before her. Splayed on the sidewalk was a man—Nathan, she surmised. Over him stood a man with a baseball bat, if her eyes weren't deceiving her.

Kendra threw open the door.

Russ, wide-eyed and mouth agape, said nothing.

"What in the hell?" Kendra darted out of the house in her

robe and bare feet, nothing but shock and concern registering. "What did you do?"

She shoved Russ away from Nathan and crouched down beside him. "Are you okay? Nathan, talk to me."

It was difficult to see between the shadows and dark sky, but Kendra spotted a snake of blood extending from Nathan's temple down to his chin.

Nathan mumbled something incoherent.

"Russ," Kendra shouted. "Help me get him inside."

Russ placed a hand in one of Nathan's armpits, and Kendra assumed the same position on Nathan's other side. They lifted with all their strength, Nathan's sheer mass causing both of them to summon every ounce of muscle to right him. Once erect, Nathan put an arm across both Russ's and Kendra's shoulders as they slowly led him into the house.

"Call 911," Kendra ordered.

Nathan outstretched a trembling hand. "No. I'll be okay. I'm just startled."

"Russ, what were you thinking?"

Russ fumbled for words. "You had visitors the other night and not for the first time. I hoped I could prevent you further harm. Honestly, I didn't realize you had company."

Kendra's voice rose, and her hand flew to the door. "Did you not see Nathan arrive? Did you not see his truck parked out front? Why on earth do you feel it's your personal mission to keep watch over me?"

Russ's shoulders slumped. His gaze remained on the floor for another long minute before he glanced at Nathan. "Hey, man, I'm sorry. I've lived in this neighborhood all my life. Kind of see it as my job to make sure all the residents are safe. Back when my wife was alive …" Russ's voice trailed off.

Nathan held his head while Kendra hurried to the kitchen to wet a washcloth and place some ice in a plastic bag. She handed

Nathan the ice pack upon her return and dabbed at his temple and cheek to wipe the blood away.

Russ stepped from one foot to the other, as if standing on a bed of coals.

Kendra left Nathan for a moment and marched to the front door. "Good-bye, Russ."

Russ hesitated on his way out the door. "Sorry, man. Really sorry."

Nathan didn't lift his gaze, and Kendra slammed the door behind her neighbor.

"That man makes me crazy. If I didn't know better, I'd say, he's the one stalking me. Now, let's get you to bed. I need to keep an eye on you. Do you think you have a concussion?"

Nathan rubbed his hand gingerly over his head. "Not sure, but this hurts like a mother. The guy came up on me from out of nowhere."

Kendra led Nathan from the living room to the bedroom. She helped him lie back and removed his jacket and shoes. "You're spending the night. No argument."

"But—"

"No buts."

"I have to work."

"Call in sick."

Nathan groaned and laid his head back on the pillow. "I don't miss work."

"There's a first time for everything." Kendra marched out of the room to grab a pain reliever and a glass of water.

After he refused a visit to the ER, Kendra spent the rest of the night focused on Nathan. Other than a goose egg on his temple, he seemed fine. She roused him every two hours to make sure he hadn't suffered brain damage or some catastrophic injury. He complained of a headache, but appeared to have weathered the assault.

Kendra thought a lot about Russ while she lay awake. He'd

been around for every one of the iffy events since she had moved into the lake house. He'd offered Jake a place to stay, warned her about "visitors" he'd seen at her place at night, been more than a little interested in her background and daily activities, and inserted himself into the process of installing the upgraded home alarm system. More than a meddlesome neighbor, he'd been intrusive and creeped her out on several occasions. She had tried to distance herself from his constant eye, but he kept showing up. Tonight's incident was over the top. She should have called the police, and when Nathan woke in the morning, she'd speak with him about filing charges. Maybe Russ had staged all of this. The *whys* remained.

Kendra couldn't sleep. Not only couldn't she sleep, but she also didn't feel like she should. After sitting on the edge of the bed for two more hours, she gave in to exhaustion, cuddled up next to Nathan and drifted off.

Nathan's movements woke Kendra at six a.m. True to his word, Nathan was showered and dressed, ready for work. He left after a lingering kiss. Kendra remained near the door, reluctant to move and break the spell of his strong arms around her. A knock startled her.

Clouded by tingling, Kendra answered the door. "This is a bad habit."

"Sorry to show up unannounced," Jake said. "Decided to catch you early."

Dumbstruck, Kendra had no idea what to say. But somehow, she found the words. "I thought we agreed you wouldn't show up unannounced."

Jake hung his head. "I know. Sorry. I won't keep you long. Just a few minutes."

Kendra sighed and let him in.

"You have photos of your wedding, right?"

Kendra knitted her brows, her eyes narrowing. *At least he got right to the point.*

She marched into her office and plucked the box of photos off a shelf, then strode back to the living room. "Here."

Kendra left Jake sitting on the living room couch and wandered into the kitchen to make a cup of tea. She glanced over at him every now and then, unable to discern a telltale facial expression. He was quite accomplished at keeping his emotions hidden when he needed to. Must be a family trait.

With the pictures in hand, he scratched his head, studied, perused, and examined, as if with a magnifying glass, looking for something. She could ask, but distance from Jake's expedition seemed judicious. When you had a pile of your own dung to deal with, no sense in delving into someone else's shit.

Kendra leaned against the kitchen counter, sipped tea, and watched Jake. Still nothing readable. No revealing signs.

When he finished scrutinizing the professional photographs, he set them on the table, leaned back against a couch cushion, and closed his eyes for several minutes. At first, Kendra worried he'd fallen asleep and she'd be stuck with him. But Jake opened his eyes at last, silent but for a breath, and leafed through the photos again.

He continued to study the images, as if he'd missed something or wasn't willing to give up his search. He didn't ask a single question or make a single remark. His face didn't betray him, but stayed even and objective. He wasn't overcome with emotion at seeing his brother married, seeing his brother's image after years of separation.

Kendra pulled further back, as if she were a fly on the ceiling, taking in her life. None of this was real. A stranger following her. This man on her couch. Even having had a baby and husband seemed like a dream. Reality crept away.

A not-so-distant experience that she'd hoped had left her behind, a panic attack, began. Her arms began to jitter with nerves, and white noise filled her head. She was so damn sick of feeling like a wimp, unable to control her emotions when faced with a conflict, as if she'd entered a portal to a thick, frightening jungle, hung with tangled vines, fallen limbs, and unexpected rushing rivers.

Kendra fought to stay on her feet. She grabbed the counter and held on, blinking, struggling to breathe, clawing her way back to the present. Only after several long minutes of consciously controlled breathing did she begin to move past the panic attack—or so she hoped. She wandered into the family room and curled up on the couch, unable to do more.

It was as if the past few months—take that back, the past two years—pressed down on her like a vise.

Why now?

What seemed like hours later, Jake rose, lost in thought, and murmured as he headed for the door, "Thanks, Kendra. I'll be in touch."

At the last minute, Kendra's brain fired. "Did you find what you were looking for?"

Jake remained pensive. "I need time to think."

A shiver snaked up Kendra's arms. "Fair enough. Could you just give me a clue? What's going on?"

"I was curious if you wore the necklace in your wedding photos. I'm wondering how brazen Joe was."

"Far as I can tell from my recent research, pretty darn brazen. And you could have asked me if I'd worn it in the photos. I would have told you I did."

"I needed to see for myself."

Kendra nodded. "I get that."

She let him out and locked up behind him.

236

Kendra woke to soft tapping on the front door and jumped out of bed, disoriented. She had to steady herself against the bathroom counter while reaching into the closet for her robe. As sunlight streamed through the transom window, she recalled Nathan's promise to return after his shift. Kendra glanced at the clock on her way to the door—seven twenty-five a.m. She'd been asleep for at least sixteen hours. She remembered lying down …

She yanked open the door and ushered Nathan inside, checking the road for car or foot traffic. The street was quiet.

"I guess I crashed." Kendra rubbed her eyes with fisted hands.

Nathan removed his coat and strode into the kitchen. He opened and closed cupboard doors, a man on a mission. Finally, he yanked out two mugs and supplies to make coffee. "Glad you slept. You needed it."

"I guess so. I wrote for a long time then went to take a nap. No idea what happened then, but I'm awake now."

A twinkle came to his eye. "So, you're rested and ready for other activities."

"After I brush my teeth and shower."

"And after coffee." Nathan poured two cups.

"I could get used to this. Busy night for you?"

"Not too bad. I never sleep well at the station though. Always listening."

Kendra tipped her head down. "Like a new mom."

Nathan squeezed her shoulder.

Nathan looked past Kendra, out at the lake as the water moved with the wind. "Grief traps us."

Kendra lifted her eyebrows. "You okay?"

Nathan took away Kendra's coffee cup, carried her to the bedroom, and set her on the bed. He stripped off his clothes and climbed under the covers, and then he reached under her pajama top and strolled his fingers from her waist around to her back, gently massaging and stroking her. She stopped him.

"Tell me a secret. One of your failings that you seldom admit."

Nathan erupted with a groan. "Your timing is perfect."

Kendra gazed into his eyes. "I need to know you. Not just all the wonderful attributes, but also your fears, your most frightful moment. Your essence."

"My essence?"

"I know I sound crazy, but I blew it with Joe. He was my husband, but only now do I realize that I never knew him. He wore a mask. He didn't let me in. I don't want to be with someone like that ever again."

Nathan bit his lip, clearly wanting to please Kendra but uncomfortable at the same time. "I'll have to think. It's not like I spend hours focusing on my weaknesses. As a man, I find it troubling to admit I'm not perfect." He chuckled uncomfortably. "At the station, the guys always tease me. I'm a softy. I'm great at initial assessment of a situation, but I tend to second-guess myself after a run. *Did I handle things right? Was I empathetic enough?* In the crises I find myself in, often life and death or at least devastating injuries, I always wonder if I could have done more. Prevented the worst."

"Seems only natural. I tend to give people the benefit of the doubt as well. I take on their personal issues as my own, and rather than protecting my psyche, I assume I'm at fault. Like with Joey and Joe."

"And Jake. Maybe part of human nature for us good guys. I'd like to say I exude confidence at my very core, but I'm not that cocky or sure of myself."

"Could be a weakness, but in my mind, it shows you're compassionate and you always want to do your best." Kendra brushed Nathan's chest hair with her fingers.

"I'm a good, steady six."

Kendra kissed him. Wanting to devour every inch of this man, she took the lead, stroking him until he was beyond thought. From touch to kiss to genuine emotion, they entwined in pure desire, learning every inch of each other's bodies, pressure points, plea-sure centers.

When they finished, they lay in each other's arms, satisfaction pasting smiles on their faces.

CHAPTER THIRTY-TWO

AFTER NATHAN LEFT, KENDRA SAT DOWN AND TYPED out a long missive to her friends. They were right about everything. She owed them more than an apology. Once she finished, she thought twice about her email. Meeting with them in person made more sense. She sent a group text.

I know it's last minute, but can everyone join at my house tonight at six p.m.?

She heard back from Jill first. *Count me in. I'll bring a snack.*

Then Molly. *In. I'll bring a bottle of wine.*

Amy texted. *Just made cookies last night.*

Kathy next. *Sounds great. See you then.*

Nothing from Erica.

But the fact that Kendra had heard from four out of five of them so quickly left her optimistic. They didn't all hate her. At least, not yet.

Kendra bustled about, attending to all those little tasks she'd neglected for far too long. She wiped cobwebs from the corners of the ceiling, dusted windowsills, and vacuumed baseboards. Polished wineglasses. She headed outside and mowed the lawn, hopefully for the last time this season, and trimmed the edges and hedges. The weather was warm enough that they could sit outside, so after wiping down the table and chairs, she blew the leaves off the deck and extended the awning.

By four o'clock, she wondered if she could stay awake until six, but she drank a cup of coffee for a wake-up and set out all the necessary items for the evening. She spent the next two hours hunched over the manuscript, writing with a fury that had eluded her for months.

When the doorbell rang, she was so involved in her story that she about jumped out of her skin.

Jill arrived first, loaded down with two bags and a charcuterie tray. Marching into the kitchen like she owned the place, she set down packages and wrapped Kendra in a lingering hug. "It's so nice to finally be getting together at your house with the girls."

Kendra prided herself in the house, suddenly pleased with the unconscious move she'd made months ago. The place presented well. Simple and well appointed in spite of the fact that she'd merely moved furniture from the much larger house in Saline and made it work in the new little cottage. Without Molly's help, she'd never have been able to get rid of all the extras, and she didn't miss anything that they'd ditched.

Soon, the house buzzed with cheerful female voices for the first time since Kendra had moved to the lake. Amy checked out the fridge, as she always did, having teased Kendra years ago for lining the shelves with paper towels. The ladies giggled over the old joke, but Kendra still insisted it saved her time with spills. Kathy inspected for cobwebs, being even more OCD than the rest of them put together. Alive with laughter, the ladies all oohed and aahed over the house before heading outside. Just like the old days, an abundance of food and drink filled the table.

At the last minute, even Erica made an entrance. "You know how I hate group texts. I wasn't sure I'd be able to make it, but here I am!"

If her friends loved the inside of Kendra's new home, they were ecstatic with the lake and the serene view it provided. After ten minutes of comments about how they'd never leave if they lived there, how it was the perfect spot, and then questions about the boat activity, the neighbors, and the size and depth of the little lake, Kendra made an announcement.

"Please take a seat. I've brought you all together for a reason." She stopped and chuckled. "No, I don't have earth-shattering news, but I do have something to say. I owe you all my sincerest apology. I've been so into myself since Joe and Joey died. I've been moody and pissy and totally crazy at times. I'm sorry. If I've ignored you and your families, which I know I have, it's not because I don't love each and every one of you, but because I've been lost for a very long time. I'm fighting like hell to get it together, and I don't want tonight to be about me. Also, I don't want to offer you excuses for my absence or my erratic behavior, but rather an explanation.

"After I lost the guys, I couldn't see straight." She paused to gaze at Molly, who nodded her encouragement. "Without Molly, I wouldn't be in this new place, and I'd have probably wallowed even longer. I'm not out of the woods yet, but I'm getting there. I want to have you here often, have this be an escape for all of us. Remember how we used to say we needed to rent an apartment together, so we would have a getaway when life became too hectic? I want this to be that place. I know the weather is about to change, and we'll all want to be in our caves this winter, but next summer, I want all of you to bring your crew out here on weekends. We can swim, paddle, fish. Whatever you like."

As Kendra glanced around the table, her friends listened and lit up at the invitation. For years, they'd been sure to meet on a regular basis, plan girls' nights out, weekend trips up north.

She longed for those days again.

When she broke for breath, she was met with a barrage of questions.

"What's changed?" Erica asked.

"She's going to that grief group," Molly said. "I think that's made a huge difference."

"Yes, Mom," Kendra retorted. "It has. But it's also learning about Joe. He wasn't who I thought he was—at least, I have good reason to think so. Jill shared with me that you all thought he was a player. I had certainly been caught up in the attention he lavished on me. But finding out he was less than perfect and most likely unfaithful has both pissed me off and given me permission to move forward."

The group nodded in unison.

"From now on, we need to make a pact. If any of us falls under the spell of a smooth-talking, fine-looking specimen, promise me we will be honest. And if we all know ahead of time that we're just being concerned, maybe that will help ease the sting of the message."

"We can't make anyone see what they're blind to," Amy said, chewing on a nail.

"I'm not blaming you," Kendra said. "And you're right. I probably would have labeled you as envious or some stupid thing. Hey, remember when we used to talk about stars? What, were we ten?" she asked Amy.

"The first time, yes. We wished upon a star. I don't remember the wishes we made, but I do recall we said we'd never forget that night."

"And none of us did. I loved piling up in the hammock together," Jill said. "Such great memories."

Kathy piped up, "I always managed to be awarded the stupidest stars while Molly amassed all the gold ones."

"Oh, you mean, those stars," Erica said.

A round of hearty laughter filled the air.

"We could make it as simple as that." Kendra thought for a moment after she spoke. "Yes. A simple *that might award you a stupid star*. Like a little knock upside the head."

"You sound like a bunch of fifth-graders right now," Molly added.

"Whatever works." Erica refilled everyone's glasses. "Now, let's get down to business. Who was Joe having an affair with?"

Kendra told them all about Jake's arrival in her life, the dead animals, and the scary visitor in the middle of the night, and then she shared the details of her trip to California. That seemed like more than enough for now. While they seemed to accept the news with some skepticism, they agreed that Kendra should be watchful.

"That's all pretty crazy," Amy said. "I'd be freaked if I were you."

Kendra felt as if she belonged again and eased into the evening.

Ninety minutes later, as the breeze picked up, they toted the food and drinks inside and sat around her family room, huddled in the tight space. It almost felt like a sleepover from their high school days. They reminisced about football games, their homecoming dances, and proms. The time Kendra had asked a boy to the Sadie Hawkins dance, who wound up kissing like a lizard.

"Hey," Kathy said. "I'm thinking about the weird things happening to you. Do you want to keep Aries out here for a couple of weeks? He's a great watchdog, and you might feel more secure with him here. He knows you even though you haven't seen him in a while. What do you think?"

Kendra hesitated for a long moment. She had grief group in

two nights and a ton of pages due to Jean. Could she handle care of a dog too? She didn't want to leave Aries alone. But then again, she had to admit, she'd feel safer.

"Are you sure you're willing to let me keep him? He's your dog. I have considered getting one of my own. My UPS man actually suggested it. Maybe I'll go to the Humane Society this weekend and adopt one. I'd hate to take Aries. The kids would miss him."

"Well, the offer stands. If you want to borrow him, the kids will understand it's a loan, not a permanent change."

CHAPTER THIRTY-THREE

WHEN KENDRA OPENED THE DOOR TUESDAY MORNing, Indian summer still seemed to have a firm grip on the weather. It occurred to her that she hadn't seen or heard from Russ in two entire days, ever since he'd clobbered Nathan over the head. He must have been embarrassed and ashamed after the incident. Relieved yet curious, Kendra wondered if he'd stop bothering her now. Nathan had acted so cool about it, as if he appreciated Russ watching out for her. Except for that part where his head ached like he'd been hit with a bat, which he had, and the prospect of missing work, which he never did.

As a side effect, Kendra wouldn't be at all sad if it meant Russ ceased to hover and make her feel like a caged animal. And if she adopted a good watchdog, that might keep Russ at bay even further. She decided she'd ask Nathan if he had time to help pick out a dog this weekend.

Speak of the devil, Nathan texted. Must be ESP.

Want me to pick you up for grief group tomorrow?

If you can, sure. Want to help me find a dog this weekend?

Only if I can name him.

And what name would that be? Kendra smiled at the prospect of Nathan naming a watchdog. He'd probably like something like Sugar or Honey.

Thor.

Kendra laughed aloud. Nathan had a habit of surprising her in delightful ways.

See you tomorrow.

Nathan sent a heart emoji. For a brute of a man, he sure had a soft heart.

Kendra reopened her email and checked it before reopening her manuscript and writing. She found a message from Jean.

Sorry to bother, but I'm wondering how the pages are coming. The last few I received were much more you, as if your voice was back, so I was encouraged. You've had a lot to juggle the past months, but I'm seeing signs of life. Good for you.

We have to have a first draft to the publisher in sixty days. From these recent pages, I think you'll get there.

Send what you have as you go, and I'll be happy to give you feedback. Hate to hound you, but I know you respond well to nudges and deadlines.

Hugs,

JJ

A bit irked—not with JJ, but with herself—Kendra closed the server and dived back into her manuscript. She played the keyboard for a solid three hours before breaking for a pit stop and a smoke. Still ashamed she'd fallen into the old, ugly habit, she decided to step out onto the deck instead of the front porch should Russ have decided to start lurking. Kendra had always been the type to hide her indiscretions from others. She hated being judged.

When she strode outside, she froze, her feet turning to lead.

Bitter bile stuck in her throat. Blood covered the deck, where just last evening, she'd enjoyed her first happy hour with friends.

After she swallowed back breakfast, her eyes trailed the blood to the mound at the edge of the deck. One of the beautiful, stately swans—graceful royalty of the lake—was nothing more than a bloody, feathery symbol of hate and destruction. It had been mutilated.

Kendra hesitated to call Russ. She'd enjoyed being away from his overprotective hovering. Isaac was working. She couldn't bother him. Nathan would come, even in the middle of a shift, but their relationship was new. *Could you drop by? Clean up and bury a murdered swan from my deck?* Didn't seem an appropriate request even if he'd already seen her at her worst.

Kendra sank to her knees, stomach roiling. *What kind of sick, deranged person would do this to an innocent creature?*

She had no real knowledge about waterfowl, except to understand that the parents kicked out their young around November. Whether this was a parent or cygnet, she had no idea. Either way, it sickened her.

Anger fueled her movements. She marched inside and tromped through the house and into the garage, pilfering a snow shovel from the hanging tools and then a large trash bag from one of the shelves. Staying outside on her return trip, she stood six feet away from the dead swan, propped the trash bag open with a stick she'd found in the grass, and went to the deck to retrieve the poor thing. She slid the shovel under its lifeless, bloodied body and closed her eyes as she lifted the carcass and inserted the tool into the mouth of the bag. Averting her gaze, she dumped the cadaver into the bag, dropped the shovel beside it, and tied the bag as tightly as possible. The thought of carrying the bag to the trash sickened her, but she picked up the shovel and sack, and then trooped to the garbage cart and dumped the bag inside. Kendra dropped on her knees outside the garage and vomited in the weeds.

She sat back on her heels after her stomach emptied and held her head in her hands. It dawned on her that she still needed to hose off the deck. Kendra swiped a sleeve across her mouth and trudged the thirty yards back to the scene. The hose hung off the deck rail, and she attached a nozzle, turned on the water, and rinsed off as much of the blood-spattered detritus as she could before retrieving a scrub brush and soap from inside. An hour of scrubbing later, no evidence of the horrific scene remained.

Kendra stepped inside and secured all the doors and windows in spite of the unseasonal warmth. She sank down into the office chair, spinning it in circles for several minutes in a feeble attempt to erase the sight from her mind and move into a different headspace.

She hammered out an email to Jean.

JJ,

You're right. I'm doing better. Last night, I had my girlfriends over for the first time since moving, and we had a nice time. I'm not as preoccupied as I've been with death and grief, but that's not to say life is great.

I just finished cleaning up the remains of a swan, which had been purposely slain and left for my discovery on my back deck. It's funny—though not in a laughable way—but this is actually the third time I've found a dead animal planted on my property with the intention of scaring the wits out of me. Success, my dear stalker! I'm caught between being terrified and fighting mad.

As you always advise me, my dear friend, use life to fuel my stories. I'm not sure how this would play in a novel, but in real life, it serves to unnerve me to my very core.

Love and hugs,

KK

Well aware of the time, Kendra poured a hefty glass of wine and stomped out on the deck. She grabbed the jar she'd fashioned into an ashtray from its hiding place as well as a pack of cigarettes, sat down, swallowed a hearty gulp of air, and lit up.

Nathan arrived early the next day. They didn't need to be at grief group until six that evening, so Kendra made sandwiches and met him out on the deck. After they ate, Kendra looked up to see Russ trailing across the lawn.

"Glad I found you two," he said. "Just want to check in on you, Nathan. I can't apologize enough for the other night. I let my protectiveness get the better of me. I never should have hit you. I should have contacted Kendra first and made sure she was all right. Trust me, I've been puzzling over this since it happened, and I can't say how sorry I am. I'll be more cautious from now on. I was out of line."

Nathan stood and shook Russ's hand. "Apology accepted. Now, do me a favor. I plan to keep an eye on Kendra. You don't need to preoccupy yourself with that task any longer. I'm quite capable of assuring her safety and security." Nathan spoke with authority.

It reminded Kendra of a face-off. A *mine's bigger* conversation. Quietly delighted yet surprised by the strength of Nathan's words and the assumption that he intended to be around to watch over her, she was at once pleased and conflicted. Needing him wasn't necessarily something she was sure she could trust or was ready for.

After Russ hung his head in defeat, he left.

On the way to grief group, they were both quiet. Lost in their own thoughts, Kendra surmised.

Nathan went to take her hand in the parking lot as they meandered into the church, but Kendra whispered to him, "Let's keep our relationship private."

Nathan narrowed his eyes, seemingly disappointed by her words.

"Just for now," she added, blowing him an air kiss.

Once in the musty basement, Kendra poured a cup of sludge and took her seat in the circle, between Gary and Cathy.

"Would anyone like to start tonight?" Mary asked.

Kendra raised her hand. "I would."

The group members' eyes settled on her.

"I'd like to talk about secrets. It's come to my attention, if there's any right way to say that, that my husband wasn't at all who I thought him to be. I evidently idealized him. Come to find out, he was a liar and a cheat."

"Maybe he—" Josh started, but Mary interrupted. "Let her finish, please."

"I'm not sure if he liked me or not, but he sure pretended to. Turns out, our relationship was a sham. I've discovered he was having an affair, and he kept far more than that little tidbit from me."

"You're hurt and angry," Mary said.

"Ya think?" Kendra was so sick and tired of people stating the obvious.

"I've been there," Gary offered. "My wife was unfaithful. And I'm not trying to turn the focus of the conversation on me. I just want you to know that you're not alone."

"What happened with your wife?" Cathy asked. "You've always portrayed her with love and adoration."

"I loved her all right. She loved me too, but she had other issues as well. After her death, I discovered she'd been involved with other men throughout our marriage. In fact, I've been delving into how to snag DNA tests on all my kids and see which ones are truly mine."

The room went dead quiet.

"We all have secrets," Nathan said. "And if you had known when your wife was alive, Gary, would it have changed anything? Or for you, Kendra? Would you have loved your spouses any less?"

More quiet as the entire group seemed to answer the questions for themselves.

Mary finally broke the silence. "It's not unusual to find out things we didn't know about our loved ones after they depart. Maybe not to the extremes Kendra and Gary have mentioned, but every one of us has things we keep to ourselves—our frailties, our ugliness, our shame, and guilt. We harbor those deep inside. Who wants anyone to know their darkest thoughts or indiscretions? My guess is that your wife loved you, Gary, as best as she could. Same for you, Kendra. But that doesn't mean we're not left with strong feelings we have to sort out in their absence. Not to have the chance to talk to them and hammer these issues out is very difficult."

Kendra let out a long puff of air. "For weeks after I lost Joe, I refused to wash his pillowcase. At night, I'd hold it close to me and inhale his scent. It made me feel like he was still here. And now, I'm really pissed I made a fool of myself like that."

"You did what you needed to do," Mary said gently. "It's okay."

"If it's okay, then why do I feel so shitty? I sleep with Joey's blanket a lot too. But it's entirely different. It's …"

"Pure," Gary interjected.

"Yes," Kendra said.

"Babies are innocent. We don't have conflicts with them," Brendan added. "Our relationships with our kids are unconditional, even when they grow up and start spouting off. It's different with spouses. We end up fighting. Or keeping quiet and shelving problems. We form resentments."

"We know our loved ones weren't perfect, except for little Joey. But when we lose those closest to us, oftentimes after they first leave, we can only remember their best sides," Mary said. "We loved them so hard … we can't and don't want to let go of them, much less admit we loved an imperfect soul. None of us are pure. We're all flawed. That's why we go through these stages of anger, guilt, and shame and even chastise ourselves for not being different or better when they were here with us. It's far easier to idealize them, and it makes grief more straightforward. We'd rather live with the sadness than those other messy emotions."

Trevor leaned forward. "I'm a bit like you, Kendra. My sister was so young, and while as siblings, neither of us had the pure relationship you did with Joey, I have trouble reckoning why I'm still here and she isn't. She was a perfect soul. Maybe we fought sometimes, and maybe we didn't talk for days after a fight, but in her youth, I don't feel like she hurt me to the core. Nothing I can't easily get over. But for you and Gary to live with deceit after the fact, that's gotta be tough."

"Do you want to go for a beer?" Nathan said as he sat behind the wheel.

"Would you mind dropping me off at home? I'm suddenly exhausted."

"Something I said?"

"No. I'm seriously feeling the weight of the past few months. It's like the table tennis game I've been playing has gone on too long, and I'm finally realizing I need to take a break and rest. I'm not upset per se, but I feel like I need to sleep for a few days, you know?"

"Actually," Nathan said, "I do." He rested a hand on her knee as he drove, walked her to the door after they arrived at her house, and placed a sweet kiss on her cheek. "Now, lock up tight, trigger the alarm, and sleep as long as you like. Text me when you wake up."

Kendra wrapped her arms around him and held on tight. "Thanks for understanding."

CHAPTER THIRTY-FOUR

As exhausted as she was, Kendra couldn't relax. It was as if her nerves wouldn't take a breath, the way electricity buzzed up and down her limbs. Kendra finally crawled into bed at about eleven, watched the nightly news, and clung to Joey's blanket. Without realizing, she rubbed the edge of the fabric between her thumb and forefinger. If anyone outside grief group witnessed her behavior, they'd be sure to lock her up.

Kendra relished being alone in her little house. Life was about to take a turn for the better. She knew it. Even though grief group had been tough tonight, Kendra had a sense she'd let go of some viciousness she'd been carrying around like a lodestone. Once she had a decent night's sleep, she envisioned turning a corner.

Kendra drifted off to the hum of the weather report, waking an hour later to shut off the television. When she did, she realized something had awakened her. Not the TV, but a premonition. She lay still and listened. After a minute or so, she rolled over. Nothing. She recounted her last actions of the evening. She'd triggered the alarm, set a wineglass in the sink, thrown the wine bottle in the recyclables, brushed her teeth, changed into pajamas, and gone to bed.

She blew out a breath and started to count backward from one hundred—an old habit she fell back on when insomnia struck. She tapped her foot against the mattress to make counting more pronounced and then blamed her earlier nerves for the sudden wakefulness.

A creaking alerted her. Kendra fought to place the sound. Since she'd moved to the lake, she'd grown accustomed to all kinds of signs of rural life—walnuts peppering the rooftop in the fall, squirrels chattering and scratching all summer long, the staccato yip-howling of coyotes in the night, roosters crowing at dawn, chain saws trimming branches. This sound was none of those.

The alarm system is on. Relax.

If Kendra didn't know better, she'd swear the side door lock tumbled. She listened harder, detecting the faintest squeak of a plank on the old hardwood floor. As hard as she tried, she could not make her brain process information.

Somehow, Kendra slid onto the floor next to the wall of windows. Tried to squeeze her body under the bed. Silent. Halted breath. Pulled the bed skirt over her body. Alert. Listening. Arms peppered with gooseflesh. Listening harder. Nothing.

Seconds passed. No sound.

A minute maybe.

Nothing.

Kendra freed a soundless breath.

The cell phone vibrated on the nightstand.

Seconds later, her phone buzzed again. A call. In the middle of the night.

Still as stone, she waited.

Footsteps padded through the dining nook, entered the bedroom.

A sharp inhale. Choking on fear.

In an instant, Kendra's leg was dragged from beneath the bed, out onto an open swath of carpet. She lay exposed under sharp, penetrating light. She squinted. The glint of a blade caught her eye. She recoiled and writhed in anticipation.

He's going to slice me.

She forced herself to look past the knife. *Josh? Grief group Josh? How? Why?* She tried to speak, but the words caught in her throat.

"Get up," he ordered, flashing a light toward the bed.

She stood. Wobbled. Fought for rational thought. *Save yourself.*

"What do you want? I'll give you anything."

"On the bed," he demanded.

He's going to rape me.

He clicked off the light. Kendra's limbs shook. Legs went to jelly. She didn't move. Couldn't move.

"Do what I say, or I'll slice you to slivers, just like I did that swan."

Kendra forced her legs to cooperate. Sat on the edge of the bed.

"You. You took him from me."

Kendra shuddered. Ice ran through her veins. Consumed her whole.

Moon glow through the transom window caught the reflection of a blade.

Kendra's brain rapid-fired. *He's talking about Joe. His partner. Joseph.*

Kendra darted to the outside bedroom door. Grabbing her by the hair, Josh pulled her back. She landed hard. Stunned. Disoriented. She clawed at his eyes. Scratched. Screamed. Kicked. Punched. He climbed on top of her. Held her down. Braced her wrists. She writhed in pain under the pressure of his weight.

"Dumb bitch."

Kendra tried to buck him off. His furious mass kept her pinned to the floor.

His hands, strong as a vise, clutched her wrists and fumbled as he tried to zip-tie them above her head. Her breath faltered.

"He hated you. He loved me. You're why he left me."

He rose slightly, and in an instinctual move, Kendra kneed him. He flew off her. Grabbed his crotch and curled in to a ball, moaning.

In a flash, Kendra unbolted the door. Ran into the night. Fought to find cover. Shook. Rattled to the very core. She sought refuge. To the east. The neighbor's tiny shed. Kendra fumbled with the door hasp.

Bare feet slid on the grass. Kendra's body splayed on the lawn. Again. He had her foot. Dragged her back to the house. Up the steps of the deck. Her head bounced. Each tread of the staircase threatened unconsciousness.

Kendra kicked. Wriggled. Fought to get away.

The world went gray. Then black.

When Kendra came to, she stayed still. Head throbbing. The sweet metallic scent of blood filled her nostrils. She swallowed. Bile rose and spewed from her mouth. Excruciating pain radiated from her legs to her abdomen. Sirens wailed nearby. She squinted toward a light. Russ. "It's okay. I've got you." She heard his footsteps traipse across the deck and into her house.

Kendra struggled to move. To stand. To free her arms. Blackness consumed her again.

When she woke, she blinked to gain her bearings. She was disoriented and aching while sharp, stabbing pains shot through her like she'd been splayed open. Beige walls. Clinking trays. White coats. All buzzed around her like a runaway merry-go-round.

She turned her head, frantic to understand. Finally, a nurse noticed Kendra had awakened, and placed a warm and gentle hand on her shoulder.

"Hi, Kendra. I'm your ER nurse, Alison. You're going be all right, honey. From what I heard, a neighbor of yours showed up just in time, kept you warm and applied tourniquets. You've lost a lot of blood, and you're going to feel crappy for a while. We're getting ready to stitch you up right now. We'll get you some pain medication and into a room soon." The nurse rested a steady hand on Kendra's shoulder. "You're okay. You'll be good as new before long."

Tears slipped down Kendra's cheeks. She didn't wipe them away.

Kendra's brain lifted from her body. She stared at the medical personnel who shrouded her and saw what they were doing reflected in the eye shields they wore. Dabbing at her wounds, cleaning her skin, injecting vials of medication into the IV lodged in a forearm.

An hour later, an orderly wheeled her into a private hospital room. He asked Kendra to scoot from the gurney to the bed, but pain made the task impossible. The orderly called in nurses and aides to help. Kendra yelped in pain as they transferred her to the bed. She felt as if she'd been sliced open without anesthesia. Her skin burned, and blood throbbed through each artery.

A nurse entered the room with several vials. "Hi, Kendra. I'm Brynna. I'm going to give you more antibiotics and the serious pain meds they couldn't give you downstairs. You should feel much less pain in about thirty minutes. Maybe sooner. These are pretty fast-acting. Would you like some water?"

Kendra couldn't stem the flow of tears. Whether adrenaline fueled them or it was the sheer bliss of survival, she couldn't say.

The nurse dabbed Kendra's cheeks with a tissue. "There now. You're safe."

Brynna left to fetch Kendra's water. Kendra lay stone still and stared at the ceiling, thanking whoever had served as her guardian angel.

A minute later, the door to the room scraped open. Nathan. Big, burly, smiling Nathan.

"Hey you."

Kendra's eyes leaked like Niagara Falls. But her body warmed at the sight of him. He pushed a chair next to the bed and leaned over to kiss her cheek before sitting down. The nurse returned and set a jug of water on a tray before leaving them alone.

"You don't have to talk," Nathan said. "You have to be exhausted. Are you in a lot of pain?"

Kendra's eyes lit on the IV bag. "Not for long."

"I'll be right here. You don't have to entertain me. Just sleep."

Kendra reached out for Nathan, and he gingerly held her hand. She closed her eyes and let the medication take hold.

Later, Kendra woke. Her head muddied by the starkness of her surroundings, she noticed Nathan snoozing at her side and felt a sudden sense of calm. Behind him stood two people, a man dressed in khakis and a sports coat and a woman in a fashionable suit.

The man took a step forward. "I'm Detective Cotter from the Washtenaw County Sheriff's Office. This is my partner, Detective Mathers. Are you up to answering a few questions?"

Kendra nodded and tried to find her voice. Nathan's head lifted, and he quickly surveyed the room. He noticed Kendra struggling for words and handed her a cup of water.

After she sipped, she spoke. "Yes."

The detectives considered Nathan.

"He should stay," Kendra ordered.

The partners had pads of paper and pens at the ready. Kendra shuddered. Memories of the night before buried her like an avalanche.

She fumbled for the bed remote and pressed the button to

lift the head. She folded her arms across her chest and inhaled a ragged breath. "I'm ready."

The female detective rested a hand on Kendra's shoulder, her eyes full of sympathy. "First of all, please know how sorry we are for your injuries. We also apologize for making you relive the ordeal."

Kendra recited what she remembered. Waking to the sound of the door. Hiding. Being discovered. Breaking away. Being dragged across the yard. Everything she could recall until the world had gone dark.

"Do you know your attacker?"

"Yes," Kendra simply said.

"Can you give us his name?"

Kendra gazed pleadingly at Nathan. She had no idea of the man's name. She'd only called him Josh. Just Josh. She remembered the first night when he'd introduced himself. A polished, slender guy but pure muscle beneath the tailored shirt. Nathan couldn't help either, she realized. He had no idea who had carved her open in the middle of the night.

"He's a member of my grief group. He said his name was Josh, but we don't share surnames. Whether he gave us his real name or not, I can't be sure. Our group is confidential, and we only share personal information if we want to. I'm sure our facilitator, Mary, would know. The group meets through Grief Angels. We get together every Wednesday evening at the Unitarian Church on Clinton Road."

Detective Mathers tented her brows, and Cotter left the room for several minutes.

Detective Mathers continued. "Do you have any idea why he did this to you?"

"He might have been involved with my husband." She watched Nathan's mouth fall open and his eyes register shock.

Detective Cotter entered and narrowed his eyes on Nathan, as if suspicious of him, or wondering about him in some way.

Kendra proceeded to elaborate on Josh's presence in grief group, only now piecing together the ties to Joe. "My husband killed himself last March. Seems I didn't know him as well as I thought. Joe had a troubled past."

"And?" Detective Cotter said.

Kendra told the detective what she knew, recited bullet points on Joe's past and details of the months after her move to the lake as if on auto play—what Sylvia had shared about Joe during Kendra's visit to California, the conversation she'd overheard at Dan's about Joe being some kind of player, the series of dead animals left to scare her silly, Jake's arrival in her life, and the complications around the Kelly brothers' parents' deaths, the necklace, and the missing knife she'd never reported.

Nathan squeezed her hand.

Kendra patted his hand. "I'm okay … I'll be okay." She said this to herself as much as Nathan.

The detectives turned to Nathan, and Detective Cotter leaned over and whispered in his ear. Nathan shook his head. Cotter said something more, and then the two detectives strode out of the room.

She watched them leave and then turned back to Nathan. He had blanched. His always-steady hands now trembled.

"What is it?"

Nathan sat back and scrubbed his jaw. Concern clouded his features. He grasped both of Kendra's hands but said nothing.

"You can tell me."

"I'm usually pretty good at delivering tough news, but when I think about it, I seldom have to share something this upsetting with someone I love."

Kendra's face contorted in confusion. "What could be so horrible?"

"Josh carved a word on your body. The detective just told me. I can't imagine."

For a few moments, Nathan stayed quiet.

Kendra clenched her jaw, attempting to ready herself for the next blow. "What word?"

"*Slut.*"

Kendra choked out a sob. "Where?"

"Are you sure you want to know?"

Kendra's voice rose, even as she choked out the words. "I can go and look in the mirror. Eventually, I will."

Nathan held her in a firm embrace for a prolonged moment before he backed away and gazed at her. "On your torso."

Kendra's eyes widened. "He tattooed me with scars."

"We'll find a plastic surgeon. Those guys do great work."

Kendra attempted to breathe, but she couldn't take in air. She spun away from Nathan and vomited. All over her nightgown, her hair, the bedsheets, the nightstand, and the floor. Horrified, she asked Nathan to leave.

"I'm not going anywhere. I've seen bushels of vomit in my lifetime. You can't scare me away so easily."

Kendra watched him closely as furrows deepened on his forehead. He ducked into the restroom and returned seconds later with a wet washcloth and a bowl.

Kendra's face drained of color.

"Bathroom," she managed.

"Bowl," Nathan directed and held it beneath her mouth.

Kendra leaned forward and continued to vomit.

He held back her hair, soothed her by rubbing her back, and uttered words of encouragement. "It's going to be okay. You'll be all right."

Kendra wouldn't be all right. Not today. Not tomorrow. But someday. She was done being a victim.

When the detectives reentered the room, they talked about charges they would level on her perpetrator once they found him.

She gazed at Detective Cotter. "Can you catch him?"

"We will."

Detective Cotter handed Nathan a business card as he regarded Kendra. "Call us if you think of any other details that would assist us in apprehending your assailant. According to the doctors, you'll be in the hospital a few days. We'll be sure to place an officer outside your room. I don't anticipate this guy will show up here, but we want to ensure your safety."

Nathan stood and shook Detective Cotter's hand. "I'll be parked here for the duration of her stay. He won't hurt her again."

Detective Cotter excused himself, and Kendra and Nathan stayed quiet as they both grasped the events of the last twelve hours.

"I love you, Kendra." Nathan gazed into Kendra's eyes, full of compassion, protection, and longing.

"I'd really like a beer," Kendra said.

"That's my girl." Nathan leaned over and kissed her cheek. "In the meantime, what else can I do for you?"

"Call Molly. She needs to know where I am. Do you have my phone?"

"No. The alarm company called the police after they couldn't reach you by phone. They deciphered a breach in the alarm. He'd hacked and disabled your system. I'm guessing your phone is still in the house somewhere."

"I never once thought about Josh. All along, I wondered about Russ or Jake. Russ had no real motivation, but Jake could have. I feel stupid. I should have figured this out."

Nathan rubbed her arm. "What, with your crystal ball? Because, far as I know, you don't have one."

"Wait. I just remembered. When I first woke up, a nurse said something about a neighbor helping me before the police and ambulance came. I have this faint memory of Russ standing over me after I was attacked, but I could have been hallucinating."

"Yep. Russ. I think he saved your life."

Three days later, an orderly wheeled Kendra down to the entrance of the hospital. Nathan pulled up his truck and lifted Kendra from the chair into the passenger seat, took care not to jostle her too much, and buckled her in.

Kendra's wounds were extensive. If she elected, plastic surgery could be performed to minimize scarring on her arms, torso, and legs. She had strict instructions to rest. No cardio. No weights. No lifting of any kind. Lots of fluids. Lots of protein. A steady dose of pain pills for the next week or so.

It required great effort for Kendra to bear weight or walk unassisted or without pain. She didn't have the energy or will to argue with any of her friends about their hovering. Rather, she welcomed it.

Kendra twisted her head slightly and noticed the suitcase in the back of the cab. "Going somewhere?"

"As a matter of fact, yes. I've got three weeks of vacation time to use before the end of the year. I'll be spending my time in a comfy, little cottage at this cozy, little lake in a quaint, little town. Maybe you've heard of it? Pleasant Lake? It's a delightful spot, walls of windows overlooking the water. Great decor. Homey as can be. The rent is practically free. Care to join me?"

"I believe I will."

When they reached Kendra's home, Nathan tentatively helped her from the cab, and then he lifted her in his arms and carried her to the front door. He set her down briefly in a padded porch rocker and unlocked the front door. He eased her inside, helped remove her coat, and situated her on the family room sofa, complete with a pillow and fuzzy blanket. He'd also placed a dozen roses on the coffee table, a mix of yellow and red, before bringing her home.

"Red roses for falling in love. Yellow for a new beginning."

Kendra's head fell back against the cushy pillow. Nathan delivered a tall glass of water and tucked her in. She slept like a hibernating bear for hours before Nathan shook her awake.

"You have a visitor."

Kendra's eyes widened at the sight of Russ Jameson. He held several photo albums in his hands and an apologetic expression in his gaze.

"I'm sorry, Kendra. Sorry for overstepping my bounds as your neighbor. I know you're recovering, and I don't want to keep you, but I thought you'd like to have these. At some point when you feel better, take some time with them. I've written out a story. I'm not an author like you, but I have a story to tell, and it might have more than a little to do with you. Nathan here tells me he'll be staying for a while. I'm glad you have someone to watch over you. And I'm sorry I didn't keep a closer eye on things. The last thing I wanted was for you to be hurt."

He shook her hand and headed out the front door. Nathan followed him outside.

Baffled, Kendra inched to the edge of the sofa and retrieved one of the books. She groaned in pain but succeeded in procuring the album. Inside, she found the photograph of a young woman. Pretty with dark brown hair and startling blue eyes, she looked to be around eighteen. This could have been a high school graduation photo.

Again, Kendra wriggled over on the cushion and winced with pain. She managed to get hold of the second book and rested it on her lap. As she peered inside, a typed page slipped from the album and rested soundly on Kendra's chest.

Kendra lifted the page with a free hand and began to read.

Stephanie Jane Jameson, beloved daughter of Anne (Sidecki) and Russ Jameson, passed away on July 5, 2001, the victim of a drowning accident. Stephanie had graduated with honors from Manchester

High School this past June. She was an accomplished soccer player and was headed to MSU this coming fall with an athletic scholarship. She leaves behind her loving parents, numerous aunts and uncles, and her precious dog, Suzie. She will be sorely missed.

Tears rolled down Kendra's cheeks. Here, she had been so frustrated with Russ, yet he was watching out for her because he'd suffered the loss of a child, just like she had.

"Nathan!" she called out.

He came zooming through the front door. "What's wrong? What do you need?"

"Is Russ still here?" she choked out.

"He's just leaving. What's up?"

"Can you ask him to come back? And can you hurry?"

Nathan leaned out the front door. "Russ? Kendra wants to talk to you."

Russ came back inside and stared at the open books and photos. When he glanced at Kendra's face, she opened her arms to him. He sat beside her, and she wrapped him in a hug.

"You saved my life."

Russ shook his head. "I didn't realize how overprotective I'd become since I'd lost Stephanie. I haven't quit living, but I'm always missing her. You gave me a chance to care for someone again. You're about the same age she would have been had she lived. Glad I was able to be there when you needed someone. I only wish I'd gotten there sooner."

CHAPTER THIRTY-FIVE

"I FEEL LIKE A FOOL," KENDRA SAID AFTER NATHAN tucked her in bed that night.

Nathan rolled his eyes. "Don't hammer yourself for this. How could you have known?"

"If I hadn't been so paranoid, I could have been more understanding about Russ. I was so mean to him."

"Can't say I witnessed that. Sure, you gave him hell after he clobbered me over the head, but in my mind at least, that was more than appropriate." His eyes glimmered in the moonlight streaming through the transom window. "You stood up for me."

"His attention was protective, but I could only see it as smothering. I kept my thoughts to myself most of the time, but I did curse him a lot in the privacy of my mind. In the end, he's suffering, just like I am. He had his daughter for eighteen years. And then to lose her …"

"Remember how Mary said we can't compare our grief to

someone else's. Just like we can't feel our pain is sharper, you shouldn't give Russ's grief any more weight than your own.

"Besides, you had a hunch—more than that really—that you were being stalked. And you had that feeling not because you were losing your mind, but because you *were* being stalked."

Kendra nodded and pointed to her head. "It's a mess in here. You seem to handle life so straightforwardly."

Nathan puffed out his chest. "It's a guy thing."

"I don't think so. There are plenty of neurotic men out there. You have a balance I admire. Maybe if I hang out with you long enough, I'll become more like you."

Nathan nuzzled her neck. "Sort of like when dogs and their owners start looking alike?"

"Not quite like that, but you've got the idea."

"Stick with me, kid. I've got you covered. And by the way, I want to get a dog for you. I'm going to head to the Humane Society this weekend. You can look online and see if you fall in love."

Kendra gazed up at Nathan, a huge grin on her face. "I know we're brand-new, and we haven't discovered all our frailties yet …"

"Hold on a minute. We met in a grief group. I've seen you at your worst, angry and bitter. You were a little like a box of chocolates at times. I never knew who was going to show up."

"So, you thought I was kind of crazy?"

"A bit unpredictable, is all."

Nathan walked around the bed and lay down next to Kendra, offering her his shoulder. She snuggled in, found a semi-comfortable resting place, and breathed in his calming scent.

"It's as if I were Dorothy in *The Wizard of Oz*, caught in the midst of a storm."

"You've been through a nightmare. That's over now. Time for healing and laughter. I'm a pretty funny guy, you know. Did I tell you about the lady and the chipmunk?"

"Please do. I love a good bedtime story."

"We got this call the other day. A woman reported a chipmunk in her home. She was screaming at the 911 operator, 'Chipmunk, chipmunk.' So, we headed over, and sure enough, she had trapped a chipmunk in her bedroom. She was shaking like a rattle, still repeating, 'Chipmunk, chipmunk,' and pointing at the bedroom door. Outside the bedroom, she'd set a hamper and a board. Good thinking, right?

"But I was thinking it was a rabid rodent, so I went back to the truck and grabbed my work gloves. I went inside with one of the other guys. We snuck into the bedroom so as not to let the little bugger out, and sure enough, he was sitting on the night table, staring at us. Except he wasn't a chipmunk. He was a red squirrel. They're pretty common in the country, especially more forested environs, like here, where you live. And they're nasty critters. They chew through attics, drywall, anything really. And they're social as heck, so where there's one, there's more. But I digress.

"My partner slowly started to position the hamper over the varmint. Neither of us were breathing at this point, and the rascal flew into the air. By some fluke, I reached my hand out just in time to catch him. Like you do, I kept my words inside my head. But I'm thinking, *I got ya, you son of a bitch.* I took him outside and delivered him to a field across the street."

Kendra heard Nathan sniffle. "Are you crying?"

"Me? Never. Just felt bad for the guy. After all, it's his nature to be troublesome."

"You crack me up."

"What? You don't feel for vermin?"

Kendra tilted her head back in laughter. "I have issues with small, fast gnawers with long tails—or tails of any kind." Then, she yelped as her head bounced on Nathan's arm.

"Did you bean yourself?"

Kendra touched the series of stair-step lumps on the back of her head. "As long as I don't touch it or lean on it too hard, I'm not in too much pain. I guess when I was laughing, I raised my head. Won't do that again."

Nathan puffed out his chest, and his biceps twitched. "I'm not going to let anything happen to you. I can't believe I never suspected that bucket-head Josh or whoever he is. Usually, I have a pretty decent radar for creeps."

"I had no idea. I guess when he said his partner's name was Joseph, I didn't make much of it. Joe is a popular name, and my Joe never went by Joseph. I never thought twice about it..."

"You need time to absorb all this, and I'll be here every step of the way. If you want to go to counseling or see a doctor to deal with the emotional piece, I can come with you. Drive you. Wait for you. Whatever you need."

Kendra squeezed her eyes shut. "I'm relying on good old-fashioned coping skills for a while. Meanwhile, I don't want to be left alone. I want to eat ice cream. Only ice cream. I want to read books and watch movies."

"And maybe drink some adult beverages," Nathan added.

Kendra's eyes filled with tears.

Wrapped in a blanket, Kendra sat outside the next morning, sipping hot coffee, nibbling on a homemade blueberry muffin Nathan had baked in the early morning hours. A lighthearted romance novel lay on the table as trees shed their leaves like a snowstorm. Luckily, Nathan had extended the deck awning, so Kendra could enjoy the nature show without being covered in leaves, and he'd fired up the deck heater as well, so she was toasty warm. Nathan had ducked inside to start a pot of soup, but she expected him to join her shortly.

A few minutes later, Nathan strode outside, accompanied by Detectives Cotter and Mathers.

"Sorry to interrupt your morning, but we took a chance on finding you at home and wanted to give you an update. We've apprehended Ian Spencer, the man you knew as Josh. Got him at a traffic stop. He's in jail, and his bail hearing will probably happen tomorrow. The prosecutor is going to request that bail be denied."

Honestly, Kendra didn't care to know a single detail about her assailant, but Mathers seemed determined to demonstrate she'd done her job.

"He's a software engineer at your deceased husband's place of employment, probably how he knew a way to hack into your alarm system. There was a report filed a few years back in which he was accused of domestic abuse with his previous partner, before he and your husband were a couple. Much to our dismay, the assault involved knives. Unfortunately, the partner dropped the complaint and chose not to proceed with charges."

Kendra pretended to listen but found solace in the branches of the white pines that danced with the wind. She nodded occasionally and passed Nathan the hint of a grin when he refilled her cup.

"It appears that Mr. Spencer's motivation was revenge. He holds you accountable for your husband's suicide. Of course, we don't hold you or anyone else responsible in the case of the suicide. Clearly, his death was ruled as self-inflicted, and the coroner was resolute in his decision. There was no suggestion of homicide."

Anger spiked up Kendra's spine, and her skin flushed. Tears threatened, but she was unyielding. She'd not award Ian Spencer that satisfaction. He'd done enough harm.

"Did you find the knife?" Kendra's eyes fell to her legs.

Nathan raised his eyebrows.

"I want to see the weapon he used."

"Not yet, ma'am. But we're looking. Just awaiting a search warrant for his apartment."

"I think when he broke into my house—and I'm sure it was

him—he stole a knife my husband had received from his father. He used it to cut me. I want the knife back."

"It's evidence, ma'am. That isn't likely to happen."

Nathan patted her arm. "You don't want the knife."

Kendra inhaled a long breath. "I'm thinking of Jake. The same knife could have been used in his parents' murders. As for me, I just want this to be over."

Nathan nodded. "Let the knife go into evidence. Let this part be done and over with."

After Nathan saw the detectives out, he came and stood by Kendra's side.

She rested her head on his hip, closed her eyes, and pressed her lips together. "I'm going inside to write."

"Look, you're exhausted. I'm sure if you email your agent, she can talk with your publisher, and they'll allow you some leeway."

"I've had plenty of leeway. If my life is full of crises and chaos, the only way to reclaim my sanity is to write."

Nathan thinned his lips, as any smart man would do. "Get to it then."

EPILOGUE

Winter ~ A Year Later

NATHAN HELD KENDRA'S GLOVED HAND AS SHE DE-
scended the icy courthouse steps. Her face had drained
of color. He detected trembling of her fingers as well. He
placed her hand in his coat pocket when they reached the salted
sidewalk and planted a kiss on the top of her head.

"You were a tremendous witness."

"Add that to my résumé. Best-selling author. Authentic witness. I could barely look at Ian. I wanted to—really, I did. I wanted
to glare at him until he caught fire. But thinking of him made me
think of Joe. Right now, I'm really angry. Joe took advantage of me.
He used me as a front for his homosexuality. Don't get me wrong
… I have nothing against gay men, and I know I should forgive
Joe, considering his abuse. But being abused doesn't give you the
right to abuse someone else."

Nathan stayed silent.

"He stole my grief for Joey. He had no regard for me or our relationship. Thank goodness Ian didn't testify. If he had, I couldn't have stayed in my seat. Damn him. Damn them both. I wonder how long they would have carried on before I found out. It's humiliating enough, knowing this is in the news every day. As far as I'm concerned, I'm done. Done with stupid memories, done with the limelight, done being the focus of local gossip and speculation."

"Seems Jake is in the same place. I spoke with him briefly when you were in the restroom. He's starting over in Minnesota. Found some long-lost relative of his mom's and decided to take up roots there. The detectives offered to talk to the courts in California and provide the knife as evidence should Jake decide to pursue further resolution of his parents' deaths, and he said he might contact you at some point about the necklace, but he wants you to concentrate solely on your health right now and to this growing baby." Nathan patted her protruding middle.

"I should have spoken with him, but there's only so much I can handle right now. I'm glad he found a place to go. And glad he's leaving us, to be honest."

Kendra stopped at the corner and sat down on the snow-covered bench. The wind whipped furiously down Main Street, stray plastic bags caught on light posts, and leftover fallen twigs zipped through the air like projectiles.

Nathan assumed a seat next to her. "You sure all this cold on your bottom isn't going to freeze the baby?"

Kendra rested her head on Nathan's sturdy shoulder and murmured under her breath, "Let's go home. Thor's waiting."

ACKNOWLEDGMENTS

To my first two editors—my husband, Don, and my dear friend, Lori Alexander—my endless thanks. If not for the two of you, I doubt any of my books would see the light of day. Your astute observations and support mean the world to me. A special thanks to Kathleen Sullivan for her astute proofreading. She's my unexpected angel.

To my faithful readers, thank you for reading and loving my books. Without you, I'd have no reason to write.

ABOUT THE AUTHOR

Claudia Whitsitt is the best-selling author of eleven books and has been published since 2012. She is a lover of the written word, mystery and romance, and includes some of each in most of her novels, no matter what genre she is writing.

When Claudia isn't reading or writing, she's spending time with family, enjoying the outdoors, traveling.

Claudia is also a lover of coffee and cabernet, depending on the time of day, and although she avoids sugar, it's a weakness she has yet to overcome completely.

To find more about upcoming events and releases,
please sign up for Claudia's newsletter.
www.claudiawhitsitt.com
cjw@claudiawhitstt@gmail.com

Made in the USA
Monee, IL
27 June 2022